THE
TWICE–
HANGED
MAN

Also by Priscilla Royal

The Medieval Mysteries

Wine of Violence
Tyrant of the Mind
Sorrow Without End
Justice for the Damned
Forsaken Soul
Chambers of Death
Valley of Dry Bones
A Killing Season
The Sanctity of Hate
Covenant with Hell
Satan's Lullaby
Land of Shadows
The Proud Sinner
Wild Justice

THE
TWICE-
HANGED
MAN

A
MEDIEVAL
MYSTERY

PRISCILLA
ROYAL

Poisoned Pen
PRESS

Sourcebooks and the colophon are registered trademarks of Sourcebooks, Inc.

Published by Poisoned Pen Press, an imprint of Sourcebooks
P.O. Box 4410, Naperville, Illinois 60567-4410
(630) 961-3900
sourcebooks.com

Library of Congress Cataloging-in-Publication Data:
Names: Royal, Priscilla, author.
Title: The twice-hanged man : a medieval mystery / Priscilla Royal.
Description: First edition. | Naperville, IL : Poisoned Pen Press, [2019]
Identifiers: LCCN 2019018756| (hardcover : alk. paper)
Subjects: LCSH: Executions and executioners--Fiction. | Abbesses, Christian--Fiction. | Murder--Investigation--Fiction. | Monasticism and religious orders--Fiction. | Cities and towns, Medieval--Fiction. | Great Britain--History--Edward I, 1272-1307--Fiction. | GSAFD: Mystery fiction. | Historical fiction.
Classification: LCC PS3618.O893 T89 2019 | DDC 813/.6--dc23 LC record available at https://lccn.loc.gov/2019018756

Printed and bound in The United States of America.
SB 10 9 8 7 6 5 4 3 2 1

"Laws are silent in time of war."
—Cicero, 106-43 BCE,
Pro Milone

"The first casualty when war comes is truth."
—Hiram Warren Johnson,
1917 speech, U.S. Senate

*In memory of Sharon Silva
and forty years of friendship.*

Chapter One

Flames from torches stoutly battled the darkness of Satan's hour as the bearers hurried toward the party of exhausted travelers.

Prioress Eleanor squeezed the hand of the moaning woman lying next to her. "We have arrived," she said gently. The cart on which they rode came to a juddering halt.

The woman arched her back and cried out in agony, then gripped the hand of the prioress with painful force.

Jumping to the ground, Sister Anne rushed to the woman servant standing at the open door to the hunting lodge, held a brief discussion, and returned to help Brother Thomas and another man ease the suffering woman from the cart.

"Take her as gently as you can to the prepared chamber." The nun pointed to the woman at the door, reached into the cart for a small bag, and hurried to the lodge.

Wiping a hand across her eyes to clear away the moisture from the heavy mist, Prioress Eleanor watched until the foursome disappeared inside.

"My lady?"

The unknown voice startled her, but then she saw a servant extending a hand. With murmured gratitude, she took it, slipped down from the cart, and hurried to a man dismounting his horse.

"Your wife is now in her chamber, Robert," she said and laid a hand on his arm. "We have safely crossed the border into England, and Welsh soldiers are no longer a danger…"

He shook his head. "We never should have listened to Hugh. Elizabeth was too near her birthing to travel." His inflection rose in pitch, and his words began to flow together. "I was wrong to agree to this journey. Surely the rebels were not so close that we had to flee." He turned toward the lodge. "I must be at her side."

She tightened her grip to hold him back. "You cannot be in the birthing chamber, brother. She has Sister Anne, the finest midwife in England. When you are calmer, you will agree that our eldest brother was right to send word that Welsh soldiers might be too close for us to remain safely at the manor."

He put his hands over his face and groaned. "This is her second birthing in just over a year. This journey has weakened her. If she dies…"

Eleanor put her hand against his cheek. "Be still. Her life is in God's hands and those of my sub-infirmarian. I will sit with you outside Elizabeth's chamber, and we shall wait together for word." She looked around and beckoned to a tall man who stood nearby, the flames from his torch struggling to stay alive in the damp air. "Is there a fire and mulled wine inside?"

"Aye, my lady, and a servant waiting to bring what you need. When we got word that you were coming, we prepared for your stay." He gestured to shadowy figures and ordered them to take charge of the horses and carts.

Nodding her thanks, the Prioress of Tyndal clasped her brother's hand and led him like a small boy across the muddy courtyard and into the lodge.

Chapter Two

Prioress Eleanor took in a deep breath of the new morning air, shut her eyes, and savored peace.

The tense and hasty journey to escape the rebel bands had been sleepless. Last night had been filled with screams of a mother giving birth and fears that Elizabeth might not live. Then, just before dawn, Robert and Eleanor heard the outraged cries of a healthy baby and saw Sister Anne's smile. At the end of their endurance, brother and sister fell into each other's arms and wept with joy.

Now the air began to bite her lungs with late autumnal iciness. Heavy with the threat of more rain, it was also filled with the sweet scent of fresh wood fires drifting across the narrow dark river that marked the boundary between Wynethorpe property and the dwellings in the small village.

Even though the land on which she stood belonged to her family, Eleanor had never visited here before. The lodge behind her was built on a high point that allowed a viewer to see some distance and observe ongoing hunts if desired. It was also a useful defensive feature common to many such lodges. Although her elder brother thought it unlikely that this border town would be ravaged, as Oswestry to the north had been some months ago, the view would provide an early warning if Welsh troops did attack.

That was comforting.

In daylight, she realized the building was insignificant in size and intended for the accommodation of small parties of guests who wished to hunt in the surrounding forest where the Wynethorpes had rights to the game. She did not know if marriage had brought it into their baronial hands, whether it had been a gift from a former king, or even how often it was used. All that mattered now was that it was a reasonably safe haven and close by when her sister-in-law suffered the hard contractions that proclaimed her second babe was demanding birth.

Eleanor blinked, her eyes gritty, and she turned back to the lodge.

Even a straw mat on the floor of the solar would feel as soft as a summer cloud, she decided, and was convinced she could dream through the roars of a hungry newborn. She was so weary, she feared she might fall asleep on her feet.

———

Sister Anne stood in the doorway.

Despite the dark circles under her eyes, the nun looked content. A woman of notable medical talent, she was never happier than when she saved a child's life or delivered a healthy baby.

"You must rest," the prioress said to her friend. "I assume Elizabeth and the child remain well and can do without your care for a few hours."

"Indeed, they can," Sister Anne replied, "but I came with a message. Your brother and his wife would like to discuss a matter of some urgency with you."

Eleanor raised an eyebrow.

"It is for them to explain," the sub-infirmarian replied, but her gentle expression banished any dread that the subject was a worrisome one.

As the two women entered the lodge, Anne chuckled. "I think you will be delighted when you see your brother. Now that his wife has finished her ordeal and is settled into her bed, I surrendered to his pleas and let him in to see her." She pointed to the stairs up to the small solar and then led the way.

"I know Robert. He must have bounded to her side like a great puppy." The prioress' smile quickly faded. "He was worried."

"As he should have been." Anne stopped and looked back at the prioress, a gray shadow of concern passing across her face. "His wife is not in her early youth, and birthing two children in just over a year is hard on a woman. It may be the will of the Church and the curse of Eve, but…."

Eleanor winced. Both she and Robert had vivid memories of their own mother's death in childbirth.

Sister Anne said nothing more. When she entered the solar, she went to the large, curtained-off area, where mother and babe rested, and pulled aside the opening so the prioress could enter.

Eleanor laughed at the sight before her.

"I fear I have lost my position in your brother's heart," Elizabeth said, pointing to her husband standing by her bed. Her face was pale with exhaustion, but her blue eyes sparkled with pleasure.

Robert of Wynethorpe was gently rocking a tiny, well-swaddled babe in his arms. Utterly besotted, he did not even look up at the sister he had summoned.

"I have never seen such perfection," he exclaimed. "Come and look at these little ears!"

Being a short woman, Eleanor did not have to bend to look at the child in order to admire the noted ears, nor did her brother have to persuade her that the baby was perfect. Her heart had been won by her new niece from the moment she heard the babe's first lusty cry.

"They are not your ears, Robert. I think God was kind and gave your daughter ones more like those of your wife."

He laughed, but his awe-struck gaze did not move from the baby's face.

Eleanor had always been able to tease this brother. She and Robert had been the closest of the three siblings since childhood. Although they loved their eldest brother, Hugh, he was much older and, as befitted the heir, reveled in war and the intrigues of a king's court. Robert was a gentler man, took joy in farming and sheep, and was now the skilled manager of the baronial estates while Baron Hugh fought the Welsh at King Edward's side.

The prioress turned to her sister-in-law. "I fear you are right. You shall have to be satisfied with second place."

"I am relieved that he is content enough with a daughter. I had hoped to bear a son." Her small reserve of energy now depleted, she lay back on the pillows and sighed.

Her husband looked up, his eyes wide with surprise. "We have a fine son and, God willing, we shall have more to content Hugh, but I may now confess I prayed for a little girl this time."

"Then I have pleased you?" Elizabeth flashed a brief smile of happiness.

"My beloved one, you could not have given me greater joy." His words were soft with the love he bore his wife.

Robert had married later than most men, but Hugh had found him a wife who not only brought the Wynethorpe family increased wealth but also shared the second son's good nature and husbandry skills. The pair had found joy in each other soon after meeting, and the marriage was a happy one.

Anne went over to the bed and put the back of her hand against Elizabeth's forehead. "You have no fever, but I advise rest. These early days after birth require it to ward off illness." She shot Robert a significant look.

"I agree, Robert," Eleanor said. "We must leave your wife for now, and the babe shall sleep easily in the crib." She gestured at a little wooden object close to the bed.

For a moment, Robert looked horrified that he must give up the child, and then he nodded and carefully handed her over to Sister Anne. "Before I leave my wife and the beautiful babe she struggled valiantly to bear," he said, "Elizabeth and I have a favor to ask of you, dear sister." He motioned for his wife to continue.

"We would like to name our daughter Alienor after you," Elizabeth said.

Eleanor was speechless. "It is too great an honor. I am unworthy."

Robert approached, put his hands on her shoulders, and looked very serious. "If you grant our wish, it is we who shall be greatly honored. Both Elizabeth and I decided, should the child be a girl, that she must bear your name. In doing so, we hoped that your niece would look to you as the example of the wisdom, faith, competence, and fairness to which all women should aspire."

Blushing, the prioress looked down at her feet. Although she had given herself up to God's service early in life, she knew how imperfect she was and believed she was no mentor for a young girl. "I think she would be better directed to look elsewhere for a guide in those qualities, brother, for I am a frail woman who is possessed of a very sinful nature."

"Nonsense!" Robert laughed. "You may have willfully ruled me when we were children. You may have shown you had sharper wits than I by often getting the better of me. But I bore my yoke with love, and now I want our daughter to be just like you and keep her elder brother, Adam, humble."

"You did train my husband well," Elizabeth said lightly, and then changed her tone to a more serious one. "He and I are of one mind and heart in this. Please grant us this boon."

Reluctant though she was, Eleanor knew it would be ungracious and even unloving to protest further. And in the deepest part of her soul, she was delighted they had chosen to name this child after her. "Very well," she said in a soft voice. "You have my permission, and I shall pray that I may become the model she needs for a virtuous life."

Before she could say more, they were interrupted by the arrival of a woman servant at the top of the stairs.

"I beg pardon, my lady," she said to the Prioress of Tyndal.

"Abbot Gerald from the local abbey seeks permission to speak with you about an urgent problem."

"May God have mercy on us," Robert muttered. "I swear that man shares a sett with a badger under the lodge so he knows the moment I arrive. Since my visits are so rare, there can be no other explanation. A tiresome man, sister, and you need not cater to his fancy and see him. You have not had any sleep…"

Eleanor closed her eyes and felt herself sway slightly with fatigue but waved away her brother's suggestion. "He has most likely come to offer Brother Thomas accommodation at the abbey." And if not, she thought, it was her duty to see any fellow religious who begged her help.

"Send word if you need rescue, sweet sister. I do not like the abbot."

Eleanor smiled, then turned to the servant. "Take him to the dining hall," she said, "and I shall meet with him shortly. Make sure he is offered refreshment."

Halfway down the stairs, she stopped, leaned against the cold stone wall, and prayed she could stay awake long enough to deal courteously with this abbot.

Chapter Three

Abbot Gerald was a square-faced, neatly dressed man who did not look like he had spent any time in a badger sett.

Eleanor quickly banished the image, steeled herself not to yawn, then welcomed him with grace.

After a brief but equally polite reply, the abbot quickly apologized. "I would have waited until later to trouble you had the problem been less dire."

Then he has not come simply to take Brother Thomas to more comfortable lodgings in his abbey, she concluded, and studied him as he worked with excruciating slowness toward his purpose in seeking this audience with her.

Although the abbot's speech was Norman French, Eleanor noted that his vowels were slightly elongated, suggesting he was either of Welsh descent or had grown up amongst them. Unlike most men descended from those who followed William the Bastard to England, Gerald was short, but that did not mean the man was Welsh. Her own brother, Robert, was of small stature as well.

"My priest has been most foully murdered. I must beg your help."

Eleanor was taken aback. She and her family had just fled

from possible capture by enemy soldiers, her sister-in-law had suffered a hard birthing, and Abbot Gerald wanted her to deal with a murder?

"The local sheriff, or crowner, is surely the one best suited to assist in this matter." She did not even try to disguise her annoyance.

He shook his head. "The death of Father Payn is not within the jurisdiction of the king's law."

Eleanor searched his face for some clue to his character. Was he sincere in assessing the dilemma, or was he trying to take advantage of her reputation for solving crimes to avoid making any effort himself?

He was most certainly an interesting-looking man, one composed of a multitude of angles from his bony fingers to his pointed chin and hooked nose. His gray eyes suggested an equally sharp intelligence blunted by worry. She found no reason to distrust him more than any other mortal, and concluded he was likely a proud man from his stiff-backed stance. Such men do not easily beg for help and especially not from a woman.

"Please explain," she said in a kinder tone. If nothing else, she owed it to a fellow religious to hear him out, even if she must find cause to refuse his request.

He picked up the mazer of wine sitting close by him on the table, took a small sip, and began.

"Father Payn was coming from the village very late at night and took the footpath along the edge of the forest to the abbey. It was there he was vilely murdered. No sooner had he been killed than a witness of good repute, a man named Bardolph, came around a bend in the path and saw the slayer kneeling by the corpse of our dear priest. When Bardolph cried out, the murderer vanished. The body was as warm as life, although the witness found no evidence of breath. The moon was full that night, and no clouds dulled the light. The witness clearly recognized the perpetrator as a man named Hywel."

Had she missed something? Had she drifted into sleep for a moment? Eleanor shook her head. She saw no problem here that required her help. "Then surely this Hywel has been arrested." I am also proud, she thought, and glad I did not betray my confusion like a weak woman.

Abbot Gerald took time to reply by taking a very slow sip of his wine.

"Hywel is a ghost," he finally said, "the spirit of a Welsh brigand recently and most justly hanged for murdering good English soldiers in a cowardly raid. Satan has apparently released his sin-blistered soul from Hell to inflict revenge on our innocent village."

Since Eleanor had yet to meet any such malign spirits, although she had most certainly encountered enough wicked flesh-and-blood mortals, she was disinclined to believe in ghosts. Not that she discounted the possibility of their existence. Satan was a wily creature. But she most certainly did believe the shadowy ones were exceedingly rare. "This ghost can be vanquished by virtuous men from your abbey. You, yourself, for instance…"

Again hesitating, he took another measured swallow of wine.

I suspect he is trying very hard not to reveal that he thinks I am slow of wit and does not wish to be rude. Or else, she thought, he is taking time to enjoy a better quality wine from a Wynethorpe lodge than he is likely to get in his abbey. With minimal fervor, she rebuked herself for such irreverent thoughts.

"We have tried all we can to rid our village of Satan's minion. We have failed."

"A messenger could be sent to the nearest bishop…" She was too tired to even remember who the man was.

Without warning, he knelt and lifted his hands beseechingly.

She gasped and stepped back.

"My lady, this noisome thing is stubborn. He has been witnessed since his killing of poor Father Payn, roaming the village streets at the height of his vile master's hour and frightening honest men. You, my lady, have been granted the gift of a vision of the holy family! God clearly looks upon you with favor for your virtue and dedication to His service."

Eleanor tried to protest, but he ignored her.

"If you and your well-regarded monk, Brother Thomas, took it upon yourselves to save us from this malignancy, God would listen to you. It seems He finds us too sinful." He looked up at her, his eyes wide with hope.

"Rise, Abbot Gerald, for I am unworthy of such homage or praise."

He remained on his knees. "Please help us! We have failed to get God's attention, although we have most zealously tried. You have His ear. He will listen to you!"

Eleanor knew she did not have the energy to argue further. If she agreed to something minimal, perhaps he would be satisfied and she could get some sleep.

"Have you buried your priest?" Quickly, she pressed a hand to her mouth to fight back a yawn. Her eyes burned with weariness.

"His body rests in the abbey chapel where a monk prays for his soul."

In all likelihood, the question of a ghost would be swiftly resolved. Brother Thomas and Sister Anne could examine the body and determine if death was caused by a mortal hand. If so, this whole matter could be assigned to the king's men. Or the death might prove natural. The only things that troubled her were the witness' recognition of the man kneeling by the body and the apparent sightings of this hanged man by others in the village. But she was just too tired now to present a logical argument to herself, let alone this abbot.

"Please alert your monks that I will send Brother Thomas to view the corpse. He will likely be accompanied by Sister Anne, who is the well-respected sub-infirmarian at my priory."

He paled. "A woman?"

"She will respect Father Payn's vows as she has always done

in her work with any men of his vocation who have needed her knowledge. I remind you that she has taken vows herself which she devoutly honors."

She immediately moved her foot, fearful that he was about to kiss it in reverent gratitude.

Instead, he rose and thanked her profusely. "I will tell the monk who accompanied me here to return immediately to the abbey with orders that those you send to examine the body of our dear priest must be given any assistance needed."

While he left to do this, Eleanor told the woman at the far end of the hall to send a man to bring back Brother Thomas, who had gone into the village after the sun rose. Then she ran up the stairs to alert Sister Anne that she must be ready to accompany their monk to the abbey chapel to briefly observe a corpse.

Chapter Four

The village square was boisterous with a confusion of sound: the laughter of women, the grievances of animals, and the shouts of men. It was market day.

Brother Thomas remained indifferent. Although the sun had finally chosen to shine after an early struggle, he neither noted it nor truly cared. A thick shroud of melancholy had so completely encircled his soul that neither light nor joy could touch it.

His dark mood had not prevented him from acting swiftly when word came from Baron Hugh that bands of Welsh raiders might be too near Wynethorpe lands on the River Wye. He joined his prioress in urging her family and servants to flee, then helped facilitate the hasty departure. The family had established good relations with the Welsh long ago, but Baron Hugh was also a friend of King Edward. In time of war, there was always merit in taking hostage anyone close to your opponent.

On their arrival at this small family holding, he was grateful that those he loved had withstood the perils of the journey, icy temperatures, and relentless rain. When joyful shouts from the attending women and the vigorous cries of a newborn reached his ears, he had thanked God with deeply felt gratitude that his prioress' sister-in-law had survived the ordeal of birthing a healthy child.

As for himself, he had not cared whether he became a prisoner of the Welsh princes, escaped, or died in the attempt. At the moment, he thought, dying might have been best as long as the others had reached safety.

Finding the din of merchants calling out to friends and customers too much for his dour mood, Thomas turned away and entered the more congenial dimness of a nearby inn.

———

The place smelled of old sweat, sour ale, and burned fat. There were few men inside. Some looked up at him under heavy brows and with unfriendly curiosity. Others turned around, scowled, and rudely stared.

The burly innkeeper came over and noted the monk's tonsure. "If you want lodging, go to the abbey. If you want to break your fast, I'll give you enough to cleanse a sin or two from my soul, but you had best be on your way to holier ground than this inn." He left no doubt that he wanted Thomas gone.

Thomas was not in the mood to explain why he had come to this village or to mention the highborn family he had accompanied. "If you have the butt of a bread loaf and some weak ale, I shall be grateful," he said, keeping his inflection meek. When he left the Wynethorpe hunting lodge early this morning to first wander in the silent forest and then to cross the river into the village, he had not been interested in breaking his fast. It was only now that he realized his body demanded sustenance despite his melancholy.

In short order, both items were thumped down in front of him by the sullen innkeeper.

The bread end was so old it might have been mistaken for a rock. The ale stank.

Thomas did not even blink at the foul offering. The meal suited his mood.

He fell into a wordless musing as he took his eating knife,

sawed the bread into bits, and dipped them into the ale to soften the hardness. Cautious of his teeth, he began to gnaw.

"You think that stranger's a Welshman," a man at the closest table said, not bothering to keep his voice down.

"He has a tonsure. The Welsh aren't Christians," the man sitting across from him replied.

"A few are," replied a third man, "or so some claim."

"Who says? The Devil?"

There was a ragged burst of appreciative laughter.

"Ah, let him be. Wido'll get the stranger off to the abbey, and that'll be the end of it."

The first man turned around briefly and pointedly glared at the monk. "Not so sure you're right. Don't trust a man with red hair. No proper Englishman has that coloring. Maybe he's a Welsh spy. We've had enough traitors here, pretending to be loyal to the king."

"And we hanged that one."

The man across the table nodded. "He won't sit there long. Even the birds can't eat bread that old. As for where he comes from and why, let the abbey decide."

The first man grumbled something inaudible.

"The abbot is loyal enough. As for that tonsured fellow, if he's honest, we should pity him. With that hue of fur on his head, everyone knows what kind of sin his parents committed to beget him!"

After another round of laughter, the trio went back to their jacks of ale and complaints over the weather, the harvest, and rumors about the war.

Thomas sighed, dipped another piece of bread into the ale, and stared out the door. The color of his hair had always been the cause of jests, some cruel and others meant with innocent humor, however misguided. He no longer reacted to the suggestion that his parents must have coupled while his mother was suffering her courses, an act deemed sinful by the Church, and he most certainly was not about to give an angry retort to these men.

His head ached with weariness. He had spent the night hours after their arrival helping his prioress comfort her younger brother whose wife was enduring a hard birthing, an agony for which the man blamed himself. Thomas liked this brother and understood his suffering. Not only did Robert agonize because Death seemed to desire his wife, but he suffered guilt over his part in putting Elizabeth into danger. God may have cursed Eve with the torture of childbirth, he often thought, but He also condemned Adam to the impotent anguish of watching her.

The monk narrowed his eyes and glared at the inn door. The mocking sun seemed determined to follow him and was now directing a beam of light that reached toward him like an imp's beckoning hand. In the brightness, dust motes danced, ridiculing his sad humor.

Thomas shut his eyes and swallowed the hard bite of stale bread.

It had not been long after Prioress Eleanor, Sister Anne, and he had returned from the Hospitaller priory in Somerset that Robert sent word that his wife was expecting their second child. Unlike the first pregnancy, she was having problems that worried him, and he begged for Sister Anne's help. Without hesitation, Prioress Eleanor set off with sub-infirmarian and monk in tow.

For Thomas, this second journey had brought him personal misery. He had not heard from the merchant, Durant, for months, even though he had sent a message through the journeyman who delivered wine from him to the priory. Because the monk had been in a relatively remote area in the Marcher lands, and was now stranded in this tiny border town, he had no hope of either getting a message from Durant or discreetly sending another. He was distraught with worry and could do nothing to ease his anxiety. All he wanted to do was return to Tyndal. In the meantime, his soul had descended into a living nightmare.

As if on cue, a shadow darkened the table in front of him.

"If you want to pray," the innkeeper said, "you'd best be off to the abbey. They have a chapel inside the walls and a church without."

Thomas felt his anger spark and fought to keep calm. Keeping his head bowed, he said nothing and rose. Silence was wisest, but he clenched his fists and longed to strike the man down.

Gesturing to a serving wench to take away the barely touched jack of ale, the innkeeper grasped the monk's shoulder, forcefully aimed him at the door, and gave him directions to the abbey. "You won't need to return here," he said.

Thomas swallowed his rage over the insults and walked back into the hurly-burly of the market square.

———

The sun apparently felt a continuing need to add to his torment. The bright light stabbed at his eyes. Thomas shaded them and turned his back on the cruel glare.

Unwilling to go back to the lodge where he would have to feign cheerfulness, the monk wandered through the stalls. Now that the more sociable aspects of setting up for market were finished, and the needs of those who wished to buy or wanted to sell took over, Thomas tried with some success to lose himself in the anonymous bustle of a crowd focused on profits and bargains.

A man tried to give him a fat pie oozing with meat juice, and, when Thomas refused, the merchant begged him to take it so he might gain some credit with God. As a kindness, the monk did and gave the man a blessing. As soon as he saw a filthy beggar child, however, he handed the gift to the lad and hurried off before the boy could even thank him.

Thomas turned away when he saw the butchers. The stench of blood made his almost empty stomach queasy. Instead, he approached the booth of a spice merchant, where the colors of the wares were as bright as gemstones. Yet staring at the wondrous hues failed to distract him from the cause of his melancholy.

Why had Durant not sent any message? Besides being a well-regarded wine purveyor to King Edward, he was also a skilled spy whom the king used when an assassin was rumored to be planning a royal death. Was Durant engaged in that work and thus unable to send word to Thomas? If he was, might this man he loved have been injured in a dangerous assignment?

The other possibility he feared was that the fraught relationship between them had become too much for Durant to bear. Although Durant had anonymous sex with other men, he could not bring himself to couple even once with a man vowed to God, nor had Thomas been willing to break his monastic oaths despite his longing to lie with the merchant. Had Durant decided it would be far easier to break all ties than struggle with this agonizing celibacy?

If Durant had not been so sexually reluctant, Thomas might have surrendered by now. What held him back was not so much that he prided himself on honoring his word—and his vows were sacred—but he feared the result of just one night in Durant's arms. His love for the man was far deeper than lust, but he also knew that such a physical union might permanently bond their two halves into one. How could one ever live separately from the other afterward?

So why had he not broken off all contact himself? Because he had never found anyone, even Giles, who made him feel so complete.

During this long silence, Thomas wondered if the Hell he suffered on Earth could be any worse than Hell after Death. His prayers had become rants at God. Hadn't he tried hard to obey and only begged for answers he could understand? What had happened to the Gospel promise of "seek and ye shall find"?

"What are you seeking, Brother?"

As if God had spoken, a chill of fear hit him.

Thomas looked up.

The man who spoke was younger than he, smooth-skinned, with golden hair and eyes so blue they looked violet in hue.

The monk blushed. "I was admiring your wares. The woman in charge of kitchens in our priory in East Anglia would give her best pots for some of these spices."

The merchant smiled. "I could send some samples back with you. Perhaps you could tell me what might please her most?"

His expression and words were so gentle, Thomas felt as if a balm had been applied to his wounded spirit. "I am Brother Thomas of Tyndal Priory in the Order of Fontevraud," he said. "I accompany Prioress Eleanor who has arrived here with her brother, Robert of Wynethorpe. His wife has just given birth."

"Then I have some herbs that might be of use for her as well. Who was her midwife?"

Thomas told him about Sister Anne.

"Her reputation is well-known, Brother, as is that of your prioress and yourself. Shall we go through my wares and see what might delight God's servants or be of help to a new mother?"

Although there were interruptions when a customer came to the stall, the two men spent some time going over the fresh herbs and pungent spices, many of which had come from Outremer.

For the first time in weeks, Thomas found pleasure in something and was grateful to this young man for easing a burden to which he dared not give voice. He smiled at the spice merchant with a gratitude he could never explain.

Suddenly, the merchant pointed to a person hurrying toward them. "I think that is a messenger for you."

"Brother Thomas," the servant said, gasping for breath as he stopped in front of the monk, "Prioress Eleanor wishes you to return with me to the lodge. She has immediate need of your assistance."

His first thought was that Robert's wife or their child had fallen ill, and he paled.

"Go, Brother, and we can continue our discussion another time. My name is Lambard, if you wish to find me later. Everyone in the village can direct you to my house and shop. In the meantime, I shall offer my prayers for the Wynethorpe family." His smile was both warm and sympathetic. "If medicine is required, I will send whatever is needed and, for the good of my soul, charge nothing." He motioned to his wares.

Feeling his face grow warm, Thomas thanked him and hurried off with the servant.

Had he ever looked over his shoulder, he might have seen Lambard watching him with great interest.

Chapter Five

When Eleanor returned to the hall after her brief conversation with Sister Anne, she found Robert and Abbot Gerald engaged in a conversation that might politely be called a very one-sided one.

The abbot spoke at a breathless pace. His hands drew great round circles in the air with evident passion.

Robert watched in silence, arms folded and eyes narrowed.

"Ah! You are back!" Abbot Gerald turned to the prioress, his eyes brightening with fresh enthusiasm. "I was hoping to…"

"You were suggesting that you take my sister on a walk through the village to your abbey." Robert interrupted with a rare sharpness.

Even in her weary state, Eleanor knew that the two men were at swords' points over something, and she was not willing to seek the reason or to kneel at their feet and beg tearfully for reconciliation as a woman was sometimes expected to do. Now that her sister-in-law was safely delivered and their anxious journey from the Marcher lands was over, she wanted sleep and was in no mood for the arduous demands of peacemaking. And that was something Robert should know, she thought with annoyance.

"I welcome the opportunity, but I fear I may not take more than a very short walk." She cast her brother a baleful glance. "Sister Anne will be leaving my sister-in-law's side for a short while, and I will take her place. I must also speak with Brother Thomas."

"I shall come with you," Robert said. "I have a matter to resolve in the village." He ignored her angry look.

The abbot nodded begrudging agreement, but his expression did not suggest defeat in whatever he had been so keen to promote.

After calling for a woman servant to accompany her for propriety, Eleanor and her companions set off.

The air was still brisk. The rain no longer threatened. Sunlight warmed the earth between the scudding clouds, and Eleanor was grateful. Her fatigue ebbed away, and she looked around at her surroundings with more interest than she had expected.

The river between the lodge and village was narrow as was the small stone bridge that bent over it.

"It is wide enough to get carts with supplies across to the lodge," Robert said as he watched his sister mentally measuring it.

She smiled at how well he often read her thoughts and nodded.

The abbot bent to look around Robert at the prioress. "I was remiss in not asking how your journey was. Am I wrong in concluding that you were forced to leave because of some danger?"

Usually, Eleanor could quickly decide how much to tell a questioner when many details might best be left out or were simply unnecessary. Her obvious hesitation annoyed her even though her fatigue was a reasonable cause.

"We had heard tales that a large number of raiders were close to us," she finally said, praying that her vagueness was not perceived as deliberate rudeness, "and my sister-in-law was near term. We deemed it wise to move to safer land."

"Of course! Baron Hugh must be with King Edward and sent you word."

Robert looked sharply at the abbot. "We do not know exactly where our brother is, nor do we know the location of the king." His tone hinted that further questioning would not be tolerated.

Abbot Gerald's look suggested that he was not about to cooperate.

Eleanor spoke before either of the men could continue. "I think I had better know more of this story about the hanged man whose spirit is haunting the village," she said, "since you have asked my help in this matter."

"It is a simple enough tale." Gerald sighed, signifying that he had conceded at least temporary defeat in whatever else he had in mind to present to Prioress Eleanor and her brother.

They crossed the bridge and now turned into the road which became the main route through the village. So small was the village that the road was the only one of note and widened into a town square, now crowded with stalls for the market day.

As she drew closer, Eleanor could see several paths that branched off from that road, although they were so narrow she could not see where most of them went. Behind the village was a thick forest that extended across the river where the lodge sat and became the baronial hunting lands.

Eleanor pointed to a low rectangular tower of dark stone just beyond the busy market. "Is that the abbey?"

"It is the church that serves the village and sits next to our abbey," Gerald replied. "It is of great age, plain and small, but it is also where all the abbots are buried in the vault under the apse. The cemetery within our walls is for the monks and priests. The abbey chapel is tiny and was only intended for our own monastics to honor the Offices and for each man to pray alone when his spirit needs God's comfort."

She nodded. "Now tell me the tale of the hanged man."

"We lie close enough to Marcher lands that some of these villagers are Welsh."

"As are you," Robert added, and then looked at his sister.

Gerald bristled. "Only half, my lord. My mother was Welsh but of high birth."

Eleanor concluded that her brother wanted her to know this for some reason, but she chose not to comment on the information. "Do continue," she said to the abbot with deliberate gentleness.

Like a wet dog, he shook himself. "The few Welsh here have always lived peacefully amongst us and never quarreled with English law or customs until recently. Such was true of this Hywel and his brothers. But Hywel became corrupted by the arrogance that infected those base men who call themselves princes, and he led a band of raiders to slaughter innocent English soldiers while they slept. When it became evident that Hywel might be arrested, he confessed to Sir William, a local knight and sheriff, and was given up for a fair and proper trial."

"Was the crime committed locally?"

"Near enough. Just over that border." He pointed to the northwest. "Methinks you crossed at the same location into England proper, for that is where this road goes from here."

Eleanor nodded. It was indeed the way she, her family, some armed men, and their small band of servants had come, but she had seen no details of the countryside in the darkness. All her eyes had strained to see were signs of the village which meant that the lodge and an easier birthing place for Elizabeth were nigh.

"The evidence against him was clear. He was easily convicted and soon hanged." He gestured to an area just beyond the village. "The gallows are on the low hill, at the boundary of the village and alongside the road. Do you see that passage next to the inn behind those stalls? That leads to the gallows." He waved generally at the crowd.

Eleanor squinted but could see nothing of the gallows. "When did the execution take place?"

"Several weeks ago. I cannot recall the specific day. There were no saints to be honored or other celebrations to bring it to mind." He frowned in thought for a moment more and then continued. "Sir William insisted Hywel's two brothers accompany him to the hangman and lead him by the noose around his neck. This was meant as a warning to others of their race who might be inclined to a similar rebellion against English law."

Eleanor winced. The man might have been lawfully tried and convicted, but she felt a pang of sorrow for the suffering forced upon the brothers whose only apparent guilt was that of kinship. She often suspected there was a thin line between rightful punishment of a heinous crime and the added extreme of sinful cruelty.

"His death was confirmed?" Eleanor knew it was a fair question. On rare occasion, a felon had not hanged long enough to choke to death and, after being cut down, had risen to his knees, gasping for air.

"The hangman is experienced and knows the signs of death well enough. He even checked to make sure the brothers had not tampered with the noose. After Hywel had dangled for the proper length of time, the hangman let the brothers take the corpse for burial." He shrugged. "I assume they found somewhere for it to rot. The villagers would never have allowed a traitor's corpse to be buried amongst loyal subjects of the king."

"Was he allowed to see a confessor?" Even though a man who had murdered Englishmen was a despicable sinner, he could still confess, repent, and find some mercy with God. If this man called Hywel had spoken with a priest, what reason would his spirit have to wander about like a hellish thing and even kill?

"Of course he did. It was Father Payn, but he was outraged because the brute refused to admit he had killed those men in their sleep. At the gallows, before Hywel was hauled up, our good priest told him he could not shrive him if he was not honest about all his sins, especially the most egregious one."

And it was Father Payn whom this ghost allegedly killed. Eleanor felt a shiver of unease as if the ghost himself had just brushed against her. "Were there many witnesses to the execution?"

"Most of the village," the abbot replied. "Should you wish to question anyone, no one will hesitate to assist. We all want this imp banished back to Hell." He looked up and gestured happily toward the other walls that were more clearly visible behind the church. "Now you can see my abbey!"

The stone wall that encircled the neighboring set of buildings was grim, austere, and black with damp. The aged and squat Romanesque-style church looked cheerful in comparison.

Suddenly, Eleanor was struck with an unbearable yearning for Tyndal Priory. It was dour and simple too, but it was her home and she longed to be back within its walls. Unruly tears crested and rolled down her cheeks. Hoping that no one noticed this frailty, she swiped at them as if a rude insect had landed there.

"You are weary, sister! Let me take you back to the lodge." Robert gently took her arm and firmly directed her toward the woman servant who had dutifully followed them in silence.

Eleanor did not argue. "Your wife needs me by her side," she replied, then looked at the mournful abbot. He looked so desolate that she pitied him. "We shall talk again and soon. You have more to tell me about this matter, but I must also send off my two monastics to examine the corpse and find out what they are able to learn." Her smile took effort but she wanted to be kind.

He bowed to her with courtesy and mumbled polite phrases.

Eleanor observed that he said nothing to her brother.

Robert seemed not to care, but his lips twitched as if he were struggling not to betray a glee common to the victorious.

And so the Wynethorpe siblings left the abbot and the village, returning across the stone bridge to their property and the shelter of the warm lodge. Although neither chose to speak, they could never remain at odds with each other for long. Their silence was companionable.

Not long after, Brother Thomas also returned. Worried that something dire had occurred, he had outpaced the servant sent to bring him back to the lodge.

Chapter Six

Sister Anne and Brother Thomas stood at the entry to the abbey chapel and waited for the monk within to finish his prayers.

"The servant should have told you that the pressing matter had nothing to do with the mother and babe," she whispered. "I grieve that you suffered so needlessly."

Thomas gently shook his head to dismiss her worry. "I could have asked. But, when I learned the urgency involved a corpse to examine, I almost laughed. After our anxious flight from the manor, and fears for the health of Robert's wife, I was oddly grateful that the new problem was just another dilemma for our prioress to solve." He looked sad. "May God forgive me for that. I owe this poor dead man's soul many prayers. He deserved more compassion than I just gave him."

She looked at him for a long moment with much tenderness. "Surely, God will not condemn you, Brother. Your heart is never cruel, and laughter is a sound we have rarely heard from you of late." She waited, hoping for an explanation of his recent solemnity or at least a clue to it.

Instead, Thomas turned toward the chapel door and nodded to the monk who was now approaching.

"You have come from Prioress Eleanor?" The man addressed

Brother Thomas and ignored Sister Anne except for a brief glance of disapproval.

Thomas read his meaning with annoyance and replied, "Sister Anne is the sub-infirmarian at Tyndal Priory, famous throughout England for her knowledge of healing and causes of death. Although her expertise is essential in this matter, she will respect the priest's body. I shall be the one to touch and view Father Payn's corpse. Nonetheless, I must consult with Sister Anne. Surely, Abbot Gerald told you to let anyone from Prioress Eleanor examine the body."

"He said nothing about a nun, and the cause of death is clear. One of Satan's imps killed him. Of course, you, Brother, may examine the earthly remains if it will help you vanquish this evil spirit." He again shot a censorious look at the nun. "I see little reason for a nun to be present, and there will be little enough time for any consultation. Father Payn's family will be here very soon, and burial must then occur quickly." The monk squeezed his nostrils together. "The body is rotting into dust rather faster than usual, I fear. That is certain proof that the Devil was involved."

"We promise to be swift in the examination," Thomas replied with gritted teeth. "It would be more efficient, however, if Sister Anne and I were both there should any question arise that requires her knowledge."

"I could summon our own infirmarian."

"It would take time to do so, and, as you said, the family will be here before long."

The monk bowed his head in defeat and gestured toward the door. "I shall remain close by lest the family arrive or you have need for me."

————

In fact, the examination did not take long.

As Sister Anne stood a respectful distance away, Thomas felt the priest's head for any obvious wounds, checked the neck for bruising or fractures, looked into the eyes for anomalies, and examined the chest and back for indications of violence. As he did so, the sub-infirmarian whispered suggestions about what to look for and then considered the facts he relayed.

When he had repositioned the body and covered it up to the neck for modesty, he turned to the nun. "I see nothing that points to murder, but you must at least look at his face. I fear I might have missed a subtlety."

Hearing the sound of people approaching the chapel door, Anne hurried to the corpse and stared down at the face with intense concentration.

"His lips are still frozen in a grimace," she said, then bent to look at his cheeks, lips, and quickly looked under the covering at his hands. "He has been dead too long for any informative color to remain. Decay has been rapid, and that hides clues to what might have caused his death." She frowned. "His face is purplish, and his fingertips are gray. I wish we had seen his body soon after death. These signs could have been his natural coloring in life."

"What do you think?"

She swiftly retreated away from the body as the voices came nearer. "There are no signs of a struggle. He is not a young man. Unless there are details we do not have time to discover, I would have to conclude the death was natural."

A loud wail erupted from a woman standing in the entry.

The two monastics glanced at each other, then hurried out of the chapel.

"The family," the abbey monk said, his hands fluttering helplessly. "Brother." He pointed to the man. "And sister." He nervously shifted one finger to the woman.

"Come with me, daughter," Sister Anne said to the sobbing woman. "We shall pray together by the body of Father Payn, and God shall bring you comfort." Then the sub-infirmarian gently led her into the chapel.

"Summon the abbot," Thomas suggested.

The monk nodded gratefully and vanished.

Thomas turned to the priest's brother. "Is it best to leave your sister...?"

The man grasped the monk's sleeve. "I need to speak with you first." His speech was rough with emotion.

Thomas suggested they step further away from the chapel entrance.

The man looked around, his eyes round with fear. "My sister knows none of this, but I live in terror for my brother's soul! He was a wicked man."

"We are all mortal and thus sinful." For once, Thomas was glad his own troubles gave these routine phrases the greater force of conviction.

"You misunderstand, Brother. Perhaps you did not know him well? I imagine there are many religious here."

Deciding there was no reason to tell the man that he was not a monk of this abbey, Thomas simply nodded.

Father Payn's brother tugged so hard on the monk's sleeve that it might have ripped had it been made of cheaper cloth. "He died with all his sins upon him. I know he was coming back from riding his whore when he died. He has been breaking his vows with her for years!"

Thomas replied with an innocuous phrase that encouraged the man to say more and managed not to betray his eagerness to hear details.

The brother looked apprehensively over his shoulder. Hearing a muffled wail from his sister from within the chapel, he bent closer and whispered, "When he was a youth, before giving himself to God, he saw the whore and Satan struck him with hellish lust. Even after he took vows, he followed the Prince of Darkness to her bed. I put my hands over my ears when he admitted the wickedness so cannot say how often she lured him to sin or how he managed to escape over the abbey walls to couple with her.

He confessed he had been caught by the abbot and whipped in Chapter many times for his lust, or at least he was until he grew too old to punish."

Will I ever grow too old to be whipped or even burned at the stake for my sins? Thomas wondered.

"And she was married! Her husband was a peddler who was rarely home and thus cuckolded while earning enough to put food in her mouth and clothes on her back."

"Did her man not know of this?" For one who covered his ears, Thomas thought, the brother has learned a great deal.

The man snorted. "A simple, God-fearing man? One who was witless enough to trust his wife? My brother pitied him but claimed he felt no guilt over how often he took the husband's spot by the whore's side in bed."

"With good cause, you fear for your brother's soul. Yet he may have given up this sin and reconciled with God before he died."

"Nay, Brother. When I came to watch the hanging of the Welsh brigand, I spoke with Payn then. He admitted he still met with her when it was safe to do so."

Letting go of the monk's sleeve, he began to scratch his ears. "Surely this itching means something evil is near," he muttered and scratched harder.

Thomas dutifully looked around and told the man he smelled no smoke and saw no signs of imps.

Payn's brother seemed relieved and stopped scratching. "There was another reason I knew she had been sent by the Devil to win my brother's soul," he said. "What godly woman can keep a man enthralled when her breasts sag and her face grows hair and warts? She had to be a witch."

"Do you know her name and where she lives?"

The man stared with horror at the monk.

"I do not ask so I might fall victim to her myself," Thomas said. The dismay in his voice at the very thought of coupling with any woman had been genuine for years. "But to know an imp's name is to have power over it, and in this way I may be able to exorcise it from the woman so others will not be brought down as your brother was."

"I refused to let Payn speak her name or where her hut was out of fear of the Devil. Even if I knew, I could not utter the words to you. My own soul would be endangered! You are vowed to God, Brother, and He will protect you. I am not so blessed!" He began to shiver and wrapped his arms around himself.

Of course he knows who she is and where she lives, Thomas thought. But he chose not to force the man to speak words that terrified him. Despite his condemnation of his brother, Thomas felt sorry for the man. Although terrified and dismayed over Father Payn's sins, he still visited him, and they spoke openly about the priest's mistress. In a way, the monk thought, he had never stopped loving his brother. That also meant he grieved deeply over Payn's death, conflicted as he was over the sins, and he cared about the fate of his soul.

"If Father Payn was known by his abbot and confessor to have committed the sins of lust and adultery all these years," Thomas said, "surely he tried to struggle against the Prince of Darkness and was given acts of penance to perform. It is therefore quite likely that the only sins of this nature on his soul, when he died, were committed that night—if, indeed, they were committed at all. It is possible Father Payn had gone to preach the virtuous path to this woman."

The man blinked. The light of hope flickered briefly.

"And so the only sins for which he must suffer are those we all commit as weak creatures of the flesh. Some time in Purgatory may cleanse his yet. Prayers for his soul would be quite useful."

Had Sister Anne not returned alone just then, Thomas feared the man might have fallen to his knees in gratitude, a gesture he could not have allowed. Unable to explain why the man would be committing a transgression by kneeling to one as befouled as Thomas believed himself to be, the monk would have feigned the virtue of humility and thus greatly compounded his own egregious sinning.

Fortunately, the man rushed into the chapel to join his sister in prayer before their dead brother's corpse. He was so eager to start his orisons on behalf of Payn, who was suffering in Purgatory, that he failed to say anything further to the monk.

Thomas was relieved.

―――――――

"Are you convinced that Father Payn died a natural death?" Thomas asked the sub-infirmarian a short while later as they stood looking down at the black river surging under the rough stone bridge.

Anne hesitated. "I believe less in ghosts."

"I agree," he replied.

Chapter Seven

Although Robert tried to persuade his sister to sleep, she insisted on waiting for the return of her two monastics.

"I apologize for keeping you from your task in the village," she said, pointedly changing the subject to let him know that further argument was useless.

He looked confused, and then replied, "Ah! That can wait." He grinned, hoping to disguise that he had forgotten the stratagem he had used to go with her and the abbot.

Eleanor smiled sweetly in return. She had always read her brother well, and the gray now evident in his hair did not mean he had grown cleverer in fooling her. With a servant in attendance, there had been no reason for him to accompany her, and he knew that. So why had he lied? She decided not to ask. Either he would explain later or she would find out another way.

A slight flush in his cheeks suggested he knew he had failed to deceive her. "Shall I leave you in peace?"

She gently touched his cheek. "Kiss my little niece and tell your wife I send my blessings."

"Have you need of anything while you wait?"

"Go, Robert! I know you long to be with them, and I am content.

Sister Anne and Brother Thomas will not be long." Playfully, she pushed him toward the stairs.

Throwing her an affectionate kiss, Robert swiftly left the room.

Rarely have I met such a devoted father, the prioress thought with pleasure. Then she began to pace around the hall to stay awake.

———————

Soon Sister Anne and Brother Thomas joined her and recounted what they had observed.

"With no evidence that Father Payn died by any form of violence," Sister Anne said, "there is surely no basis to pursue this matter raised by the abbot."

Eleanor knew she must disappoint her friend but struggled to find words to make her thinking clear. "I agree that is reasonable," she said, after a long pause, "except that Abbot Gerald will not accept your conclusions as adequate proof that nothing untoward happened."

Brother Thomas stiffened. "If he will not accept conclusions based on knowledgeable observations, what could possibly convince him that a vengeful spirit did not kill the priest?"

Eleanor was surprised at his impatient tone, then realized that he, too, was suffering from grinding fatigue. "He claims there was a credible witness to a ghost. If we can prove the man really saw nothing, or that he saw someone else and mistook him for Hywel, that would be a forceful argument. There are witnesses to subsequent sightings of this alleged phantom. Prove them wrong, and we will have won our case."

"Perhaps Father Payn was visiting his mistress that night..." Sister Anne stopped and looked at Thomas.

"And the peddler husband returned to find them together, killed the priest in a way we were not able to detect on such a superficial examination, and dumped his body in the forest?"

He shook his head with evident regret. "I apologize for offering such a weak argument."

Anne concurred.

"I wonder where the hanged man's brothers are," Eleanor said. "Might one of them have been mistaken for Hywel by this allegedly competent witness?"

"We do not know where the men are," Sister Anne replied.

"We must still question others, or at least some more thoroughly." Eleanor looked sympathetically at her two monastics.

Anne understood exactly what her friend meant. "I shall talk to the priest's mistress. She is more likely to confide in a nun of simple birth rather than a prioress from a baronial family." She smiled at Eleanor. "Gentle though you might be, you would terrify her."

"And I shall seek this Bardolph," Thomas said. "As for any others who might have seen the ghost, I spoke with a friendly merchant today. He might know more of this haunting, or else lead me to men who have witnessed the creature. I think it best if we do this immediately before memories fade further or rumors that we are seeking information cause people to improve on the stories they might tell."

Eleanor shook her head. "You have both slept little since we left my brother's manor."

"I slept while you were all awaiting the birth of little Alienor. Not all my time was spent in prayer." Thomas smiled to hide his lie, and then added with greater honesty, "I am delighted with the choice of name, my lady."

Eleanor blushed.

"And I napped after you returned to talk with Abbot Gerald and before Brother Thomas came back from the village. That rest was adequate enough." Noticing Eleanor sway on her feet, Sister Anne put a firm hand on her friend's shoulder. "It is time for you to sleep. If you need me, you can send a servant. The village is small enough that anyone can offer direction to the woman with whom Father Payn stayed."

Try though she might, the prioress did not have the strength to argue. After arranging for a reliable woman, long in her brother's service, to accompany the sub-infirmarian, Eleanor sent them off to discover what they could.

Brother Thomas had already left to find Bardolph.

Then Eleanor climbed the stairs to the solar and found the tiny room her brother had made ready where she could sleep without hearing the babe. The moment she lay down on her straw mat, the Prioress of Tyndal fell into the gentle arms of deep sleep.

Chapter Eight

Sister Anne had no doubt that everyone in such a small village knew Father Payn had a mistress and who she was. Nonetheless, she chose diplomatic phrasing when asking directions to where the woman lived.

Smiling modestly, she waited for the baker, who had been promoting the freshness of his bread as well as the honest weight of the loaves, to respond. From the delicious smell, she doubted he lacked customers.

"You'll be wanting the house in the middle of that close with the wall at the end. Just ask for Mistress Berta, the peddler's wife." He pointed to a lane so narrow only one person could walk through it.

"Is her husband home?"

He laughed. "He so rarely is that many of us call her widow. I'd take you there, but I must stay with my wares. Just knock on any door nearby if you want. We all know her well."

Anne did not get the impression that Mistress Berta was condemned for her union with Father Payn. Such was often the case with the mistresses of priests in small villages, especially if the relationship was of long duration and both were from local families.

The first door she knocked on was opened by an elderly but

spry woman who glanced at the servant by Anne's side, then at the nun.

"Well, I know neither of you," she said, but nodded amiably at the servant and then turned her gaze on the nun. "You haven't come from the abbey, that's for certain." She tilted her head and waited for an explanation.

"I arrived late last night with Robert of Wynethorpe in the company of his sister, Prioress Eleanor of Tyndal Priory. My prioress has learned from Abbot Gerald of the death of Father Payn. She sent me to speak with Mistress Berta about some matters pertaining to that sad event and…"

The woman scowled. "You needn't say more, Sister. The abbot's been wandering about, wringing his hands, and wailing about evil spirits. I shooed him off when he came here. The mistress is grieved enough without having to face this nonsense about imps and phantoms. And if you want to worry her with talk of souls back from Hell, you can just turn around, walk back to that hunting lodge, and tell your prioress that the abbot needs to find something else to fret about and leave sorrowing folks alone."

"I have no intention of that. I am more concerned with his mortal health when Mistress Berta last saw him. If I may ask a few questions, I will be on my way and not trouble her again."

The woman's forbidding gaze wavered but did not concede defeat.

"Perhaps it would give her some comfort if she and I prayed together for Father Payn's soul. Such was my prioress' hope and command to me. I swear to be gentle with her grief."

"Aye, it would." She almost smiled. "That is more than that mewling abbot offered. Come in. I shall let her know you are here to offer consolation."

Mistress Berta was a surprise.

Unlike the description suggested by the priest's brother and passed on by Brother Thomas, this woman was of agreeable enough appearance, albeit with plain features, wrinkles, and gray hair. No warts were in evidence, although she was missing a few teeth. She most certainly did not fit the common image of a seductive whore, sent by Satan to lure a priest into breaking his vows, but neither was she ugly. Her charms were a mouth circled by deep furrows, suggestive of a natural merriment, and a youthfully soft skin devoid of scars or other disfigurement. Her eyes, however, were red and puffy from weeping.

Sister Anne introduced herself, then reached out to take the woman's hands.

An instant later, Mistress Berta was in the nun's arms, sobbing with grief.

When her tears subsided, the woman looked up at the sub-infirmarian with much embarrassment and begged her pardon. "He was a good man," she murmured and called out to the elderly servant to bring fresh ale.

Sister Anne talked soothingly and avoided questions until she was given a mazer and Mistress Berta had calmed further. "You were long acquainted?" Anne asked, and then sipped. The ale was surprisingly good.

"Our families lived next to each other. We grew up together." Berta drank. Suddenly, she hiccupped, and her face turned scarlet. "I should never drink when I've been crying."

"Take a deep breath and hold it for a moment. Press your hand against your chest, just here." She showed her. "Then drink very slowly. It will ease a little of your pain." The nun waited until the woman swallowed without ill effect and then continued. "You were friends from an early age, then."

"Aye! More like brother and sister, or so many said. Our parents jested, saying we were like pups from the same litter when we ran out the door and saw one another. Our families decided we would marry one day." She rubbed her eyes and struggled not to weep again.

Anne did not ask why this had not occurred, hoping she would soon learn.

"When we were older, we wanted to marry and even lay together, assuming God would forgive us for anticipating the wedding day we expected soon." She looked at the nun as if seeking forgiveness.

"A deed not uncommon amongst the young," Anne said gently. In truth, she found no sin in that, having bedded her own husband before the marriage vows were uttered. Even after her spouse became Brother John, he never claimed that they had sinned in so doing, for a betrothal was as binding as the later church door vows.

"And so we all believed, until a vile plague hit our village and many died. Payn's family survived, as did mine, but his father decided he owed God a gift for His mercy. His offering was to give his son to the abbey." Mistress Berta turned her head away to hide a sorrow she had never shaken off.

"Had he no other son to give or had Payn discovered a calling after surviving death?"

"At that point, he was the youngest, and his only future would have been to work for his father as a baker and, later, the older brother." She covered her eyes. "Afterwards, his mother bore another son and a daughter, but, by that time, it was too late to change their decision. The daughter was allowed to marry. The youngest brother was apprenticed to the smithy after that man's own son died. Opportunities in the village had changed."

Anne decided that the last two children were the ones she and Brother Thomas had met at the abbey. The eldest must be the baker from whom she had asked directions, unless he had since died and another taken his place. A village this small would only have one.

"So Payn was sent to the abbey, there being no other trade he could have followed here. He argued that he had no religious vocation, wanted to marry me, and would take on whatever labor there was to earn our keep. His father insisted that giving up the world and taking vows out of gratitude for God's mercy could be any man's calling."

"And thus he became Father Payn."

"His parents rejected much of the world too. His father turned the bakery over to his eldest son. The parents spent most of their time kneeling in the abbey church, other than the times they lay together to bring forth two more children."

Anne noted the bitterness in the woman's words.

Mistress Berta bowed her head and sighed. "Forgive me, Sister. I should not offend your vows and blessedly chaste life by speaking of such matters. I have no right to criticize them, for I am the worst of sinners."

Anne touched the woman's shoulder. "We all sin," she said, "and I entered the religious life after being married for several years. Remember that God loves a kind heart, faults and all. It is the sanctimony of hypocrites that He curses."

"I confess I resented them for not draping themselves in celibacy and still finding solace with each other in bed when they demanded that Payn and I deny ourselves the same comfort."

The sub-infirmarian nodded.

"He and I were unable to stay apart, although both of us spent hours begging God for the strength to do so. I even married a man who needed a wife to cook and mend for him when he came home from his travels on the road. The peddler is a kind man but has spent little enough time in my bed. For my sins, God has also cursed me with barrenness."

With no warning, she began to sway.

Rushing to her side to keep her from toppling, Anne eased Mistress Berta down on a nearby bench and put an arm around her for support.

Berta seemed confused and put her hand to her head. "My head hurts," she mumbled.

Anne called for the servant who took one look at her mistress and poured another mazer of ale.

"Drink," the maid ordered and held it to the woman's lips. "She's done this before," she said to the nun. "She'll be all right soon. It started after Father Payn's death."

The nun knew the symptoms all too well and suspected that Mistress Berta might not long outlive the man she had loved since childhood.

"I think she needs to be in bed," Anne said. "Shall I help you?"

After the two women had settled Mistress Berta into her bed, the peddler's wife fell into what appeared to be a tranquil rest.

"I think you eased her soul," the servant said. "Whatever the world might say, I call her a good woman who never hurt anyone." The look she gave the sub-infirmarian dared her to say otherwise.

"She told me her story," Anne said. "God may hate the sin, but she said she had struggled. He would have seen that."

Taking the nun's arm, the woman led her further away. "Their bond was chaste enough of late," she whispered. "Surely God noted that too."

Sister Anne raised a questioning eyebrow.

The servant shrugged. "Payn had lost his manhood. When he arrived at night, he was usually short of breath and red of face. I don't think he was well. They lay together, for sure, but all they did was hold each other in comfort."

Nodding, Anne realized she had gotten what she had come for. Father Payn had most likely died from heart failure on his way back to the priory, and, she suspected, Mistress Berta would soon follow.

"You and your mistress are very close," the nun said. "Have you served her long?"

The woman smiled sadly. "I am her elder sister. When my husband died, Berta took me into her home so I would not starve. Aye, I serve her, but we eat together and confide our thoughts as the sisters we have always been. As for Payn, I liked him. He made Berta as happy as she could be, given the circumstances."

"Shall we spend a few moments praying for their souls and that God will find goodness enough here to forgive all sins committed in this house?"

The two women knelt in front of the door where Mistress Berta now slept very much alone with whatever dreams it pleased God to give her.

Chapter Nine

Brother Thomas had a less fraught task ahead of him. Finding the young merchant was easy. As he walked into the aromatic shop, Lambard greeted him with a merry look.

"Welcome back, Brother! I feared I had seen the last of you." Then his expression turned grave. "I pray all is well with the family of your prioress."

"It is, but I need your help. May we speak in confidence?"

The merchant nodded, excused himself, and went to explain something to an apprentice.

"Please come upstairs," he said to Thomas when he returned. "It is easier to discuss serious matters over a little wine." He grasped the monk's shoulder companionably and then led the way.

As Thomas followed, he prayed none in the shop saw him blush. The man's brief touch had warmed him with a pleasure that was utterly forbidden and one he believed he had successfully banished. For a fleeting instant, he felt happy, then begged God to forgive him.

When the men entered the rooms above, a pink-cheeked manservant greeted them and took his master's orders for refreshment.

The living quarters were small but neat, and the room where Lambard took him was furnished simply with a bench and table, both smoothly planed, scraped, and apparently rubbed thoroughly with beeswax.

The merchant invited Thomas to sit on the bench and then sat at the opposite end.

"Your wife orders the house well," Thomas said.

"I am not married, Brother." The man tilted his head and smiled warmly. "I have been too busy with my efforts to expand my spice and herb sales beyond the village and so have had little time to woo a good lass. Instead, my manservant must take credit, for it is he who takes on the responsibilities of any wife."

The aforementioned young man arrived with a sweating ewer of wine and a platter of bread and cheese.

"Our guest has praised your skills at running this house," the merchant said to the servant and winked.

Turning to Thomas, the man curtly bowed and left without a word.

Although the servant's response had been just polite enough, Thomas felt he had somehow done something wrong. Or perhaps the young man was simply taciturn by nature? Concluding he was overreacting from fatigue, he dismissed the thought.

"How may I assist you?" The merchant poured the wine and handed a cup to the monk.

Thomas took a long drink, cleared his throat, and proceeded to explain how Abbot Gerald had come to Prioress Eleanor and begged her help in banishing a ghost that seemed to be haunting the village.

Hesitating, he looked at the food but felt no hunger and chose to drink again more deeply. The wine is good, he thought, almost as good as the ones Durant sold. The thought of the wine merchant sharply cut into him, but the warmth of the wine just as quickly began to chase the raw pain away.

The merchant waited for the monk to say more, then said, "I have heard tales of this ghost, Brother, although I have not seen it myself." He frowned, lowered his head, and folded his hands against his mouth as he thought.

"Who is telling the stories? Do you know any who have seen the spirit?"

Lambard glanced up.

He has the most beautiful eyes of such an unusual color, Thomas thought. For just an instant, he imagined them to be a sea of violets in which he might happily float. Then he squeezed his eyes shut, realized the wine should have been watered, and swore not to drink more of it. He set down the cup and reached for cheese.

"I usually meet with friends at the local inn once or twice a week. If you came with me, you could question them about the ghost."

"If it is the inn just over there," Thomas gestured, "the innkeeper was not welcoming to a strange religious breaking his fast there."

"Wido?" Lambard laughed. "He'll sing another ditty if you come with me and are welcomed by my fellow merchants. He's an innkeeper, Brother, and loves his coin. Wandering religious rarely have much of that, and he balks at the charity of giving gifts of his fare, even if it is for the good of his dark soul." He laughed again.

Thomas winced. The sound reminded him of Durant's laugh.

Reaching over to lay his hand on the monk's, the merchant grinned. "He earns enough from us all on a night like tonight, and I shall pay for anything you drink." He hesitated. "My soul is in greater need of help than Wido's and welcomes the opportunity to offer that small pittance, Brother."

Thomas silently prayed that the man would remove his hand. The merchant did.

"Where shall I meet you?"

"Here, when dusk comes and the shops are closing. Or you could stay in my house until this evening. Perhaps you would like to pray or even rest since the night may be a long one?"

"You are kind," Thomas rose quickly. "I have one more task to perform for my prioress," he said, grateful he was telling the truth. "Do you know a man named Bardolph? I must speak with him."

"A man well-known in the village, Brother! I can direct you to where he lives."

Thomas looked down at his cup, sitting abandoned on the table, and then drained what little was left. It felt like an act of rebellion, but he wasn't sure whether he was defying God or himself. The liquid burned his throat as if he had an open wound.

"Shall I take you there?"

"I would not keep you from your business any longer. If you tell me where to go, I doubt I will get lost in this village." Thomas did his best to smile and fought to hide his sudden need to flee.

With that, the two men walked down the stairs to the door where the merchant explained how to reach Bardolph's hut.

As Thomas walked away, he felt his back tingle as if Lambard was still watching him. What troubled him most was his hope that the spice merchant was.

Chapter Ten

Bardolph lived on the very edge of the village near where the gallows stood. His wood-framed hut with its turf roof was tiny but in good repair, and there was a garden next to it that showed evidence of recent harvesting. On the edge of the plot sat a woven willow basket filled with onions, white beets with bright green tops, and parsnips.

Thomas knocked on the rough wooden door and was surprised when he saw the man who opened it. Because he had been described as such a reliable witness, the monk had imagined that Bardolph would be a person of more venerable age, the kind usually accorded more respect. Instead, he was closer in years to Thomas.

The monk explained he had come about the ghost.

Bardolph tilted his head in surprise but invited him in. "Some ale? It is fresh."

"I would welcome it." Ale, he decided, would counter the aftertaste of Lambard's wine which had turned bitter in his mouth.

Thomas looked around. The inside contained only one room. The floor was covered with a fresh layer of straw, and whatever few possessions the man owned must have been stored in the small chest near his narrow bed. Although there was no indication of any woman living here, the place was neat. The small, carefully contained fire in the center provided a dim, albeit cheerful light, and there was a smoky smell of recently roasted meat.

Bardolph gestured to a spot on the floor near the fire for them to sit. Handing a filled mazer to the monk and placing a clay pitcher between them, he sat with legs crossed, then folded his arms and waited for his uninvited visitor to speak.

"Abbot Gerald has approached my prioress, Eleanor of Tyndal Priory, who has come here with her brother, Robert of Wynethorpe, about the death of his priest."

Bardolph nodded. "And he has told you that I found the corpse and saw the killer."

"Did you see a ghost or a mortal?" Thomas liked that the man was plain-spoken without being rude.

"Indubitably a ghost." He smiled. "Lest you think I am wont to spectral imaginings, Brother, I assure you that I am not. It was Hywel. No doubt about it."

"Not an angry husband or anyone else with a grievance against the priest?"

"Most certainly not, nor was he either of Hywel's two brothers."

Thomas had already come close to insulting the man by questioning his observations. With some, those who lied or evaded questions, it did not matter if he was abrupt and suspicious, but Bardolph had shown a willingness to reply and seemed a reasonable man.

As if reading the monk's mind, Bardolph grinned. "If I were you, I would question how I could be so convinced. Am I correct?"

Thomas laughed and nodded, then complimented the man on the quality of the ale.

Bardolph refilled his guest's mazer and poured more for himself. "I didn't just know Hywel because he lived here, Brother. I hanged him." He jerked his thumb in the direction of the gallows. "I'm the town executioner, which is why I live on the edge of the village and so close to my work."

Thomas was too surprised to speak.

"Oh, we don't have that many who need my services in such a small place. I earn bread enough by carpentry, mostly for the abbey, when the gallows are empty. But we have had a few more hangings now that the war is so close to hand. If Welsh rebels or raiders are caught near the border, it is simpler to hang them here."

"Can you tell me about Hywel's hanging?"

Shifting to get more comfortable, Bardolph settled in for a tale. "It was an odd execution. Not one I'd likely forget. There were two men sent to hang that day. Father Payn was the accompanying priest. The first man, a rapist and murderer, confessed his sins, and was given absolution swiftly enough, but Father Payn denied forgiveness to Hywel because the Welshman refused to confess he had helped slaughter the English soldiers. That was the crime for which he was condemned."

"Was there anything to explain why he would go to God's judgment with a deliberately befouled soul?"

"None. Hywel may have been Welsh, but he was a Christian and a dutiful one at that. He begged Father Payn to grant him peace, but the priest refused. How could he grant complete absolution, the priest said, if he failed to be truthful?"

"Surely there was some privacy for the confession. How did you hear it?"

"The two men shouted at each other. Anyone close to the gallows would have heard it, not just me, although I stood as far away as I could out of respect to both priest and penitent. My job is an efficient death. I have no right to be involved in what comes after for the souls."

"And no one wondered if there was a good reason why the Welshman refused to admit the crime for which he had been convicted?"

Bardolph shrugged. "He had been tried and condemned on good witness, Brother. There was no cause to doubt the justice of the conviction. Besides, the Welsh aren't like us, are they?" He fell silent for a moment, then looked away. "Well, maybe they are. Hywel was well-liked here, as was his dead wife. The verdict was a shock. I felt sorry for the man, but there was nothing I could say or do. Sentence had been set, and I saw no cause to doubt its fairness."

"Was the king's man there to represent justice?"

"The sheriff, Sir William? He did not attend the execution but did send a man on his behalf."

"So Hywel was hanged."

"Oh, there is more to the tale! I hanged him first and, while he finished thrashing in the air, I hanged the second man. Because that fellow was very fat, it took two of us to haul him up. When we did, his weight, with that of Hywel's, broke the gallows beam!"

"And both men fell to the ground?"

"Hywel was dead by then. I checked. The other man was screaming for mercy while I repaired the beam. Claimed he should be released because God had intervened and saved him. The crowd shouted that the Devil must have done it because God was on the side of England. He shat all over himself and was a mess to haul up again, but we managed. This time, the beam held. The crowd loved it, but I prefer neater executions."

"Hywel was definitely dead?"

"I was sure. Not only were the signs there when he dropped to the ground, but he didn't move during the long wait between hangings. But I pulled his body up after we raised the fat man that second time. The crowd wanted to see both felons swinging in the wind, especially Hywel, and I didn't cut him down until the other man had stopped jerking around. Hywel was dead, all right. Tongue dark, protruding. Bowels and bladder emptied. No breath."

"Was the body still warm?"

"It takes a while for a corpse to cool, Brother. Neither body was cold. I look for other signs."

"After you cut him down, who came forth to bury him and where did they take the body?"

"His brothers took his corpse. I heard they took him somewhere to prepare his body for burial. No idea where that was, though. My job ends when I confirm the death and release the corpse. There is a plot of ground near the gallows where such bodies are usually put. I assumed he'd be buried there, yet I never noticed freshly turned earth. I don't know where his body rots."

Thomas saw no reason to doubt the man's competence. The job might be a grim one, but Bardolph seemed to know what he was doing. He chose another issue to direct questions.

"Why would Hywel's spirit want to return to kill Father Payn?"

The man raised his eyebrows. "Were I refused absolution, I would come back to haunt the priest too. In Hell, does a soul care if the denial was just? The condemned have no reason not to indulge in great wrath, and Satan does love his wicked ones. As a man vowed to God, surely you have seen how he indulges them to spite the good."

Thomas chose that moment to drink ale.

"As for Father Payn, we all knew he had a longtime mistress in the village and never honestly repented the sin. We are all kin and neighbors here, so easily forgave them both, but God might not have been that eager to protect him when the Devil let Hywel's soul loose to wreak revenge."

"Explain how you saw the ghost, if you will."

"I was coming back from the village myself that night. It was a full moon, almost as bright as morning light. When I rounded the bend, I saw a man kneeling beside a body stretched on the ground. He heard my footstep, looked up, and stared at me, which is why I recognized his face. Clear enough in that light."

Thomas nodded.

"I did cry out, then closed my eyes against th sight. No mortal wants to see things from Hell lest our eyeballs fry." He offered the monk more ale but did not pour himself another. "Although I had had little enough to drink, I thought I must be imagining the scene. Indeed, I prayed I had. When I opened my eyes, the spirit was gone. I ran to the body on the ground, saw who it was, and determined he was dead. The corpse convinced me that I had dreamed nothing. Then I rushed to the abbey and told them what had happened. The abbot sent men to retrieve the corpse of their priest."

"Could anyone else have killed Father Payn?"

He shrugged. "I cannot imagine who had cause, other than Hywel on the gallows. Amongst us, there were some who had a quarrel with the priest. He had a sharp tongue on occasion, but no one hated him enough to kill. Even Hywel before his execution. In fact, he least of all. The stonemason was a good man, or so we all thought."

"Not the family of the woman the priest treated as a wife?"

"If this had occurred years ago, I might have conceded the possibility. But after all these years during which they coupled? Maybe her husband didn't like the horns she put on his head, but he is rarely at home." He smiled. "And he looks nothing like Hywel."

"The ghost has been seen since?"

"Others have claimed so, but I saw him only the once and that was enough. Lest you think me prone to such sightings, let me remind you that I have been the village hangman for many years. If there were enraged ghosts, I would be the one most likely haunted by those I have executed." He shrugged. "Yet I walk safely enough at night and have never awakened to any black-faced corpse bending over me with hellfire blazing in his eyes."

"Do you remember the names of those who say they have seen the spirit?"

"Men do not confide in the hangman, Brother. I may overhear much as I wend my way through the stalls on market day, but I never hear the full tale."

Thomas finished his ale, thanked Bardolph for his hospitality, and left more troubled than he was before he had spoken to the man.

Chapter Eleven

Eleanor was angry.

Surely it was too early for the next Office. Had she believed otherwise, she never would have begun this intricate review of her accounting rolls. Now that she had, she dare not stop. It was too important. Who was responsible for this terrible error? She must find out!

Yet the bells were still ringing incessantly, somewhere.

She fought to ignore the noise. She tried to scream for them to cease. No words came. She pounded the table—except it was too soft to be made of wood.

Slowly, the Prioress of Tyndal unclenched her fist, opened her eyes, and looked around.

"How long have I slept?" she murmured to the silence around her. Groggy and disoriented from her troubling dream, she struggled to regain her wits.

Sitting up, she realized the sun had moved far to the west since she had returned from the village with Robert. He had urged her to lie down for just a little while and insisted she do so in this small enclosed space, far from the cries of her new niece. She had been too weary to argue. Hadn't he promised to wake her in time to pray at the next Office?

Rubbing her eyes, she wondered if someone would soon knock at the door. Or had her brother decided to let her sleep, a kindness that honored the demands of mortal flesh more than strict duty to God?

Robert owned a kind heart, but he was as much a man of the soil as Hugh was of war and intrigue. The two were dutiful about the rituals of faith, but their first concerns were always worldly ones. It was only she who had chosen God to serve above all else. Yet that division of labor amongst the trio of their parents' children must have found favor in His eyes. Despite all their sins, the Wynethorpes prospered.

She rose, brushed straw from her habit, and walked over to the basin where she splashed cold water on her face to completely rouse her from the stupor of dreams.

Now more fully awake, she looked heavenward and decided God would probably forgive her for sleeping through the Office and Robert for letting her.

After drying her hands and face, she slipped out of the room, peeked at her sleeping sister-in-law, and then hurried down the stairs to find someone to tell her what had happened while she slept.

Had Brother Thomas returned, or Sister Anne?

––––––––

Most of the few servants in residence at this small lodge had left to perform whatever duties they normally had. The ones who had accompanied the Wynethorpes to safety had chosen to assist others where they could. Only one woman stood at the bottom of the stairs in case she was needed. When she saw Eleanor, she smiled.

The prioress stopped. "Have you checked on your mistress? I saw she was asleep and did not wish to disturb her."

"She is well, my lady," the woman whispered. "And the babe is a wonder! She rarely cries." A look of besotted adoration warmed her face.

Eleanor was both touched and amused. According to Hugh, she had been like a pack of hunting hounds in full cry herself at the same age, a description that would fit most babies that young, including her new namesake.

"And is Sister Anne here?"

"Not yet returned." The voice behind her was masculine.

When Eleanor turned around, she saw her brother, a fond expression on his face.

"Our Alienor looks like you at that age."

"And you remember what a baby looked like so many years ago?" She pressed her fingers against her lips to keep from chuckling. "I would have thought you'd have been outside, digging up weeds wherever you could find them, and not in the least interested in your new sister."

He gestured for Eleanor to follow him some distance into the hall. "I must speak with you," he said, his voice dropping into a grave tone.

The servant discreetly vanished up the stairs to the solar.

"And perhaps explain why you insisted on accompanying me to the village with Abbot Gerald, when you clearly had no errand there and I had a woman servant by my side." Now that she was rested, she was more curious and eager to know his purpose.

"You and I have always understood each other well." He briefly touched the tip of his finger to her nose in the affectionate gesture he had often used when they were growing up. "I do not trust Abbot Gerald."

"In what respect?"

"I did not fear for your virtue. According to all reports, the man adheres to his vows with impressive rigor. You had an older woman with you and are no innocent after all these years of ruling a priory and dealing with earthly wickedness."

"I was in even less danger on a market day amongst a crowd

of villagers, nor had I any intention of taking a leisurely tour of his abbey grounds."

"His sins lie in another area," Robert said, then shrugged. "He is an ambitious man who feels his talents have been ignored because he is half-Welsh, although half-Norman as well. Every time I come here, he finds a way to meet with me and beg that I speak to Hugh on his behalf."

"I assume he wants our brother to use his friendship with King Edward to urge our liege lord to offer the abbot a fine office, even a bishopric?"

"Has he also mentioned his treatise on how to conquer the Welsh, and how the king should rule them once he has put down their rebellion, while also offering himself as the best advisor in such matters?"

Eleanor's eyebrows shot up.

"He has already begun that campaign with me."

"He is not a man without wit…"

"But his ancestry curses him. We do not trust the Welsh, and it is quite clear from this recent rebellion that the Welsh do not much like us. A man born with a foot in each camp will be trusted by no one, no matter how valuable his insights might be."

"You do not think he has proven his loyalty by writing a work on how to dominate a conquered people, some of whom may be his kin?"

"I meant only to say I do not trust the force of his ambition, not his allegiance."

"Very well, but it is also possible that his choice may be temporary if we do not listen to him or he is dissatisfied with his rewards. Were that the case, he may change his allegiance to the other side and preach ways on how to conquer the English to the Welsh."

He stiffened. "A treachery that…"

She held up her hand. "Robert, I do not know the man well, nor am I suggesting he will become a traitor. I meant only to demonstrate the thinking of others, even our Hugh, in deciding whether to promote the ideas and future of such a man of mixed heritage while a war is going on between Wales and England. Should anyone suggest the abbot might be a spy, for instance, I would probably scoff. This village is not even on a well-traveled route. Yet men of great fear and little wit will suggest that to the king, as well as the other reasons to dismiss Abbot Gerald's views. It would be difficult to promote the abbot's ideas and even harder to suggest any lofty recompense. Not impossible, mind, but unlikely."

"If our nephew, Richard, takes after his aunt, he will make a fine lawyer in due course. You argue both sides convincingly."

"What I might question most is the likelihood of a man, who has spent his life serving God, having practical ideas on military operations."

"There have been bishops that rode into battle with mace in hand."

"Abbot Gerald? He has the strength of a sparrow before it learns to fly. I doubt he has ever lifted a mace. Again, I think him too ignorant of the reality of war."

Robert laughed. "Very well, but do you think me wrong to distrust him for his ambition?"

Eleanor shook her head. "No, but I think we must consider how he is handling his longing for advancement. He seems to be a very clever man and that suggests two things. The first is my purer conclusion. This work he wants us to forward to Hugh, so he can send it with his blessing to our king, may have worth, at least in part. I would be willing to consider its merit, especially his recommendations about successfully governing the Welsh once we conquer them. Even if we send his efforts on, however, we must make it clear to him that we cannot offer any promise that the king would even listen to his ideas."

Robert nodded. "From what you and Hugh have both said, I doubt King Edward will bother with the abbot's proposals. His anger over the lack of gratitude by the Welsh, after his generosity five years ago when they last rebelled, is profound. Moreover, he sees them as oath-breakers and traitors. The king is more likely to use the armored fist than an open hand of conciliation after this war. But what was your less pure conclusion?"

"Is there any way this tale of the ghost feeds the purpose of his ambition? I cannot see how it would, but there is much I do not understand about what is happening here. Could he be using it to his own advantage?"

Her brother thought for a moment. "It is truly a very odd story, yet I cannot cast any light on the matter myself. I do not come to these lands often enough."

"Although I have not told either Brother Thomas or Sister Anne about this particular concern, it is another reason I want to make sure we reveal what is truly happening in the village. Once the phantom is given form and either banished to whatever part of Hell it came from or exposed as mortal fantasy, I can decide if our abbot has used the creature as part of a scheme. If he has not, I shall directly address his more honest, if not strictly admirable, ambition."

"I wish you had not had this problem to add to your others."

She smiled. "The ghost may yet prove to be the illusion I originally thought it was. We also have much to be grateful for." She gestured in the direction of the solar. "Our new mother has borne a healthy daughter and both are gaining in strength. We, along with many of those who served us, have escaped any contact with southern raiders." She folded her arms. "Considering much, sweet brother, we have all had far worse problems than an ambitious abbot."

As they walked toward the stairs, a servant ran up to them. "Brother Thomas and Sister Anne have returned, my lady."

Eleanor softly clapped her hands. "And, if God is especially kind, we may be rid of the ghost, based on what my monastics have discovered."

Chapter Twelve

"This will not be as easy to resolve as I had hoped," Eleanor said after hearing what both monk and nun had to tell.

"The priest's death seems to have been God's will," Anne replied. "Men who show the symptoms Mistress Berta's servant described often die when the heart fails. If he saw something that startled him, he might have died of fright. Nothing we saw on the corpse suggested violence. What I learned points to a cause of death not uncommon among men of his time on Earth." She frowned. "I cannot understand why that would not satisfy Abbot Gerald and prove that no evil spirit committed any crime."

Eleanor looked at Thomas and shook her head. "I fear that the testimony of Bardolph, the hangman, still supports the idea of a ghost."

The monk nodded. "Although I wish I could say otherwise, Bardolph is as credible as the abbot claims. He does not seem to be a man inclined to fantastical visions and even jested that, as a hangman, he should be accompanied everywhere by a hissing mob of irate souls. Yet he has seen only one phantom in his life and that was Hywel, kneeling by Father Payn's body."

"And thus we must prove that the man lied, was drunk, or perhaps saw someone who resembled the hanged man." Eleanor sighed. "Is there anything the man said that might suggest any one of those three things was possible?"

"He claimed he had little to drink that night, an easy enough statement to confirm if he was at the only inn in the village. He swears it was Hywel and no one else, not even one of Hywel's brothers. The light of the full moon was bright enough, and, apart from the fact that Hywel had lived in the village for a long time, Bardolph did hang the man. As for lying, I thought he told the tale in a simple enough fashion. I detected no signs of evasion, but, being mortal, I am very capable of flawed judgment."

"You said he jested about ghosts. Might he have spread the tale to make the villagers seem foolish?" Eleanor hesitated. "Might he be sympathetic to the Welsh cause himself and have some reason to make people uneasy about hanging another such marauder?"

"With a name like Bardolph, he is not likely to be Welsh," the monk replied.

"Abbot Gerald is half-Welsh, and his name suggests a Norman ancestry," the prioress said. "Nor does English birth preclude someone from agreeing with the cause of Llewellyn and Dafydd. Some Englishmen distrust King Edward and may believe that the two Welshmen were treated badly by him. We mortals are prone to seeking justification for our dislikes, whether the tale is true or not, because it pleases us."

"Although I agree that not all Englishmen admire our king, it is treason to join with rebels. I saw nothing that suggested Bardolph was in sympathy with the Welsh or with Hywel. Although he had liked him well enough before, the man had been convicted at a fair trial for the deaths of defenseless men. Bardolph even hanged him a second time, although he believed he was dead after the first."

"You are most likely right, Brother," Eleanor replied, "but I mentioned the possibility only because we are flailing in ignorance, and we do not know the man well. Yet Bardolph's firm testimony does have a ring of truth, and he does seem to be a man disinclined to seeing what is not there."

"Ought I to confirm if others agree with Abbot Gerald that the hangman is a reliable witness?"

"It would be wise, Brother," the prioress said.

"It may be difficult. Bardolph was probably right that most people in the village do not view him with fondness. He seems to have no friends."

Eleanor noticed that her monk's skin was gray with exhaustion. "Do what you can," she said, "but I also trust your perception of the man's character."

Sister Anne shook her head with annoyance. "Despite Father Payn's death being natural, we must now verify that the witness to the ghost is reliable? How does that help banish the idea that this phantom killed the priest?"

"Unless we discount the tale that a ghost was seen next to a freshly killed corpse, there will be those who continue to claim that the Devil can make anything look natural and therefore the ghost still managed to kill the priest despite the evidence you have obtained. I had assumed that the priest likely died as God would have it and that the spirit sighting would prove an easily discredited illusion." Eleanor sighed. "Instead, it seems, the hangman appears to have been temperate in drink and in control of his wits. The villagers may not like Bardolph, but, if he is seen as a rational man, it is hard to dismiss the ghost."

"Yet he showed unreliability in one aspect of this strange tale," Thomas said. "Experienced though he is, he failed to prepare for the weight of two men on the gallows, one of whom was apparently quite fat. The beam did break."

"That does not mean he was fallible in what he witnessed that night. The beam could have been weak but flawed in a way the eye could not detect." Eleanor chewed her lower lip in thought. "What happened to the two brothers of the hanged man after they took his body away?"

"You still think one of them might have been the person kneeling by the priest?" Sister Anne brightened.

"If either resembles the hanged man, he might have been the one to blame for the priest's death. Bardolph confused the face of the hanged man with that of the live brother, and, if proven, we could dismiss the idea that a cursed spirit returned for vengeance."

"Confused in the light of a full moon?" Thomas was surprised. Had he not just told his prioress that Bardolph had denied that the ghost was either brother? "He seemed certain it was not one of the brothers."

"No matter how bright the moon, it will never match the clarity of God's sun," the prioress replied. "Did you ask Bardolph for a description of the two men compared to Hywel?"

Thomas shook his head. "I did not. He seemed so convinced that it was neither of them that I did not pursue it. I will try to find the two brothers," he said. "The spice merchant has also offered to take me to the inn tonight and speak with his friends. I intend to find out if others have sighted the spirit, and perhaps learn who has spread the rumor that the ghost walks in the village. I can talk to them more about Bardolph, Hywel, and the brothers."

"Do not drink too much ale, Brother." Sister Anne laughed.

"It promises to be a long night," he replied and forced a smile to hide his unease about this meeting.

"You have my permission to drink as you must, Brother. I trust you to remain alert," Eleanor said. "We must all confess our failures to observe the Offices as we ought as well as our engagement with worldly things that goes against the normal rules of our vocation. In fact, I believe God both understands and shall forgive. Why else would He continue to send crimes our way to solve?"

"And what more can I do?" Anne asked. "I believe your sister-in-law could do without me for a few hours."

"Then accompany me," the prioress said. "I think we should visit the sheriff, Sir William. He arrested Hywel and sent him to trial. There may be something in those events that points to a solution to this odd problem." She smiled at her two monastics.

"But now we should all rest, including you, Brother Thomas, until you meet the merchant. If this investigation grows any more complicated, we will need the sum of all our God-given wits."

Chapter Thirteen

The sheriff's house was easy to find. It was one of the few with two levels and the only one where armed men hovered like a cloud of flies. A few sat on the ground and shouted wagers as they tossed uneven brown dice in the dirt.

When one of the gamblers saw the two women in religious dress approach, he nudged his fellows. They jumped to their feet in respect.

One man carefully placed his boot over the abandoned dice.

"We seek an audience with Sir William," Eleanor said, carefully ignoring the sinful lumps of bone peeking out from under the man's foot. "Abbot Gerald has already sent word to vouch for the importance of our request."

It took only a few minutes for the man to return and escort Prioress Eleanor and Sister Anne into the sheriff's presence.

Sir William bowed to honor the vocation of the two women and the rank of the prioress.

Standing just behind him, with her head bowed, was a woman Eleanor guessed was his wife.

While the knight introduced the Lady Mary, and they all exchanged common courtesies, refreshments were offered but refused.

The prioress scrutinized the couple before her.

Sir William was no longer young but had not quite slipped into that age when other men had little cause to be wary of his strength. His rounded belly and reddish complexion suggested a fondness for meat and wine. Noting the man's swollen fingers and how he winced when he stepped on one foot, the prioress wondered if he had some pertinent health issues but knew Sister Anne would tell her later.

However, it was Lady Mary who especially caught Eleanor's interest. The woman was many years younger than her husband and carefully groomed in the fashion of the day. Her head covering was a spotless and fine white linen. Her robe, dyed a striking deep fern green, was made of soft wool. Those two items alone, the prioress thought, cost more than a simple knight could usually afford.

Although the wife's eyes were modestly lowered, and the lady remained dutifully silent, she had picked up a wiggling black-spotted white lapdog of indeterminate breed and held it in her arms.

Eleanor took an uncharitable dislike to the wife and quickly turned her attention back to the husband.

"Forgive me for saying so," Sir William was saying, "but Abbot Gerald spends too much time on his knees alone in dark chapels. Do not misunderstand me! Prayer is most efficacious, but surely even that can be dangerous when practiced to excess by one whose race is inclined to preternatural imaginings." He fell silent as if waiting for what her response might be.

Eleanor raised an eyebrow.

"He's half-Welsh, you know. They live like beasts in the woods and worship devilish spirits that hide in trees."

Eleanor was beginning to regret she had refused a cup of wine. "You say that the abbot is well-known for seeing ghosts and other things that no one else does?"

The sheriff pursed his thin lips. "I am an honest man, my lady, and therefore confess I have not heard that he has been so inclined. Yet I cannot set aside the influence of half his ancestry, even if it was on his mother's side and thus a weaker influence than his father's. At least she was Christian, and her family had wit enough to recognize the superiority of English laws and practices. Amongst the benighted, there are sometimes flickers of light." He straightened his back and looked very pleased with the excellence of that observation.

If she wished to achieve her purpose here, Eleanor knew she would be wiser to stay silent about her time spent in Wynethorpe Marcher lands and her familiarity with the native people. The rebellion against King Edward was a political issue, and she stood firmly with the English king, but otherwise she had always been rather fond of the Welsh.

"You do not believe the tales that the ghost of the hanged brigand, Hywel, is haunting the village?"

He snorted. "Seen after the sun has long set and, I would point out, when men are coming back after a night of drinking? As for the death of Father Payn, I blame his unchaste life. That was more likely to have killed him than some errant spirit." He studied his fingers for a moment. "Abbot Gerald is fond of repeating the wisdom of St. Paul about the wages of sin being death. Perhaps our abbot would be wiser to conclude that sin was the cause of his priest's death and forget about some hell-spawned phantom."

The Lady Mary began to pet her dog which yapped with pleasure.

"Why do you think Bardolph swears he saw the spirit bending over the priest's body?"

Sir William shrugged. "I cannot say, having had little direct contact with him other than to order executions performed. Nor can I suggest anyone else who might know him better. He is not well-loved in the village. What hangman is? Even I, a man used to bloody battles, would hesitate to raise a cup of wine with him." He straightened his back and raised his chin to suggest a martial stance.

Eleanor thought she saw a fleeting smile on his wife's lips.

"Were I to guess why he might have claimed such a thing, I

would say that he told the story to get attention and enjoy the rarity of people talking to him."

Realizing he had nothing more to say on that subject, Eleanor switched to another. "I have heard that this Hywel lived here for some time. What was he like?" Glancing at the Lady Mary, she noticed that her pale skin had turned quite pink.

Sir William shrugged. "If you had asked me that several weeks ago, I would have said he was a decent enough fellow and a competent stonemason who did work for the abbey as well as for me. If you need more detail about his work, perhaps Abbot Gerald can answer your questions, or even my brother who oversaw the man's labors on my land. I am too busy to be both steward and sheriff. But Hywel generally did have the reputation as a quiet man, one who honored the king's law, and he was married to an Englishwoman." He turned to his wife with a frown. "Your maid, Eluned. Didn't she know her?"

"Indeed, my lord," the woman murmured. Her lapdog, objecting to his mistress' change of attention to something besides him, vigorously squirmed.

"It was his two brothers I never liked or trusted," Sir William continued. "When our soldiers were butchered in that raid, I had them arrested. They had never hidden their traitorous sympathy for the Welsh rebels, nor did they have any witnesses besides each other to where they were that night. If they weren't the leaders in that barbaric slaughter, I believed that they most certainly were in the forefront of it."

"All of Hywel's family lived in this village?" Eleanor observed that the man's face was turning an interesting shade of vermillion.

"I cannot be expected to know his entire history. As sheriff, I maintain a residence here, but it is not my land. As for the parents, you must seek that information elsewhere if you think it pertinent," the sheriff snapped. "The brothers came to my attention because they got into fights with other men in the village after too much drink. The reason was usually how badly our king treated the Welsh. But Hywel was never a trouble until...well, it's often the quiet ones, isn't it?"

The prioress politely nodded.

"After I threw them into a cell, Hywel came to me and said they were innocent, and that I ought, perhaps, to arrest him instead. I was shocked, but what could I do? I sent word to release them and then jailed Hywel."

Eleanor frowned. "He confessed to the crime?" There was something about the phrasing of that story which concerned her. Hywel must have been more precise about the details of his actual guilt than what the sheriff had said.

"How could anyone not understand that as a confession? 'Arrest me instead'? No man would say that if he weren't guilty."

She bit her tongue from saying that she would have probed a great deal more.

"But I am a fair man, my lady, and would never send a man to the gallows without seeking confirmation."

She nodded but knew mortals well enough to conclude that any man who announces his virtues so loudly and often may well be lacking the ones he claims.

"And I found one of impeccable character."

Eleanor smiled with encouragement.

"My younger brother, Rainold, who had been one of the few to escape the slaughter. He told me that he had seen Hywel there, bloody sword in hand, but had not seen the two brothers. That doesn't mean they weren't there, but there were no other witnesses to their presence, the brothers denied guilt, and Hywel had, after all, confessed." He shrugged.

"Your brother had said nothing about the brothers' innocence until Hywel confessed?" Eleanor realized she should have phrased that more diplomatically and not so blatantly exposed her reservations.

"He was still recovering from his wounds," the knight replied with no indication that he had taken offense.

"Of course," Eleanor said, making sure sympathy was evident in her tone. "You said your brother was one of the few who escaped?"

"One died of his wounds before he could give evidence. The other said he saw nothing, although he knew the raiders were shouting in Welsh, and he fled to save his life. My brother remained long enough to kill one of the raiders, was wounded, realized he could accomplish nothing by dying, and also retreated. I found him in his bed the next morning with a bloody bandage on his head."

The prioress thought for a moment. "When Hywel had his trial, did anyone speak up in his defense?"

By this time, the sheriff's face was a regal purple, and he seemed reluctant to reply.

Realizing he would not tell her unless she insisted, Eleanor said, "If there was someone, who was it, and what was claimed?"

"I am an honest man, my lady, and I will let anyone speak if it is fairly done." He turned to the Lady Mary.

He is actually grinding his teeth, Eleanor thought.

"Ask my wife," he snarled, barely opening his mouth.

Lady Mary did not react and continued to stroke her dog.

Sir William abruptly bowed to the two religious. "I must beg your pardon, but I have duties that demand my immediate attention and may be delayed no longer over this matter of imagined malign spirits. I have real and dangerous mortals to capture, men who are traitors to our king, as well as others who destroy the peace of decent men."

With grace, the Prioress of Tyndal thanked him for his help and patience.

With a more respectful bow, he muttered promises of future cooperation and stomped out of the room.

The Lady Mary remained, and then kissed her pet.

The lapdog began to whine.

Chapter Fourteen

Lady Mary put the dog down and called for her maid.

Eleanor and Anne watched the dog rush to a wall, lift his leg, and let loose a pulsing yellow stream of warm urine.

Lady Mary giggled as she pointed at the growing puddle. "Clean it up, Eluned," she ordered when the maid walked in. "My lord husband will be ever so angry if he steps in dog piss." She turned to the two monastics. "He wants his floors dry," she giggled, "just like he keeps his sword clean." The lady widened her eyes, pressed her fingers to her lips like a child caught saying something bad, and simpered, "Was that naughty of me to say?"

Eleanor glanced at her sub-infirmarian and wondered if Sister Anne was finding this woman as easy to dislike as she was.

Eluned had knelt and was wiping up the mess.

"Wash the rag out right away. We mustn't waste cloth." The mistress of the house bent down, and the small dog raced back into her arms.

At least she seems to love something besides herself, the prioress concluded and chose not to ponder whether she was being too judgmental.

The maid left the room with her hand under the dripping rag.

"You had some questions for me?" Lady Mary blinked with excessive innocence.

The woman's long black eyelashes were pleasingly curled, the prioress noted, and her hazel eyes had a gold tint. A hue that honors her fondness for rich attire, Eleanor thought, and then asked, "You were the one to speak in the brigand's defense?"

"Speak in his defense?" The lady looked confused. "Do you mean the deposition I sent with my husband's younger brother to the trial?"

"Most certainly that. If you spoke on his behalf, I…"

"I dictated a few comments. There was no reason for me to do more. But begging for at least some mercy is expected of a woman, and I am the sheriff's wife." Her tone was as uninformative as her expression.

Eluned slipped back into the room, softly shut the door behind her, and stood in silence with her back to the wall.

"Do you remember what you said in that affidavit?" Eleanor had not forgotten Sir William's reaction when she asked if someone had spoken in defense of Hywel at the trial. If the Lady Mary had only performed the perfunctory duty of asking mercy because she was the sheriff's wife, he would not have stormed out in a rage, a response that suggested more than a hint of jealousy.

"I said nothing that would help you in this strange matter of ghosts. Indeed, I had had no contact with the man myself." She gestured at Eluned. "You were the one who knew him," she said to her maid. "I begged for compassion on the man's behalf as a favor to you."

The prioress decided that mistress and maid were well-matched. Neither showed any hint of authentic emotion or opinion. If Eluned was angry, embarrassed, or otherwise upset, there was no traitorous color that washed over her cheeks to betray her. The Lady Mary resembled an overindulged child dressed up in adult robes.

"You were gracious as you always are, my lady," the maid said after a brief hesitation, then turned to the prioress with a steady gaze.

Eleanor liked that directness and was relieved that the maid was not another simpering fool. "What did you know of Hywel?"

"Hywel was the widower of a woman in the village with whom I had long been friends. She and I were like sisters. I had always thought well of the man for the loving kindness he bore her and the care he gave after she fell ill and until her death."

"He was Welsh and she English?"

"Yet her family offered no true objection to the marriage, although they might have preferred a different match. He was a talented stonemason with much work at the abbey and other places nearby..."

"Including for my husband," Lady Mary interjected.

Eluned bowed her head as if especially grateful for that favor. "He was never one to tarry at the inn or seek the company of men who were better known for their sins than their craft."

Putting the maid's accent together with her name, Eleanor smiled. "You are Welsh?"

A wary look flashed in Eluned's eyes, but she quickly countered it with a gaze of appropriate humility. "There are a very few of us here, my lady. We came with our English masters from Marcher lands. My family continued in service to our English lords. Hywel's kin was freed to practice the stonemason craft for all who needed it. This is a small village, and no one else nearby could offer the skills he and his dead father had." She shrugged. "We have always lived together in peace, but this last rebellion has caused a rift of suspicion. Nonetheless, Hywel's skills were still in demand."

"And my husband has kept you on in his service." The Lady Mary pursed her lips, not in contempt but more like a child who was prone to sulking even when there was nothing about which to pout.

"As a great kindness," Eluned replied with a look of gratitude at her mistress, and then she turned back to the two religious. "My parents and siblings are all dead. Were it not for the charity of Sir William and his good wife, I would be starving and forced to find my shelter in the forest."

Eleanor wondered if Sir William had another reason for keeping the woman in his service. Eluned owned some beauty with her pale skin, gray eyes, and black hair. She looked back at the man's wife and repeated her question about what the lady had said in her offered testimony.

"All I did," the Lady Mary said with a hint of annoyance, "was offer my testimony that Hywel, although accused of treason against our king, had always been known in this village as a sober man, a skilled craftsman, and a faithful husband to an English wife. As such, I begged some mercy for him in the sentencing." She lifted her chin in defiance. "No one thought it odd that I did so."

Except your husband, the prioress thought. "You are certain you never had any actual contact with him?"

That question was waved away with a lazy toss of the woman's hand. "Of course not! I do not interact with stonemasons. Rainold, my husband's younger brother, had dealings with him and had no issue with the simple statement I offered on the brigand's behalf. That was all."

Yet he was the one who testified against Hywel. Eleanor thought that was an interesting twist to the tale.

Eluned coughed.

Her mistress' cheeks flushed a charming pink. "Oh, I forgot that! At the time, I did ask my husband if he could just let the man die in prison rather than hang him. Rainold had once said the fellow had never shown any rebellious tendencies. His two brothers, on the other hand, were rogues and had always been troublemakers." She lifted a hand to her mouth and tittered. "They once stole a horse from my husband's family and ran it almost to death before releasing it into a nearby field. My husband swears the horse was never the same after." She giggled again. "Maybe he never forgave the crime, and that's why my husband insisted on hanging Hywel."

Men had been murdered, let alone hanged, for lesser reasons, Eleanor thought with disgust, but she refused to be dragged off the subject. She was sure the Lady Mary betrayed discomfort in tone and manner when forced to admit she had taken the defense of Hywel a step further than what any noble's lady might offer.

The deposition was simple enough. No one would think anything was strange about that. It was likely a kindness by a woman of rank on behalf of any remaining kin of Hywel's dead English wife. That it might have been a favor to a maid as well was irrelevant. The men at the brigand's trial would listen to it read, pity a woman's benighted heart, and then proceed to ignore her plea by ordering the man's death.

Yet her husband seemed to think his wife's gesture was a little more than social custom. Perhaps because she had gone a bit further and begged him to spare the man's life?

Sir William's brusque departure, when the matter of his wife's defense of the Welsh stonemason arose, made Eleanor think. Might the husband have had cause, real or perceived, to be jealous? Perhaps he caught his wife peering through a window at the probably muscular Welshman with a less than innocent smile on her lips? After what she had already observed about this woman, that would not surprise her.

It was unlikely that the sheriff had actually found his wife in bed with the Welshman. Had that been the case, he would never have allowed the affidavit to be sent and most certainly would not have allowed her time to speak alone with two nuns. By now, he would have sent the Lady Mary to a nunnery, announcing with profound sadness that it was her desire to do so as penance for her many sins. No man wanted to be fitted with horns in the jests at the local inn.

"You must be thinking it is time for us to return to the lodge, my lady," Sister Anne whispered to the prioress.

"Indeed," Eleanor replied, realizing she had fallen silent too long and had no further questions. "You must look in on my sister-in-law." She smiled at Lady Mary. "My brother's wife has just given birth."

The woman raised both hands to her mouth in affected delight. "Your brother has been blessed! God never answered the prayers offered by my husband and me for a son." Again, the Lady Mary giggled.

Eleanor forced her grimace into a more courteous look of sympathy.

"But we have not given up hope. Abraham's wife laughed when His angels said she would bear a child although she was already aged. Soon after, she bore a son." Then she arched her back so that her youthfully high breasts became more prominent. "And I am not yet old!"

"I shall add my prayers to yours that this wish will be granted in the near future," Eleanor dutifully replied.

Then the two religious gave courteous farewells and were accompanied to the door by the stone-faced Eluned.

Soon after they left the house, Sister Anne turned to her prioress. "Sir William may suffer from gout and a tendency to diseases of choler, but treatment for that is the responsibility of his physician. Yet he was not pleased that the Lady Mary spoke on behalf of the rebel. I think there is far more to be learned about her and the stonemason. A pale skin is often the best detector of lies, and her cheeks turned quite rosy when Hywel's name was mentioned."

Eleanor laughed. "And we must also find a way to talk to the maid without her mistress present. Her responses were better masked, but I think she may have much to tell us as well."

Chapter Fifteen

Wido, the innkeeper, showed no sign that he recognized Thomas. He greeted the band of cheerful merchants as if they were old friends invited to his house, chatted briefly with them about family and business, then sent his smiling wenches to tend to their needs.

This time the drink was of good quality. The evening grew brighter, jests seemed cleverer, and Thomas began to care less about ghosts.

He forced himself back to his task. "Is it true that your village is haunted?" He very carefully enunciated his question to the man sitting next to him.

The man belched. "Aye, or so I've been told." He was a balding, red-faced man.

As if this were a vital clue, Thomas strove to recall if the high color had been evident earlier but could not. A tiny voice deep inside his head whispered that he had drunk more than was needed to share in the jollity and the man's red face didn't matter.

"Master Spicer! What do you know of this?" the man bent forward and gestured at the young merchant sitting on the monk's left.

Lambard leaned against Thomas and put his hand on the monk's thigh as if to maintain his balance. "All of you! Tell what you know. I already have." He leaned back and looked around the table. "Have any seen this spirit or heard others speak of it? I understand that Abbot Gerald is profoundly concerned, and our good brother here will take your tales to him."

The red-faced man laughed. "The abbot is the man to solve the problem. He speaks to God. What need has he of us?" He raised his cup with a flourish.

"To better learn the nature of the spirit so he can banish it back to Hell," Thomas replied and knew his speech was slurred. Although Lambard had removed his hand, the spot on his thigh still felt warm.

"Very well, Brother, then I will say that I have never seen the sprite, but I have heard of it." The red-faced man leaned over to grab the ewer and poured himself the last of the ale.

Lambard gestured to a woman for another and, when it was quickly brought, he poured a fresh drink for the monk.

Even though Thomas knew he should stop, he drank deeply and felt a rare contentment. For the first time in weeks, the black dog of melancholy had not only left him, but the void was filling with an increasing appetite for uncomplicated pleasure. He smiled back at the spice merchant in thanks.

"I have heard the tale too," another man at the end of the table said and thumped his jack firmly on the table in emphasis. "Might have seen it once on the way home from here after the last market day." He elbowed the merchant next to him, and they both laughed.

"What did you see?" Thomas knew his words stumbled against each other but doubted anyone noticed. They all seemed beyond caring—as was he.

"Well, she wasn't a pretty sight, Brother. Smelled like a ram in rut, owned a beard to match, and had teats down to her ankles." He winked broadly to show he jested.

"I thought that was your wife!" another man shouted.

"And I that she was your whore," the first man retorted.

Thomas waited for the ensuing roar of laughter to pass. "Has no one seen the ghost?" he asked when the gaiety ended.

"Come, my friends," Lambard said, patting the monk's back in sympathy. "This is a serious dilemma. We are all too wicked not to dread emissaries from Satan." He pointed to the man who had started the jest. "You made a mockery of Brother Thomas' question, but we all have good reason to fear such a thing hiding in the shadows, waiting to steal our unshriven souls and then carrying them back to the Dark Master. It is our Christian duty to aid in the abbot's fight against hellspawn if any have made a home here." He scowled. "Now who has seen signs or heard tales?"

The men fell silent. A few looked sheepishly at Thomas but shook their heads. A few admitted they had heard tales of the ghost but struggled to recall who had told them. None confessed that he had actually witnessed it.

"What have you heard about it?" Thomas looked down at his cup. The leaping joy he had so briefly felt was beginning to wane, and he longed to hold it close for a while longer. He drank more of the ale.

"It always appears at night, Brother," one man said, before taking a deep swallow from his own jack. "Or so I heard told." He looked around at his fellows. A couple nodded in agreement.

"And who told you the stories? Someone must recall." Thomas' small yet stubborn core of sobriety kicked at him with impatience. Why do they all deny knowing the source of the tales, yet insist they have heard them from someone?

Again, the men looked at each other. Finally, one of younger merchants said, "I think my wife mentioned that her neighbor told her that her husband had witnessed an odd creature skulking about in the shadows at dusk after the death of the priest."

The blacksmith frowned as if lost in weighty thought. "The sheriff's brother joked about it once when he came to my smithy to have his sword repaired, but, now that I think on it, I don't remember if he said he had actually seen it."

"My wife said Eluned, Lady Mary's maid, asked her what she had heard about the creature too. But my wife doesn't go out at night so cannot have seen it. She claims she heard tales of sulfurous imps from the baker's wife on market day."

"Sounds like the tales are just women's fantasies, Brother," another mumbled, "and we should all be ashamed that we have listened to their foolishness."

The company lowered their eyes, a few colored in embarrassment at their folly, and silence fell.

Thomas knew he would hear no more from them.

Lambard looked around, then raised a coin, and shouted to the serving women for more ale.

His fellow merchants cheered. All discomfiture vanished, or even any residual terror over Satan's imps, and their voices rose once again in jest. Witty stories quickly replaced tales of phantoms.

Thomas stared at his cup of ale two finger-lengths away. His hand looked outsized as he reached out, pulled it close, and gulped down the little left in it. The room felt unnaturally warm, and he was beginning to feel the weight of how much he had to confess in the morning. And what had he achieved for his sins? Nothing of use. The monk bowed his head.

"Pay no attention to them, Brother." Lambard whispered into the monk's ear. "I think you have learned all you can from them tonight. No one knows who started the tale, or else they blame it all on their women. The only thing they do know is that the story is being bruited about."

With the warm brush of the man's breath on his cheek, Thomas felt a jolt of long-forgotten pleasure. Hidden by the table, the merchant slipped a hand into his groin, and Thomas knew there was nothing he could do to hide his obvious longing for more than a mere touch. Nor, he suddenly realized, did he care to do so.

The merchant removed his hand and sat back, but his smile never wavered. "Let us leave, Brother. If the ghost is abroad, I know from rumor where he is most likely to be seen."

Not trusting himself to speak, Thomas nodded and rose. When he almost lost his balance, the merchant steadied him, tossed a fat purse on the table to pay for more drink to cheer his fellow merchants, and led the monk from the inn.

The men raised their jacks and shouted thanks.

As the two men walked out the door, the chill air embraced Thomas but did nothing to calm his lust. As if content to leave his body to sin, his soul seemed to have fled upwards, perhaps intending to join those cold stars that glowed with such a hard light. With no conscience, he was utterly bereft of any strength to resist temptation.

Lambard put a hand on his shoulder and directed him into a dark space between two buildings. When he gently pushed him against a damp stone wall, Thomas raised his eyes, stared at the star-speckled blackness above, and moaned.

The merchant knelt in front of him and slid his hands up the monk's thighs.

The sky above was as grim as death and as bleak as eternity without hope. Thomas knew he was weeping, but the sorrow was not about the transgression he was committing. It was because Durant was not the man with whom he was sinning. "If you insist on going to Hell," an unknown soft voice murmured inside his head, "then go hand in hand with him to the eternal flames. Do not do so with this man."

Thomas cried out and shoved Lambard away.

Sobbing like a wounded child, Thomas fled from the narrow alley. His body now shivering with the cold, and a grief that had completely vanquished desire, Thomas ran as if chased by the Prince of Darkness himself.

Any joy he had felt that evening abandoned him, and the black dog of melancholy howled with fiendish abandon as it clawed its way back into his heart.

Chapter Sixteen

Despite the bitter wind, the sharp night air, and the fleeting appearance of the cloud-scarred moon, Bardolph was in a merry mood.

He had drunk little ale tonight, being a temperate man by custom. Only twice a year did he drink more than was meet. The first was before his confession on Shrove Tuesday, the day after which Lent began. The second was on the night the Hallowmas season began, a period of three days when all the dead were honored.

Some claimed that the curtain between the worlds of living men and the souls in the afterlife thinned during Hallowmas, and mortals could communicate with the dead. True or not, he chose to honor the idea and drank to salute those he had hanged. He bore no malice toward most of them. Some were weak-witted or possessed by the Devil and blinded to the enormity of their acts. Only a few did he haul up on the beam with satisfaction.

His mistress always asked him, as she handed over that first jack of ale, if he truly feared the hellish things that might return to the Earth and haunt the ones remaining on Earth who had sinned against them. Although her tone was always jesting, her eyes betrayed worry that those he had executed might seek to do him harm. He inevitably laughed. It wasn't he who had condemned them, he retorted. He was simply doing his job.

What had made him happy tonight was the time he had spent with his mistress, Maud. A few hours with this jovial woman always brightened his spirit. Had he not become the village hangman, they would have married years ago, but he didn't want people turning their backs on her because her husband was an agent of death.

She didn't deserve that. The villagers all knew the two of them were lovers, but they could ignore that he slipped into her home in darkness and left before the sun turned the sky rosy. Sadly, he didn't even earn his bread primarily with a noose in hand. He was a carpenter, but only the abbey had steady work for him in that trade—and, occasionally, the sheriff.

Bardolph shrugged away that longtime complaint, as he was wont to do, and began singing a song he and his mistress had always loved, "Merry It Is." The lyrics about birdsong changing into fierce winds were melancholy, but neither of them was prone to sadness and the tune especially delighted them.

As he walked, he began to hum other songs and mused that all the talk of ghosts, coming after he had seen the specter of Hywel bending over Father Payn, had caused many villagers to come to him as if he could explain why the creature was haunting the town. Perhaps they thought his close connection with violent death made him an expert on malign spirits?

At first he had been amused. As he had told that red-haired monk, he didn't believe in such things. Of all the people here, he should have been the one surrounded by angry souls, damned by their own sins, whom he had thrust into the arms of the Prince of Darkness. But he could not deny what he had witnessed. Hywel, it was, and he knew the man was dead.

Then he grew annoyed by the queries. He was no expert, he began to reply when questioned. Go to the abbot, he advised. Gerald was the holy man to consult, now that Father Payn had been murdered and no new priest had arrived.

A gust of icy wind from the rain-soaked earth and nearby river struck him with such force that he almost toppled.

With no reason, he suddenly felt as if a bony hand had steadied him and something, not quite human, was close behind.

He spun around.

There was nothing there but darkness, or at least nothing corporeal.

Shivering, he forcefully reminded himself that he had walked this way many times. He was passing by the gallows and was almost home. Never before had he been bothered by anything from the Devil's realm. Why should he now?

Perhaps he would allow himself a rare mazer of ale when he got home. The thought cheered him a little but did nothing to warm the chill that enveloped his pounding heart.

On a slight dip below the road where the gallows rose, he saw his hut silhouetted against the ashen moon. Once inside, he would forget this unsettling experience. Forcing himself to laugh, he decided he must tell his mistress that she was, once only of course, quite right. This night he might have been stalked by something hostile from the world of angry spirits.

Bardolph reached out to open his door when he felt a touch on his shoulder. He froze. This time he had imagined nothing.

He turned around, slowed by terror.

A silent dark form stood there. Slowly, the creature lifted a hand and pulled back a hood.

Bardolph stepped back. "Why are you here?"

That was the last thing he would ever say.

———

The night watchman sighed with relief. It had been a quiet night, albeit a desperately cold one, and his work was almost done. If she were feeling well enough, his wife would greet him at the door with a cup of mulled wine when he came home. If not, she would have left something in the warm ashes of the fireplace for him to eat.

Trudging up the main road through the village, he braced himself for this last part of his required route. Sometimes he thought he would be wiser to patrol this arduous part first. Most of the time, he could never bear to start his night by walking past the gallows and the few huts on that sparsely populated side of the town. Tonight, he had chosen to do it last. If nothing else, he could then run down the hill away from the execution site and toward his home. Should anyone see him, he would explain that he was trying to warm himself, not flee any lurking ghosts of the dead.

But, as he approached a wooded bend in the road, he heard an eerie squeaking as if a door was swinging open and shut.

When he rounded the bend, he saw the cause.

Bardolph, the hangman, was swinging back and forth in the wind, hanged from his own gallows.

The watchman screamed.

Chapter Seventeen

"She looks like a small angel." Eleanor gazed down at the tiny face in the crib.

Little Alienor was smiling in her sleep.

"Not when she's hungry or wet," Elizabeth replied. "It is then we all become quite aware that she has a will of iron."

"Just like her aunt." Standing next to his sister, Robert winked mischievously at her.

Eleanor affectionately tapped her brother's shoulder and went over to her sister-in-law. "How are you feeling?"

"Weak but otherwise well enough. God was kind to hold back the birth of our daughter until we arrived here. I might have had the babe in the forest," she said, "and who knows what imps dance there to add even greater danger to the birthing of a new soul into God's world?"

"I have delivered babes in harsher circumstances." Sister Anne turned from where she was preparing a drink. She passed the mazer to her patient. "It is time for your steeped mint and nettle drink."

"Ugh," Elizabeth replied, but her expression betrayed her good humor and she drained it readily enough.

In passing the cup, Sister Anne casually touched the woman's forehead, hesitated, and looked at her more closely. "Do you need another cover? I wondered if you were cold."

Elizabeth shook her head. "I feel a little warm."

"I will come back, but I think I have another medicine that may help you heal faster."

Eleanor watched her sub-infirmarian leave and had noted her expression. It was a brief shadow passing over her face, and she hoped her brother had not seen it. Perhaps there was nothing to fear. Sister Anne was always cautious and very knowledgeable, which is why she was so successful in the healing arts. Nonetheless, the prioress felt a chill that had nothing to do with the temperature of the day.

A servant slipped through the curtains and came over to the prioress. "Forgive me, my lady, but Abbot Gerald has arrived and begs a word."

"The man's a buzzing fly," Robert grumbled.

Sighing, Eleanor turned to follow the servant. "He most likely wants to know what progress we have made on the ghost."

"Since he could not solve the problem, and put all burden on you, he should leave you in peace until you have settled the matter in your own good time."

"He has cause to worry, Robert. This is not as simple as it first seemed."

He tilted his head. "Not a ghost then? Perhaps this should be placed before Sir William. He is sheriff here."

"Whether or not there is a ghost remains a question. The priest most likely died a natural death, yet a man who was hanged not long ago was seen by his side. The witness, with whom Brother Thomas talked, swears he saw this Hywel. Others have apparently claimed seeing the hanged man since the priest's death as well. We are trying to find out what happened and what has actually been seen. In that, we have lacked success, although I have not yet conferred with Brother Thomas, who spoke with several village merchants last night. He has been sleeping soundly, and I chose not to disturb him after a very long night."

Robert shrugged his shoulders, then looked at his wife. Elizabeth had fallen asleep.

He looked over at his sister and whispered, "Then go and content this abbot. The sooner done, the sooner he will leave us all in peace."

———

Abbot Gerald clapped his hands with joy when Prioress Eleanor walked into the hall.

"I fear I have little enough to tell you," she said, then saw a large roll resting on a nearby table. With a silent groan, she suspected what it was and the purpose of this special abbatial visit. "We believe Father Payn's death was a natural one but remain troubled…"

"Oh, I have no doubt that you and Brother Thomas will solve this problem. What I came to speak with you about today is another issue entirely."

Eleanor closed her eyes and prayed the abbot would have vanished by the time she opened them.

As she knew would be the case, she was profoundly disappointed.

The abbot now stood with the mysterious document in his hand. "I have here a remarkable work that will be of immeasurable benefit to our lord, King Edward." He lifted the object heavenward.

"Indeed," she said, regretting that courtesy demanded she listen to him.

"Allow me to explain a few important facts." He took the stance of someone intending to enter into a long speech, feet spread and roll pressed to his heart.

Although she knew permission was not actually expected, Eleanor dutifully gave it.

"While my father came from a family who accompanied the Conqueror to this isle and fought valiantly by his side, my mother was Welsh." His expression changed into one of stony gravity. "Some men, even those of good faith, question my loyalty. Yet I swear to you that I am unswervingly loyal to our king. My mother and her family were as well, despite their heritage."

Eleanor nodded and prayed that God might be generous and grace the abbot with brevity.

"Although many say that my mixed birth can bring only sorrow, I have found the curse to be a blessing." Once again, he lifted the roll. "In this hand, I hold a work, a rare gift to our king, that none of his subjects of pure English heritage could give him. It is..."

"May I see it?" Eleanor reached out her hand.

Offended at the interruption in his well-practiced plea, Gerald drew back and clutched the document as if her touch might set it on fire. "It would be of no value to you. It is written by me in the finest Latin..."

"A language I both speak and read," she replied in the tongue under discussion.

The abbot's mouth dropped open, and he almost let the precious document fall to the floor. "I did not know that you..." Further speech failed him.

"Few women do," she conceded with a modest smile. "My aunt, Sister Beatrice of Amesbury Priory, raised and educated me in ways that would be of aid were I ever to lead a priory."

"Sister Beatrice? She whose husband was..." He gulped in embarrassment.

Eleanor simply confirmed his guess. Her aunt had married a man of greater rank than any owned by her own family and produced fine sons before her husband died and she joined the Order of Fontevraud. After her retirement from the world, she spent her days teaching young girls many skills, some of which were controversial. Learning Latin was one.

Clearly not a man who could be deterred from his purpose for long, Gerald did not surrender the document. "Even knowing the language in which it is written, the subject is a difficult one to grasp. It would take anyone, unfamiliar with the subject, much time to read. Let me explain it to you!" His eyes brightened with anticipated pleasure.

Eleanor agreed. There was no point in arguing another petty issue. She had shocked him with her comfort in Latin. She would let him believe she was of lesser wit because of her sex.

"It is a well-argued treatise on how best to defeat the Welsh as well as a guide in how to rule them once they have been vanquished. Who better to know all this than I, a man who respects the Welsh for their strengths but knows their flaws equally well?"

As she listened to him go into detail, she realized that his suggestions might actually have merit. His mixed ancestry had most likely been a reason he had never advanced in Church hierarchy, and she could understand his frustration when he saw lesser men lifted in rank above him. Despite his insistence that she resolve this question of cursed souls returning to kill mortals, the abbot was not lacking in intelligence, competence, or knowledge.

Eleanor held out her hand. "Let me have the roll, Abbot Gerald."

He actually blushed. "You will make sure the king sees it?"

"I cannot promise that. King Edward is in the middle of a troubling war. Although his eventual victory is in no doubt, both you and I know he has little time to concentrate on other matters now."

He opened his mouth.

She raised her hand. "As for giving this to my brother, Baron Hugh, I am sure you understand that he is no more at liberty to appreciate and enjoy the subtle strengths of your logic than the king at whose side he fights."

He looked devastated. "Then of what use is it if you take the work from me?"

"So that I may hold it until such time as my brother can consider your ideas and decide whether he thinks it merits a king's time to consider."

"That is little enough of a promise. I must be able to present my arguments to your brother so he is able to grasp the full importance and value."

She lost patience. "My brother is a man of wit and perception, Abbot Gerald. I can assure you that he will give your work to a learned monk who will translate it for him and answer any questions…"

"Translate? Explain? The former takes time, and no simple monk could possible grasp the sophistication of it by reading." He snorted. "I would be wiser to take it directly to King Edward and present it myself!"

"If you attempted to do this, there would be no guarantee that you would get an audience. If you did, you cannot be certain the king would agree to hear you explain all of it in sufficient detail."

He stared at her.

"I shall therefore promise you one more thing. I will ask Brother Thomas to read your work as soon as possible. He is a thoughtful man, thoroughly educated in Latin and Church law. As a devoted student of Aquinas, he is well able to understand subtlety and will present your work to my brother in a manner I believe you would find acceptable. If my brother agrees that the king would benefit from your work, nay even consider it, Brother Thomas will do all he can to assist."

Recognizing defeat, the abbot only hesitated a moment before agreeing to her proposal. He even did so with grace, although his eyes were moister than usual.

"For now, Brother Thomas and I must concentrate all our wits and faith in solving this problem of the damned soul returned from Hell. Once that is done, we will work equally hard to gain a hearing for your work, which, from what you have told me, is thoughtfully done and observes the demands of our faith for compassion to the conquered."

He bowed his head. "You are right to take one step at a time. The malign spirit haunts our village." Then he looked down at his roll and hugged it as if it were a small child who had skinned his knee and needed comfort. "I shall keep it for a while longer and read it again," he murmured. "Perhaps I can refine my arguments further."

Oddly touched, Eleanor assured him that his gift was not being rejected, only set aside until a more auspicious moment.

With luck, she thought, I may even have time to read enough of it to decide if it is truly worthy of Brother Thomas' efforts and a king's eye or whether I must find another excuse for delay.

Abbot Gerald took his leave with the sad grace of a man who believed he had been rejected as he always had been.

Watching him walk out, Eleanor felt pity for him. Had his mother been of the same ancestry as his father, he might well have been a bishop by now.

Then she turned to the servant who had remained in the hall with her and asked her to summon Sister Anne and send a man to awaken Brother Thomas. She could not delay hearing what he had learned any longer.

Chapter Eighteen

Prioress Eleanor and Sister Anne had just finished discussing observations from their meeting with Sir William and his wife when Brother Thomas arrived.

When the prioress turned, a smile on her face, she froze when she saw the monk.

Thomas had always been a fastidious man. Today he looked and reeked like a man who lived in taverns and disregarded the usual practice of washing away the stench of mortal clay that monks and nuns were wont to do. He stank of sour sweat, ale gone bad, and his eyes were an angry red.

Eleanor hoped the information Thomas had gotten at the inn last night was worth what he was clearly suffering. Her heart ached with concern, but she found that her mind was less compassionate. Her smile forgotten, she looked up at him with a mildly censorious expression and waited.

Thomas hesitated, looking at his prioress with a vague expression as if he had no idea where he was or why. Rubbing his eyes, he cleared his throat. His eyes slowly focused, and he said, in a speech made husky by the smoky fire in the inn, "I learned little enough last night, my lady, for the grievous sins I committed."

Eleanor melted in sympathy. "I asked you to get information

from residents of the village. I knew you were going to the inn. If you drank too much for a man vowed to God, I have no doubt you did so with cause." She knew she could no longer be severe with him, and her voice softened. "Confess when you get back to Tyndal, Brother, but I must also admit to my confessor how I helped lead you astray."

Instead of the expected calm response of gratitude before telling her what he had learned, he suddenly knelt and bowed his head to the floor. "I spent the rest of the night in the abbey chapel praying and wrestling with demons. When the sun rose, I left for my cot, knowing that forgiveness was impossible." Raising his head, he let his tears flow as he gasped in sobs. "My lady," he groaned, "I am a monster most loathed by God."

Horrified, Eleanor instinctively reached out to touch him in comfort, and then quickly drew her hand back. That was not a gesture she was permitted to make.

What had happened last night? He should not be this devastated by a rare overindulgence in ale, especially when any penance would be mild under the circumstances. He had always been a monk of moderate habits and pleasant manner, although she knew he had had long periods when melancholy owned his soul. Of late, he had grown unusually silent again, a sign she feared meant that he was suffering the darkness. Yet he had always fought against it. Why had he succumbed now?

She glanced at Sister Anne, but the sub-infirmarian's expression suggested she was as confused and shocked as her prioress.

One thought did occur to Eleanor, one that first struck her with dismay and then with a burning jealousy born of her own sins.

In his drunkenness, had he lain with a woman?

Eleanor felt her face grow hot and hoped that Sister Anne had not seen her reaction. Her friend was far too observant not to wonder and even correctly conclude the reason for her flushed cheeks. Looking away, she tried to stifle her selfish and wicked envy and argue against her fear.

Never once had her monk been accused of breaking his sacred vow of chastity. Several women had remarked that his virtue was saintly. In the many years she had known him, he had worn that vow like a comfortable robe. This was not a man who was likely to so easily break a vow, one he had steadfastly honored, because of one night of drunkenness.

She took a deep breath and felt her distress and hot jealousy fade. "Brother, rise..."

"My lady!" A servant, her face deadly pale, stood in the doorway to the hall.

The distress in her voice startled the two women and caused Brother Thomas to sit back and wipe the tears from his face.

"Are my sister-in-law and babe well?" Eleanor's voice trembled with a far greater concern than a monk drinking too much.

"They are, my lady. Forgive me for entering without permission."

"It is of no moment," Eleanor replied. "But what message do you bring?"

"The sheriff has sent his servant and begs that you return with the man forthwith. Sir William says that the matter is urgent, cannot be set aside, and requires your immediate attention."

Chapter Nineteen

The sheriff thanked Prioress Eleanor for answering his summons so quickly.

Eleanor noticed that he lacked his previous choler and arrogance. In fact, she concluded with some surprise, his sweat smelled distinctly of fear.

"Bardolph, our hangman, has been found dead," Sir William said, then turned a greenish pale as if he were about to vomit.

The man standing at his side clapped him on his shoulder. "He was hanged on his own gallows," he said in an oddly buoyant tone.

"My brother, Rainold," Sir William muttered as he gestured vaguely and turned away to regain his composure.

"Let me tell the story," the younger man said. "I know it best." He raised his hand and motioned to a servant just behind him for more wine.

Prioress Eleanor had already refused refreshment for the three of them, noting with relief that Brother Thomas had looked horrified at the offer.

Rainold waited for the servant to pour wine into his cup, sipped his drink, and savored the taste for a very long moment.

Feeling a sharp sting of impatience, Eleanor cleared her throat.

Rainold blinked as if he had just realized this might not be the time to muse on the quality of his brother's wine cellar. Rather than immediately getting to the tale, however, he grinned and waved his raised cup as if inviting her to join in a playful moment.

"You found the body?" Eleanor's tolerance had been tried enough that day. She didn't need this childishness.

Rainold put his cup down. "Bardolph was found by the watchman last night when he was finishing his rounds. He immediately informed me." He made a face. "Well, he intended to awaken my brother, but he saw me about to enter the house. I urged him to tell me instead, hoping any investigation of the crime could wait until the morning." He again took time to drink. "Why not let my brother continue to sleep? I was already awake, having enjoyed a meal and a pleasant evening with a friend. Does his name matter?"

"Tell the story!" The sheriff barked and then turned to face his guests with the gruffness noted in the earlier visit.

Rainold shrugged. "I had enjoyed my friend's wine, but I was sober when I left him."

"Did you notice anything odd on your return from his house?" Thomas had remained silent until now.

Eleanor was surprised by his sudden question but was grateful he had asked it instead of her. She wanted more time to step back mentally and study this younger brother who had testified against Hywel.

"On my way home, and just past the inn, I thought I saw a figure hiding in the shadows. I stopped. Even though thievery is rare in our peaceful village, thanks to the firm rule of law, a wise man remains wary." He bowed to his brother. "As I looked more attentively at the figure, I could not see his face, but I would have sworn that the light from the inn passed through what was visible of his body as if it owned no substance. Of course, the light was weak, yet I was uneasy."

Eleanor noted that he did not swear on his soul or by any saint. Then she wondered why she should be so troubled by that. He had taken no oath and was simply relaying what he had observed. She dismissed her concern as petty.

"I am not a man prone to seeing nonexistent things and decided everything was just a trick of light and darkness. In fact, he raised a hand and gestured as if summoning me. Assuming he had honest cause, I approached. The inn door was open. Many could come to my aid if the man had some ill intent. I felt safe." Rainold looked down at his cup, turned to the servant, and requested more wine.

"Get on with it," Sir William growled.

Eleanor almost thanked him.

His cup refilled, the younger brother drank deeply and then said in a tone that suggested fright, the depth of which he would likely deny, "To my dismay, when I got closer, I recognized the man as Hywel!"

"When was this?" Thomas was scowling.

Eleanor noted with relief that her monk had regained his wits and sounded fully recovered from whatever had caused his recent disturbing collapse.

"I cannot say, Brother," Rainold said. "When my friend and I are recalling our youthful errors, we do not listen for church bells or seek the position of the moon and stars. Nor did I care about such observations after I left him. I can only confirm that it was most certainly long past my usual time for sleep."

Eleanor liked this man no more than the absent Lady Mary. Had she not known Rainold was Sir William's brother, she would have guessed that he was kin to the wife. Each is inclined to an irritating superficiality, she thought.

Immediately, she rebuked herself. Her annoyance with them was probably due more to her inability to easily solve this spectral problem after she had concluded it would take her little time to do so. Chastising herself for pointing to the sins of others to disguise her own wicked pride, she chose to remain silent.

Sir William snorted and told his brother to continue. But even he summoned the servant for wine and quickly drained his mazer.

Rainold extended his own cup for more but drank more moderately than his elder brother. "I was shocked by the sight and stepped back in terror. In doing so, I tripped and fell. The cause was a drunken oaf who was coming up behind me. Foolish man! He could have called out and I wouldn't have soiled my favorite robe on the filthy ground." With a fatuous grin, he pointed at his elder sibling. "Really, brother! Is there nothing you can do about keeping the streets around the inn cleaner?"

"That is not my job as sheriff, you fool! Find another way home from your debauches!"

Good-naturedly, Rainold shook his head in mock dismay. "But I managed to get back on my feet. No help from the lout! He staggered off to the inn, oblivious to my plight. The specter had also vanished. I confess I shivered but concluded I might have drunk more deeply with my friend than I had thought."

"Did you look for the man?" Thomas tilted his head as if merely curious.

"There was no sign of the creature."

Eleanor was quite aware he had evaded her monk's question with an inadequate reply. Had Rainold been more frightened by the phantom than he dared confess? Had his pride prevented him from admitting he had no wish to look for a ghost that might have been luring him to Hell? Had Rainold even seen the creature? If not, was there a reason he would lie? A longing to step out of the shadow of his brother? She could not ignore the latter. Or was there another reason entirely?

"What did you do instead?" Thomas' eyes narrowed slightly. The prioress was pleased he had also observed the equivocation.

"I went home where I met the night watchman."

"Did he see Hywel?" Thomas smiled as if jesting.

"The man stank. He'd pissed himself," Rainold replied with a short burst of laughter. "I thought at first he had seen a ghost, but it was the hangman's corpse that scared him. He was quivering like a loose feather in a high wind when he approached me. I didn't question him. He was too terrified by Bardolph swinging on the gallows to see anything else."

The prioress lifted her hand as a sign to Brother Thomas that she wished to pose a question, then asked, "Did he take you to the gallows?"

"I insisted." Rainold raised his cup as if saluting himself. "It was Bardolph, all right. We cut him down, and I told the watchman to have the corpse taken to Abbot Gerald. Since I assumed Hywel's last victim had been buried, there had to be room for another in his chapel." He smiled at what he clearly thought was clever reasoning.

"And what did you do next?" Eleanor refused an offer of wine from the servant.

Rainold languidly raised an eyebrow as if he thought the question was too idiotic to answer.

The prioress chose to ignore the rudeness and repeated it just to annoy the man.

"Well, I made sure the watchman followed orders. Would you believe that he actually wanted to go home and leave the body for the morning? I set him right about that! I guarded the corpse until he brought some men to carry the body, and then I followed the company to the abbey. At least the watchman had sent someone to awaken the abbot with the news, and he was waiting for poor, dead Bardolph with a few sleepy-eyed monks."

"Well done, brother," the sheriff muttered. "We must be firm. There is little respect for duty and responsibility these days. Mark how a man like Hywel, taken to the bosom of our village, turned into an ungrateful rebel. Young people now disrespect their elders…"

Eleanor let him mumble on as she addressed Rainold. "After you had the corpse taken to the abbey, what did you do next?"

"Woke Sir William and told him the tale."

"And when morning light arrived soon after, I sent a servant to fetch you," the sheriff said.

Now the younger brother looked at his elder with a more solemn expression. "You know, I had always thought Hywel to be a decent enough man, hardworking and reliable. Rarely remembered he was Welsh. Even knowing I was right to tell you that I had seen him kill soldiers, I regretted that I had to tell this sad truth at the trial. Now that his angry spirit has apparently come back from Hell and killed two innocent men, I fear he must have been wicked all along." He shook his head. "Yet I grieve. It is well his wife has been long dead. She would have died of shame at his hanging."

"Her only remaining brother came to me and swore they were all deceived when she married him or they would have refused to allow it." Sir William shook his head.

"You are now convinced it was Hywel you saw last night? Might the phantom have had the opportunity to murder Bardolph?" Eleanor was interested in how Rainold replied.

"I saw something, my lady," he said. "I have never seen a vision, suffered dreams while awake, or been inclined to imagine things when I have drunk a little wine. I hesitate to confirm these tales, but I most certainly recognized Hywel's face. When I walked closer to him, there was enough light from the inn to see more clearly. And who else would have killed Bardolph? People here avoided the hangman, but he wasn't hated."

"Could the crime have been committed by one of his brothers, whom you mistook for Hywel in the dark?" The prioress tried hard to disguise how much she hoped he would agree.

"Nay. Hywel looked nothing like them. They are ugly brutes, low-browed, and hairy as Satan. They are twins, yet survived to manhood." He scowled with disgust. "But the Welsh are beloved by the Devil so their survival should not surprise."

Eleanor knew that both babies in a birth of twins rarely survived, but such births were believed by some to mean the mother had lain with two different men or even the Devil.

The sheriff began to pace in a tight circle. "I have never believed in ghosts, never seen one, nor gagged on the Devil's sulfurous reek on a dark night either. Yet two men connected with the brigand's death have met tragic ends. A priest? The hangman?" He stopped and glared at the monastics. "Bardolph was a good servant of the king. He was experienced, and the condemned died fast enough. He didn't deserve this any more than Father Payn. Both may have been sinners, as all sons of Adam are, but each was a dutiful servant to his respective master."

Eleanor was suddenly struck by a thought. The priest, who had refused absolution, was killed with all his sins on his soul. The hangman was hanged on his own gallows. Might there be a meaning in these methods of death? But were they revenge by an angry spirit released from Hell and seeking retribution? Would Satan even care about this comparatively minor event in a small English village when he had many other condemned souls with greater cause to wreak a more devastating havoc on the Earth? Some had claimed that the Prince of Darkness had a fondness for the Welsh, and thus would have favored Hywel's cause. But Eleanor believed that such a conviction was more firmly grounded in the biased passions of war than in anything proven.

Sir William slammed his cup down on a table. "I want answers!" he shouted. "Abbot Gerald isn't the only one who wants this evil spirit sent back to Hell!"

"And we shall do our best," Eleanor replied with dignity and far more calm than she felt.

"We have given our word to God, and sacred vows cannot be dismissed," Thomas added.

May it be so with you as well, Eleanor said to herself as she glanced up at her monk.

Chapter Twenty

Brother Thomas and Rainold walked in silence through the village to the abbey chapel.

Even though Sister Anne had wished to return to the lodge to tend Elizabeth and the child, and the prioress had chosen to accompany her, the monk insisted on seeing Bardolph's corpse.

Rainold could not understand any reason to do so and asked why Thomas doubted the manner of death. Was there any question that the man was found hanging?

But Prioress Eleanor supported her monk's request and insisted there was good cause. Ghosts often left a unique mark, she argued, something that might be helpful in making any required exorcism successful.

Hearing that, Sir William ordered his brother to accompany the monk, lest there be any further questions after viewing the body.

"What more can you tell me about the spirit of Hywel you saw last night?" Thomas knew he was abrupt, but he longed for sleep and was annoyed by having this man accompany him.

Rainold looked at him in surprise. "What do you want to know, Brother? I have told you everything."

"Did you know Hywel well?

"As you may have noticed, this is a small village. Yes, his face was well-known to me. I had had dealings with him when my brother needed his skills on family properties." He pursed his lips. "Although the light from the inn seemed to shine through him, his head was clear enough although very pale. I saw his features plainly."

Thomas nodded. Although it had not been a full moon, he remembered he had found his way through the night easily enough after he fled from the merchant. "Had he cousins or brothers other than the twins?"

Rainold laughed. "None that I ever knew. Besides, I could see the dark mark left by the noose under his chin that extended back to his ears on both sides. I will swear, if need be, that the creature I saw was the phantom of the man hanged for murder."

A man shouted, and Thomas stopped to look toward the abbey.

Abbot Gerald was hurrying toward them.

"Well met!" Rainold called out. "No sooner are you able to bury one corpse than the village sends you another, Abbot."

Gerald paled except for two scarlet marks of anger on his cheeks. "I would gladly abjure such secular generosity in exchange for more coin to the glory of God," he said, each word sharply enunciated. He turned to the monk. "I had been given hope that the evil spirit would be banished quickly before it could steal any more souls for his hellish master."

"I am here to examine the corpse," Thomas said with surprising meekness. "Perhaps Bardolph was killed by more mortal hands."

The abbot pointed at the sheriff's brother. "He saw the ghost of the hanged man last night near the inn."

"I fear I did relay the news." Rainold looked embarrassed. "Perhaps I should not have mentioned that when I sent word to Abbot Gerald?"

"There was no error in what you said," Thomas said, "only in your suggestion that the dead man and the second sighting of Hywel were linked."

"But surely they are!" Abbot Gerald was sputtering.

"Forgive me," Thomas said, "but I do wish to confirm that there is no reason to suspect the king's justice, not the Church's rule, applies here. If I may examine Bardolph's body, I will do so as quickly as possible." His swift smile was intended to hide his irritation. "If God is merciful, I may find that Bardolph either died by his own hand or with the aid of a common mortal who held a grudge against him."

The abbot's eyebrows shot up with hope. "Then examine him, Brother! Although I would grieve if he died by a mortal hand or committed self-murder, I would be grateful to be relieved of any fear that Hell's pollution infects our chapel."

––––––––

It did not take the monk long to discover the likely cause of the hangman's death. As he examined the man's head, he felt a thick crust that had dried in his hair. Stepping over to a dying torch that offered some light in the darkness, he took it back to the corpse.

With better light, Thomas could see where the blood that formed the crust had come from. Just above the ear, he felt an unnatural indentation that was most likely the result of a heavy blow. God apparently had chosen to grant the abbot's prayer, he thought, although he had noted no lesser sense of evil in the discovery.

"A ghost does not need to strike a man before he hangs him," Thomas said to the sheriff's brother and showed him the wound. "Without a more thorough examination, I cannot be certain this blow did not kill him. I would like the opinion of Sister Anne, but I am inclined to believe he might have survived it."

"Perhaps another hit Bardolph, robbed him, and the malign spirit then came by and hanged him?"

Thomas bit his tongue to keep from expressing utter disdain for that logic. Also resisting the temptation to repeat what he had just said in a mocking tone, the monk continued. "Would Bardolph have carried anything so worthy of theft? Robbers are more likely to strike drunken merchants on their way home through darkened streets than the village executioner who must be far poorer."

Rainold reluctantly agreed, and then quickly added, "Nor would they take the time to hang a victim they had robbed."

Thomas nodded, thankful that the sheriff's brother had finally shown he owned some wits. "A man who wishes to disguise the death as self-murder, however, might well render his victim senseless and then hang him."

Rainold sighed. "I am relieved, Brother. May I assume you have concluded that these two recent deaths are a coincidence?"

Hiding his actual thoughts on the matter, Thomas simply laid his hand on the corpse as if to suggest concurrence. Then he turned back to briefly check if he had missed anything else, decided there was nothing else to discover, and said he was done.

As they reached the chapel door, Rainold looked back at the corpse. "Sir William will not be pleased that he has a murder to solve, Brother." He coughed as if trying to disguise a laugh. "He might have preferred that the spirit of Hywel had done it. It is easier to let God handle those things."

"Surely, he has ideas about likely suspects. Bardolph must have had a few enemies. In his profession, how could he not?"

"Perhaps he did, but I fear there are many Welsh hiding in the shadows of the local forest these days, Brother. They might have resented the death of a fellow rebel, and they tend to be more elusive than Satan's other minions." He nodded with satisfaction over this idea.

Thomas chose not to reply, and the two men walked on.

As they neared the village square, Rainold stopped and pointed toward the inn. "I meant to warn you of something, Brother, for you do not know the people here well."

"I thank you," Thomas said. "What should I know?"

"Not long after I picked myself up from the ground near the inn last night, I saw you leaving with the spice merchant."

Thomas felt his face turn as cold as ice.

The sheriff's brother chuckled. "I drew no conclusions," he said, emphasizing each word, "but I was concerned by what happened next. Since Lambard is a local man, I was surprised he led you to that dark alley." He paused, smiling as if amused by something in the monk's eyes. "It is, shall I say, a very dangerous area. I pray you came to no harm..." He stared at Thomas' face as his words trailed off.

Thomas prayed that he not betray his dread at what this man might have witnessed. "I am grateful for your warning," he said with an effort at mild embarrassment. "I fear he and I had too much ale, and we needed a place to relieve ourselves, but we were also seeking the ghost. Perhaps that is why he took me where he did. In truth, I think he mentioned there had been a sighting of the imp nearby. God was kind, and neither of us came to any harm."

Had he spoken too quickly? Had he sounded too casual? Thomas could not meet Rainold's eyes for fear of what the man might discover in his soul.

"So you did not see Hywel?" Rainold's speech hinted of mockery.

"We did not."

The sheriff's brother smiled.

Or was it a sneer, Thomas thought.

But Rainold walked on, and the two men said nothing more on their walk back to Sir William's house.

Chapter Twenty-One

Prioress Eleanor and Sister Anne did not wait for Brother Thomas' return, choosing instead to go back to the hunting lodge.

Sister Anne did not want to miss any early signs of illness in Elizabeth. Although the sub-infirmarian assured her friend that there was no significant cause for concern, both knew that postpartum mothers often developed fevers. Sister Anne did not need to mention that the results were commonly fatal.

"I have observed that frequent bathing before the birthing to ease a woman's pains, suggested by a manuscript from Salerno, also seems to reduce the chance of fever later," she said to her prioress, "but your sister-in-law spent too much time in that cart on the journey here when neither bathing nor calm were possible."

"Then there is reason for us to worry." Eleanor spoke slowly to keep her inflection calm.

Sister Anne shook her head. "I simply do not wish to be complacent or unprepared. I have been told that there is an excellent spice merchant in this village. One of the lodge servants said he will immediately send anything I need and is willing to be awakened if herbs are required at night."

"Then you have prepared as well as any mortal can. May God have mercy as well," Eleanor replied and bowed her head.

When they had walked just a short distance further, Eleanor looked back and saw Eluned leave the sheriff's house and walk toward them.

Putting her hand on the sub-infirmarian's arm to catch her attention, she tilted her head in the direction of the maid. "Now might be the time to question her, if you believe the delay is safe enough. We can do so on our way, since she seems to be going in the same direction."

Anne agreed.

Eleanor called out to Eluned.

The maid had been walking, head down, as if deep in thought. When she heard the voice, she looked up, first startled and then displeased. The latter sentiment was quickly banished as any servant would wisely do.

"Let us walk together," Eleanor said. She pretended to ignore the guarded expression on the maid's face and gave her a disarmingly warm smile. "I have no wish to keep you from your tasks, but I would like to gain a better understanding of the problem we have been asked to solve."

"My help will be inadequate to your needs, my lady, but I am willing to share what little is possible."

Briefly, the prioress let the woman's phrasing echo in her mind to discern any hint that Eluned might have given herself leave to equivocate. She decided the woman had, but also concluded it would be prudent to keep that conclusion to herself. "Any tiny detail may be useful," she replied.

Eluned modestly bowed her head.

"You were friends with Hywel's wife. What do you know of the man?" It is an easy question to answer, she thought, and her manner of reply might be as important as the information she gave.

Eluned blinked. "I rarely spoke to him at the time, my lady, but his wife was a good woman and loyal to the king. I doubt very much that she would have stayed with her husband had he been a traitor."

This surprised the prioress. "Once married, what woman has that choice?"

"She had a brother still living. He would have protected her if she had left her husband for good cause. In truth, the parents hadn't liked her marriage to the Welshman, but she convinced them he was worthy."

"Had he lived in the village long?"

Eluned bobbed her head in agreement. "Since birth. When his parents died of a fever, he raised his two younger brothers, found them craftsmen to teach them trades, and set them on a good path."

The prioress watched the maid's face turn pink. What had caused the flush, Eleanor wondered, yet she found no hint in that short tale, nor any particular reason to question the truth of what she had just heard. It was a detail she chose to set aside and ponder later.

"Why, then, do you think he led the marauders who killed the soldiers?" Eleanor asked.

The maid's eyes narrowed with instant and outraged anger. "I never thought he was guilty."

Eleanor stopped. "On what do you base your conclusion, my child?"

Now the maid's face was scarlet. "Why should you believe me? Does Welsh blood not flow thorough my veins?"

Eleanor might have been offended by this rudeness from a woman of such low rank, but she was not. "I have no reason to doubt your word on that basis alone," she replied, both her tone and words intending to calm. "My family has property in the Marcher region. When I was growing up, my father never spoke ill of the Welsh. Indeed, he found them a clever and talented people. Although my allegiance is firmly with King Edward and I believe the current war is misguided, I see no reason to assume all Welshmen are as benighted as a few. But in violent times, passions grow hot and often burn away cooler logic. So I must ask you again why you think Hywel was innocent. Why might he not have found Dafydd's cause compelling and joined a band of raiders?"

The surge and range of emotions that flowed across Eluned's face shocked the prioress. Then, after so much unexpressed feeling had exhausted the maid, Eleanor was surprised anew by a look that suggested the woman was ready to confide in her. Sadly, that expression quickly vanished.

"I can offer you no satisfactory answer to your question, my lady. As I said, I rarely spoke with him. Yet he might have gone to Wales after his wife's death. He did not, nor did he ever utter a word against our king. Had he done so, it would have been spoken of on market day." She looked over her shoulder as if hearing something behind her.

But Eleanor had seen tears building in the woman's eyes. She chose to ignore that and changed the focus of her query. "Sir William seemed upset that his wife had shown support for Hywel."

"He most certainly did not favor Hywel, although that displeasure was recent." Eluned had turned back but did not look directly at the prioress.

This was an unusual departure from the expected loyalty to masters, and Eleanor chose to set it aside but not forget. She also decided to encourage the deviance and see where that might lead. "Was this change before or after the accusation of treasonous murder?"

"Before, my lady. Sir William is much older than his lady wife and, I fear, owns an older man's jealousy of any younger one."

"He thought his wife was…?"

Eluned franticly waved the very suggestion away. "Lady Mary's greatest sin was looking on the man once! Indeed, I saw her smile at the sight of him that day, and she sinned no more grievously than that. But I am ignorant of all the ways we women can commit grievous errors. As a prioress, you would know better than I if her husband should have felt his head for horns and if she committed a dire infidelity with that single glance."

"And you would have cause to know if she ever lay with the stonemason?" Eleanor chose bluntness and carefully watched the maid's face.

Eluned did not even blink at the question. "I share her room on those rare nights her husband does not join her in the marital bed."

Eleanor knew that couples, eager to lie with each other, could find many locations and times to do so without waiting for a soft bed. Yet she truly doubted that such effort had been made by the Lady Mary. Not only did the sheriff's wife seem disinclined to exert herself in any fashion, Eleanor would be surprised if she was able to sustain an interest for long, even a flash of lust.

"Do you know if Hywel viewed your mistress with equal delight?"

Eluned laughed. "He couldn't have pointed her out in a group of her equals on the major Rogation Day when we all process around the village and pray."

An interesting remark that suggests that the maid knows him better than she claims, Eleanor concluded.

"Or so he told his wife once."

And thus she takes care to explain her knowledge, the prioress thought. Yet why would the stonemason even comment about Lady Mary to his wife? What had occasioned it? Had Hywel's wife reason to question his fidelity?

With a hint of pride in her eyes, Eluned straightened her back. Then she lowered her gaze to show the proper humility in the company of her superior. "My lady, unless you wish to detain me further, I must leave you here. My mistress has sent me on an urgent errand to speak with the man who has ordered some furred gloves for her. The delivery is late, and she is profoundly distressed."

"Go, my child. I am grateful for your answers. As a stranger,

I know nothing of the village and those who live here. You have taught me well. Should your mistress criticize you for any perceived delay in following her command, please tell her that it was I who kept you from your tasks. She may ask me if she wishes."

Bowing with murmured gratitude, Eluned hurried off.

"Did you find that conversation as interesting as I did?" Eleanor turned to Sister Anne.

The sub-infirmarian smiled with some sadness. "I find that I like her, but she has secrets," she replied, "ones that may well involve the hanged man."

Chapter Twenty-Two

Rainold and Brother Thomas saw the prioress and Sister Anne at the same time and hailed them.

"Well met, my lady," Rainold said and bowed with courtesy. "Brother Thomas and I have just left the abbey chapel and were about to part." Flashing a smile that might thaw the eternal northern ice, Rainold then quickly scrutinized the state of the ground beneath him, knelt, and begged a blessing.

Although Eleanor was well aware of the dangers of beguiling men, and was not immune to their appeal, she no longer feared the impact on either her heart or reason. Instead, she chose to match his attempt to charm with an equally agreeable smile and gave the requested gift. If Rainold believed he had blinded her to his faults, so be it. She still thought he was a foppish man.

After a profuse expression of gratitude, Rainold did not stay longer but chose to return quickly to his brother's house.

Eleanor wondered if his swift disappearance might be a good metaphor for the substance he lacked and turned her attention to her monk.

Brother Thomas looked as gray as the sky. If anything, she concluded sadly, the time since their last meeting had increased the sourness of his morning after a night of drinking.

Remembering her fear that he had broken his vow of chastity with a woman last night, she knew she was blushing and grew angry over her reaction. Was she not willingly vowed to God? She might grieve over his sin, but she had no right to be jealous.

Yet, if she had been his earthly wife, she would have had no problem remaining faithful to their marriage bed. He was the only man for whom she suffered this unshakable longing.

With determined firmness, she reminded herself that she was not his wife. If this monk had broken his vows with some wench at the inn, it was a matter for his confessor. If it were but one lapse in a life otherwise known for virtue, it was not her concern and she did not want to think any more about it. Penance would be served. Forgiveness was mandatory. Resolved to comply, she gritted her teeth and ordered herself to do so, but jealousy, as she well knew, was a malignant thing and not so easily cut out.

"I have examined the corpse of Bardolph, my lady." Thomas winced as if his throat was sore.

Not yet trusting herself to speak, she gestured for him to continue.

"He was murdered and not by any spectral liegeman of the Prince of Darkness. A mortal struck him unconscious with a heavy blow and then hanged him. Or so I believe. I doubt the blow would have killed him, and do not know if he was conscious after being hanged, but I find it ridiculous to conclude that an imp would have done this."

Sister Anne asked for details of what he had observed, and then said, "I concur with your opinion, Brother."

"It seems we are dealing with a killer of one man, possibly two, although the death of the priest is less likely to be murder," Eleanor said. "I am puzzled by this. Two men are dead who had a connection with the hanging of the brigand. One seems to have died a natural death. The other was certainly murdered."

"I share your puzzlement," Brother Thomas said. "In addition, Rainold now claims that he saw the ghost of Hywel outside the inn before the night watchman told him of Bardolph's death. The coincidence of that and the sighting of this hellish creature worry me."

Eleanor raised an eyebrow. "The sheriff's brother has seen the ghost? Bardolph was a witness to the spirit kneeling near the corpse of Father Payn. He is now dead. Is Rainold in danger because he saw this vision of the hanged man? Will there be other deaths?"

"Perhaps others have seen the spirit," Thomas said, "although I have yet to find a man who actually has besides Rainold and Bardolph." Thomas colored in embarrassment. "These merchants began to claim late last night that the stories all came from women, who gathered the tales from other women on market day, or else in idle chatter."

Eleanor bit her tongue. Brother Thomas had always been reliable, never disappointing when she asked him to gather information. This time, he had failed her. He should have pursued the questioning of the merchants with greater diligence. Instead, he had drunk too much and let the moment pass for getting answers until the men had all decided to blame women for the tales, an excuse she considered hypocritical. Eve might have much to answer for, but she did not bite that apple for Adam.

And why had he not pressed harder to learn what she needed to know? What wench had brushed her breasts against him and filled him with blinding lust? As jealousy burned through her again, she clenched her fist, and heard the Devil's mocking laughter.

Bitter and embarrassed, Eleanor looked away, pretending to be lost in thought.

It was then she saw Eluned walking toward the abbey with something bulky in hand.

The prioress frowned. Hadn't the maid said she had been charged by Lady Mary to check on a glove order? If so, why was she going to the abbey and not back to her mistress? Was the item she carried the ordered gloves or was it something else?

Forgetting her anger with him, she turned back to Brother Thomas. "I think you need to question more of the villagers, Brother."

He shifted uneasily. "The largest number of men was together in one spot last night, yet I failed to discover anything of value."

"Perhaps you chose the wrong time to query them. The men seemed to have had too much time to grow merry with drink. Or perhaps you did not ask the right questions. I fear you must pursue this issue with greater thoroughness," she replied as she kept her eye on the disappearing maid.

He blinked and lowered his gaze. "I shall try harder, my lady."

"There is another who holds secrets," the prioress said and told her two monastics about seeing Eluned just now walking toward the abbey and why this made her so curious. "She is hiding something. One or both of you should wait and see if she leaves Sir William's house tomorrow and follow her." The prioress asked Sister Anne if she thought she might be able to do so.

"If there is any reason why I should not, I will let you know," the nun replied.

"If Sister Anne cannot, Brother Thomas, you can still follow the maid, but do not let Eluned see you and do not ask her questions unless you deem it prudent. If my suspicions are ill-founded, we should know soon enough."

Sister Anne and Brother Thomas agreed, and the trio left the village.

As they crossed over the bridge, Sister Anne looked at Brother Thomas with sympathy but chose to say nothing.

Prioress Eleanor deliberately separated herself from the other two, walking slightly ahead of them with a determined tread and an even more unusual silence.

Chapter Twenty-Three

In the tiny room set aside for any priest accompanying a hunting party, Thomas bent down over the basin, splashed water on his face, then poured water over his head from a pitcher, and roughly dried himself. Taking a rag and some salt mixed with crushed mint, he rubbed his teeth and gums to cleanse them and freshen his foul breath.

His body felt better. His spirit did not.

Although he had never owned a profound faith, and did not take vows out of any desire to do so, Thomas had spent over ten years in a daily and ardent quarrel with God. More recently, he had come to believe that God was giving him answers to his agonized questions, albeit slowly and in tiny bits that took yet more time to comprehend in all their complexities. The replies were not what he would have preferred to hear, but some had given him far more comfort than he had expected.

A sexual union apparently remained forbidden, but he was beginning to think that God otherwise had no objection to a bond of committed love between two men. When Durant came into Thomas' life, they struggled with lust, yet the monk had also discovered a peace he had never felt before—even with Giles, his first love.

Now, with his relationship with Durant in question, Thomas had lost that fragile peace he had found, as well as all hope and confidence that God had ever listened or cared. Looking back on last night, he was terrified at the depth of his despair and how he longed to cast himself so willingly into Hell. Perhaps he had not technically broken his vows to God, for his lust had remained unsatisfied, but he had sullied them. Even after the loss of Giles and his torments in prison, he had retained some sense of honor. When he gave his word, he kept it. Last night, he had lost even that trace of integrity.

Thomas slid to the floor and knelt, head in hands. "What happened? Why have I not heard from him? Other than wishing to couple, we have not sinned." He struck the floor in anger. "How have I offended to deserve this torment? Have I not begged for enlightenment and tried to comprehend what little guidance You choose to give me? I need direction and wisdom, not this mockery of granting comfort, tempting me with peace, and then casting me aside! That is Satan's way. I thought You were kinder to the honest seeker of truth."

As was often the case when he begged for help, he was enveloped in stillness. Today, it was stifling.

He sat back on his heels. Were a sharp enough knife near to hand, he would be tempted to commit self-murder. If he must live in such despair and his soul was doomed to Hell anyway, why not?

Inexplicably, he began to laugh. Raising a fist heavenward, he shook it with bitter mirth. "Last night, I was willing enough to go to Hell if the circumstances were right. Yet now I hesitate to kill myself." He slammed his hands on the floor. "Durant is elsewhere, has remained silent, and I have no hope of ever seeing him again. Why should I not go the Devil?"

He stopped laughing but continued to look upward with defiance.

Was it his imagination or had the silence turned softer, as if a gentle hand had just caressed him? His rebelliousness subsided. He had lost the passion for it, if not the reason.

Thomas sighed, shook his head in defeat, and rose. "Very well," he said with resignation. "I have a murder to solve. It seems You still require me to assist my prioress in that matter, but I do so only out of my respect and love for her. Until we have returned to our priory, I shall make no further decisions on whether to leap into the eternal fires with a dagger in my heart."

He headed out the door.

———

The afternoon air was still damp, but the autumn sun gave some warmth. That hint of comfort slipped under the embedded melancholy in his soul and opened a tiny passage that allowed in a hint of light.

One decision he did make now, one to which he felt God would have no objection. Thomas swore not to return to Wido's inn, and, if He were kind, the monk hoped he would not have any further contact with Lambard, the spice merchant.

He walked across the bridge and glanced down at the river, but the churning black waters did not tempt him.

Brother Thomas had a duty to perform for Prioress Eleanor.

———

Although there was no market today, the square was crowded with villagers.

A party of horsemen arrived at the inn, dismounted, and went inside. As the horses were led to the stables, they seemed eager to rest, and one brown palfrey looked around, perhaps hoping for a meal. Closer by, two women waved their arms and laughed as they shared a tale. Weaving in and out, children chased each other, heedless of those around them. One elderly man slipped, as he avoided their charge, but caught himself before he fell.

"Brother?"

Thomas turned and saw a merchant approaching. He had been one of the company at the inn last night.

The monk forced a smile.

Clutching his hands together, the man swallowed first, then said, "I fear we did you a disservice last night, Brother. We often drink to a congenial merriment after a profitable market day. By the time you asked your questions, we were in no state to take your need for information as seriously as we ought."

"Nor did I ask the right questions," Thomas replied, "and, I fear, I drank far more than my vocation permits. My sin is far greater than any you might have committed."

"You are kind, Brother, but I beg you to ask your questions of me now. In the brighter light of a more sober day, I want to make amends and perhaps help you."

Thomas brightened and explained his problem. "Abbot Gerald is worried about the death of Father Payn. Now Bardolph the hangman has died. There have been two admitted sightings of the spirit of this hanged man, Hywel, and the abbot fears he is haunting the village and may be the assassin of these two men. Exorcism has failed to banish any phantom. My prioress offered our services to help, but to do so we need reliable information." He chose to hesitate and wait for a response.

The man bowed his head. "I grieve over Bardolph. He was not a bad man. Someone has to be the king's hangman, and he showed reasonable mercy to those he executed."

"The abbot says that many others, not just two, have seen the ghost. Is this true? Is so, what are their names?"

"I have no names. No one of my acquaintance has seen this evil spirit." The merchant looked around and stepped closer to whisper. "This morning I spoke with some of my friends. They confirmed that they knew of no one who has seen the creature, although a few fear it walks the dark passageways at night."

"Any names at all?"

"No one claims to have seen anything, Brother."

"But the rumors continue."

"They do. Perhaps we want to believe the ghost has been seen to give reason to our fears. We no longer walk out at night without someone with us. I have also advised others to take care. Some point to their wives as the ones who tell the harrowing tales, but I am afraid and cannot blame a wife, for I am a widower."

Thomas scowled, not because of the lack of information but because he was beginning to wonder if he had deliberately been duped last night by the spice merchant. Did Lambard already know that no one could help? If so, why had he suggested otherwise?

Looking back on the evening, he realized that he had been distracted from asking questions until both he and the others had drunk beyond need. And all the while, Lambard's hand had frequently rested on his thigh until lust became more insistent than any longing to get answers for his prioress. Had seduction been the plan all along and the claim that others might know about the ghost only a means to accomplish that?

"Brother?"

Thomas realized he had just growled. "Forgive me," he said. "I am eager for this thing to go back to Hell, if it indeed walks the Earth."

But the man looked uneasy. "I was also concerned about whether you encountered anything untoward after leaving the inn last night." Nervously, he licked at his lips. "It was dark, and I thought you had gone...in the direction of the gallows."

He and Lambard had most certainly not gone that way, but Thomas realized that this man might have been aware of the seduction going on despite the drink. Or perhaps this merchant had also once been fondled by Lambard after too much celebration.

Thomas wrestled the memory back. "Since Bardolph died last night, your concern is warranted. We had hoped to see the ghost, innocent as we were of the murder, but quickly grasped that we were in no condition to seek it out. We emptied our bladders, parted, and I went back to the Wynethorpe lodge and my prayers. I hope the spice merchant made it home safely as well?"

The man looked relieved. "I spoke to his servant this morning and heard nothing untoward." He took a deep breath. "If I hear anything more that might be of interest to you, Brother, shall I send word?"

Thomas thanked him, then watched the man hurry away. As he looked around the square, he decided there was no one else likely to be this cooperative. Wives would hesitate to gossip with a monk. Of the men, this penitent merchant had probably spoken with most of them this morning. It was unlikely Thomas could glean more.

He turned back to the road leading over the bridge.

As Thomas proceeded to the lodge, he decided it would be wise to seek his bed, but he must also escape into prayer. Despite his quarrel with God, it was an act that sometimes gave him needed distance from problems. In particular, he must face the events of last night and think clearly about why the spice merchant had distracted him from his purpose. Was it just a longing to sate his lust with him after too much ale, as Thomas had first assumed, or was there another reason having far more to do with the sin of murder than that of lechery?

Chapter Twenty-Four

The next day, Sister Anne found Brother Thomas in the lodge chapel, and the pair hurried toward the sheriff's house, hoping the maid left at approximately the same time after tending to her mistress' early needs.

With such a small village, there was little they could do to hide their inexplicable circling of that house, nor could they pretend to be on their way to the abbey church for prayer. That was in the opposite direction. Sister Anne solved the problem by suggesting they visit the spice merchant for the purpose of finding a seasoning that would improve the appetite of the new mother.

Of all places, this was the last one Brother Thomas wanted to go, but he could find no excuse to avoid it. He had to agree.

Fortunately, Lambard was not in the shop, nor did Thomas see the servant who had grown so cool when he was obliged to bring refreshments after Lambard invited the monk to his residence above the shop.

This icy glare by a servant had bothered him at the time. Now he suspected that the man might be the merchant's regular lover. Yet what did the servant have to fear? Under no circumstances could Thomas threaten his spot in Lambard's bed. He was a monk from a priory on the other side of England.

A horrible thought struck him with painful force. What if Durant had found another man, one who meant more than his usual casual encounters, and that was the reason for his silence? The pain Thomas felt was so sharp he almost cried out.

Determined to recover his composure, the monk turned around and stared out the shop door.

While the sub-infirmarian begged the help of the apprentice, asking many questions to which Thomas knew she had the answers, he pretended a captivating interest in the ways of the world which a religious might well exhibit, despite his vows. The open door also provided an excellent view of the sheriff's house.

He glanced back at the sub-infirmarian.

She gave him a pained look. It was clear that she was running out of questions to ask.

He shrugged.

She settled on a spice. The apprentice took out a small box and filled it.

Suddenly, the monk saw Eluned emerge from the house. He looked back over his shoulder and said, "We must return, Sister. I fear we will be late for prayer!"

"I have finished here, Brother," she replied and, eyes modestly lowered, thanked the youth.

Eluned had not gone far by the time the pair emerged.

It was difficult enough to follow the maid without her realizing they were there. What was harder was complying with two separate villagers who stopped them and begged blessings from Brother Thomas. While Sister Anne tried to keep her eye on the woman who was walking at a swift pace, the monk did his best to satisfy pious longings but still avoid any subsequent discussions of a troubling or profound spiritual nature.

When the last man asked for help in determining when he could put the last bite of meat into his mouth before the Lenten season began, Sister Anne announced with evident sorrow that their prioress would put a heavy penance on them if they delayed their return any further.

"We have not lost the maid," Anne whispered to Thomas. "She is on her way to the abbey."

"And, as she did yesterday, I think she is carrying something," he replied, and they increased their pace.

Eluned hesitated at the entrance to the abbey church that served the village. After a brief look around, she vanished through the doorway.

It did not take long for Anne and Thomas to slip out of the wooded area, in which they had tried to hide themselves, and follow her inside.

The abbey church was short and square. The entry was decorated with an outer stone arch, chiseled with images of fruits, vines, and leaves. The inner arch was made of large stones, the base of each side resembling a pillar. On one side there was a crude image of a lamb while the other portrayed devils with suffering souls, although age and weather had dimmed the clarity of their misery.

Inside, it was dark, the air chill. A narrow window on each side and high above the altar directed weak beams of light down on the cross. A few other slender windows, widely spaced along the walls, welcomed less daylight but invited rain and damp. Near the altar, candles smoked and flickered. A few cresset lamps sat in niches along each wall.

Squinting as her eyes adjusted to the dimness, Anne looked around. "Where has she gone?"

Thomas sought the maid as well, but the only person he saw was a man kneeling in prayer close to the altar.

Cautiously, the pair moved further into the church, their eyes growing more accustomed to the shadows. Agreeing to search separately, Sister Anne went to the right, Thomas to the left.

The sub-infirmarian disappeared into the gloom.

As he slipped along the side, he found no places for the maid to hide. Then he looked at the kneeling man who was so deep in his orisons that he seemed unaware that anyone else was in the church.

Thomas bit back a gasp with such force that his lip bled.

The man praying was Lambard.

Shaking, the monk begged God for calm as he retreated as quietly as he could. At a safer distance, he stared at the man. Had Lambard so regretted their sin that he had come to beg God's forgiveness? Had the spice merchant also suffered from the same unbearable loneliness Thomas did? If so, perhaps that was the only reason for the seduction.

For a moment, Thomas felt some relief. It was one thing to fall into sin out of hopeless sorrow. It was another to deliberately take advantage of someone's weakness to wantonly destroy a soul.

Yet a small voice, sneering in tone, murmured inside his head that the man had never shown any hesitation about the seduction. Nor was he likely as alone as Thomas if the merchant was regularly swyving his manservant.

Thomas struggled between a surge of anger and a wish to regain reason. Did he have good cause to suspect the merchant might be involved in the deaths of two men and the seduction was a trick to distract him from investigating further with greater vigor? Or was he trying to cast Lambard into a far more evil role because he had violated his honor and wished to blame another for his own wickedness? He could not cast aside either possibility.

The merchant's head remained bowed, and he still had not moved.

Thomas worked his way around to the other side of the church, keeping to the rear so the merchant could not see him without turning around, and waited for Sister Anne.

It did not take long for her to join him.

Thomas pointed to the kneeling man, put a finger to his lips, and gestured for her to follow him outside.

When they had walked around the side of the building, he stopped.

"I did not find her," Anne said. "Behind the altar, there is a dark, narrow passage, but I needed light to see all that is there and failed to see Eluned. What did you find?"

"Nothing," Thomas replied. "There was no spot she could hide on that side of the church. It is a simple structure."

The sub-infirmarian gestured back at the entrance. "Shall we go back? Perhaps your eyes are better than mine in the dark."

Thomas shook his head. "I do not want to disturb the penitent there." But he did wonder if she might have escaped when they were looking for her.

"As you said, Brother, it is not a big church. It is unlikely we would have missed seeing her if she was there, nor could she have passed by one of us on the way outside."

"Let us stay a little longer. If she is in there, she must surely leave."

"Might there be an entrance for the priest?"

"It is unlikely," he said. "Father Payn lived at the abbey and would have walked here with others. Yet there is often a side door."

"If you stay here, you can watch for Eluned at the entrance. I shall go to the other side and see."

Thomas agreed. All they needed to know was whether the maid was inside. It would not take long to get back together and follow her from here.

Anne quickly returned. "I found an entry. It is securely locked. Unless she has a key, it is unlikely she left from there. And, if she did, why enter by the main door and leave by the other one?" She shrugged. "And for what reason would she have a key?"

While she was talking, Thomas was peering around the corner of the church. He raised his hand and gestured to Anne.

From the entrance of the church, Eluned emerged. Nothing was in her hands. She took the path back to the village.

As the pair started to follow, Thomas suddenly stopped and whispered to Sister Anne to wait.

The spice merchant had left the church and was rushing to catch up with the maid.

"What is it?" Anne looked worried.

"Nothing," he replied. Indeed, he could not explain to the sub-infirmarian why he suspected the merchant of being involved in murder. Outwardly, there was no reason why Lambard could not walk with Eluned, and, this being a small village, everyone knew each other. "My only concern was that we must be careful that no one sees us, including that man who has been praying inside."

Sister Anne agreed but something in the monk's tone made her wonder if something else was bothering him.

Chapter Twenty-Five

"I could find no way she could have vanished," Sister Anne said to her prioress, "but she did."

The trio of monastics walked slowly along the crest of the hill near where the lodge house sat. The changing autumnal afternoon now flaunted a suggestion of summer warmth and mocked the impending winter. The only clues that those suggestions were false were the sharp bite of a breeze that turned their cheeks pink and the rotting leaves that lay under damp trees.

From the grave expression on Sister Anne's face, Prioress Eleanor knew her sub-infirmarian blamed herself for her inability to find where the maid had gone. "There is a rational explanation, and we shall find it," she said, then smiled. "I could always ask the abbot. He knows the secrets of the church and seems eager to engage me in conversation about the ghost, as well as his plans on how to conquer and rule the Welsh."

"Perhaps we should not encourage him. He might find he has yet a third task for you." Sister Anne briefly smiled.

Eleanor did not seem to hear her friend. She was gazing out at the small piece of land her family owned. Then she turned to her companions. "Were it not so close to the dangers of war, I would find this place restful." Shaking her head as if to cast off her distracted thoughts, she continued, "Were there any others in the church? I ask in case someone might have witnessed her frequent visits there, know the cause, and what she does."

"I saw one," Sister Anne said, looking at Thomas who had remained quiet. "Did you notice any others?"

He turned to his prioress. "Only the man. The light was poor, but I think he was the spice merchant I spoke to at the inn. He remained in prayer the entire time Sister Anne and I were looking for the maid, left just after Eluned did, and hurried to accompany her on the path back."

"They knew each other?" The prioress raised an eyebrow.

"I do not know," he replied, "but, in such a small village, they might well. I did not think it suspicious that they walked together."

"Merchant and lady's maid?" Eleanor thought about that for a moment. "A woman of Welsh descent and an English merchant?" She looked at her two companions with a questioning look.

Thomas frowned. He had not thought about that, especially the differences in ancestry during a time of war between the two peoples. Silently, he cursed himself for his inability to banish the blinding distraction of his own misery.

"That may well mean nothing. I am grasping for anything out of place, no matter how small," the prioress replied. "We have so little solid information and less that is new. The two victims are connected to the hanged man. Although one death was not likely caused by violence, Bardolph's was."

"Father Payn, whom some might say lacked a heart for refusing absolution, died because his heart did," Thomas said.

"If we assume there is a condemned soul back from Hell to wreak vengeance, it must still be murder if that liegeman of the Devil causes a man's heart to stop." Anne frowned with puzzlement. "But surely that crime is beyond the authority of any earthly justice."

Thomas continued. "The hangman is found swinging on the same gallows where he executed the brigand. Might the manner of these two deaths point to the killer?" He waved his hand as if an annoying fly was buzzing too close. "Other than Abbot Gerald's ghost, that is."

Anne hesitated. "We can never discount Satan's minions, Brother, but I saw no signs of violence on the priest. Even the Prince of Darkness leaves his mark."

"So Father Payn's heart ceased its work," Thomas replied. "Someone might have known his heart was failing and chosen to frighten him to death."

Eleanor acknowledged the validity of their points but was still pondering why the merchant rushed from prayer to walk so companionably with Lady Mary's maid. Unable to come to any reasonable conclusion, she said, "If there is this link between the deaths, we should worry that the second witness to the presence of the ghost, Rainold, is in danger."

"But the other two were directly connected to the dead man's execution." Thomas frowned.

"So is Rainold," Eleanor said. "It was he who gave testimony at the trial that caused the Welshman to be hanged."

"I had forgotten," the monk replied with evident irritation.

"If we conclude that some mortal, not the brigand's soul, is stalking the village, there does seem to be a pattern to the deaths." Sister Anne's expression showed she shared the monk's frustration. "Yet why would someone want to kill those who caused the stonemason's death?"

"An excellent question," Eleanor replied, then looked at the monk. "You have spoken with the spice merchant. Has he a wife?"

Sister Anne blinked, perplexed by the prioress' question. Then she realized that Eleanor was wondering if the merchant and maid were lovers.

Thomas felt himself grow weak. "No, my lady. He told me that he has not been able to take time from his prospering business to woo."

"As for Rainold," Eleanor said, "I may dislike the man, but I accept that he either witnessed something eerie or had another purpose in telling that story. What think you? Might it be significant that his claimed sighting occurred near the inn?"

Thomas winced and hoped neither woman saw it. He most certainly would not reveal that another purpose might include what Rainold possibly witnessed happening between two men in a narrow passageway nearby. Thomas could only hope that Rainold, as a soldier, held the fighting man's general disdain for those who prayed, especially their weak adherence to any vow of chastity. With luck, the man's mockery, on their way back from viewing Bardolph's corpse, would remain his only mention of the sin he might have observed.

He realized that both Prioress Eleanor and Sister Anne were looking expectantly at him. He shook his head. "I do not know why the inn would have any significance. The light from the open door, according to Rainold, might have made the identification of Hywel easier."

"Yet do not ghosts and wandering souls from Hell eschew light?" Sister Anne looked to the prioress who nodded.

But now Thomas realized that his prioress might be right about something she had mentioned. Wasn't the friendliness between Lambard and Eluned odd? Was there a treasonous link? Did Father Payn suspect such a thing and might that be why he had to die?

If that were the case, the monk could not see how Bardolph was involved. The man had mentioned nothing to him about any traitor besides Hywel when they had talked. He had simply insisted he had seen Hywel's ghost. Thomas put a hand against his forehead. His head felt ready to explode.

Sister Anne grimaced as if she suffered the same affliction. "I can see no significance in the sighting at the inn, although I am now concerned about Rainold's safety as well as that of all the men who condemned Hywel at his trial. Half the men in this village might be in danger for some involvement in that case."

"Another man I spoke to has assured me that all who must go out at night now do so in pairs. I think caution has taken hold of everyone here," Thomas said.

"But I am thinking that your concern over Eluned and the secrets she holds are crucial. What involvement might she have?" Sister Anne folded her arms in thought.

Eleanor nodded. "Something is amiss with her. You and I agree on that. I cannot explain exactly why I think so, but I am convinced she knows more than she has admitted. We know she was friends with the wife of the hanged man and is of Welsh blood. How well did she know Hywel and his family? Might she have some knowledge of his two brothers? I still wonder what happened to them. It would not surprise if they are rendering their own form of justice against those who executed Hywel." Eleanor looked from monk to nun in hopes one might offer some fresh insight.

Sister Anne spoke first. "Eluned believes Hywel was a good man. Does she think that because she is Welsh, because she was friends with the man's dead wife, or because she has some reason to think he was wrongly executed?"

"Her frequent visits to the abbey are interesting," Eleanor said. "I had wondered if she and the spice merchant were lovers and met at the abbey."

"That would not explain why she disappeared during his prayer and they only met together on leaving," the sub-infirmarian said.

"Unless they were both aware that someone was in the church with them and decided to meet privately another time when there were no witnesses." Eleanor shrugged. "Perhaps I am making the reason for their meeting too complicated."

"Interest in her actions has merit," Thomas said. And so does mine in Lambard's, he thought, but had to remain silent about his reasons.

"I am also curious about the original source of the rumor that the brigand's ghost is haunting the village," Eleanor said. "Now the rumor has gained wings after Bardolph's death, but it began with Father Payn's. Where did it come from? Why was it started? Why did it continue while Bardolph remained alive?"

"It occurred to me that Bardolph, like Father Payn, might have had a woman in the village, my lady," Thomas said. "I can find out and talk to her." And, he thought, perhaps she might have more information about Lambard's reputation and loyalties.

"That would be helpful," Eleanor said, and then turned to the sub-infirmarian. "As for Eluned, we need to question her further. Would you…?"

Someone called out to them, and they looked back to see a servant running in their direction.

The woman's face was pale. "I fear you are needed by the Lady Elizabeth, Sister Anne."

The prioress froze. "Something is wrong?"

"A slight fever," the woman replied.

"How slight?" Both Eleanor and Sister Anne asked at the same time.

"I do not know, my lady," the servant said, but her eyes betrayed her distress.

The sub-infirmarian put a calming hand on her friend's arm. "The spice merchant will have a good supply of willow bark needed to bring it down, and there is wine enough to make an infusion."

For a long moment, the prioress looked at her in worried silence.

"With God's help, I believe she will survive this, but I do not want to leave her side until I am certain."

"Then I shall remain there as well," Eleanor said.

"Your prayers are needed, but so are your efforts in this crime," Anne replied. "Let me know where I can send word, should you be needed, and I shall send a servant if your sister-in-law's condition worsens." She put one hand on the simple cross she wore around her neck. "I swear it!"

Eleanor's jaw set. "I shall remain at the lodge. When you need rest or must prepare any remedies required to heal her, I can sit by Elizabeth's side. And I will pray for your success as you care for her. If Elizabeth dies…" Her eyes grew moist.

Anne put her fingers against her prioress' mouth. "Do not even speak of it. We must pray instead and have faith in a swift recovery."

But the nun was also well aware that Eleanor was torn. She might long to tend to her family needs out of love and concern, yet she must also solve this problem of an ephemeral ghost. She had given her word to the abbot, and it was her duty to honor it.

Chapter Twenty-Six

Brother Thomas left the lodge the next morning after the sun had just crept into the sky above the treetops. The scent of smoke from the village, filled with the promise of roasted fowl, rich pottage, and the lingering scent of fresh bread, made him smile. At least he still had moments when the darkness of melancholy lifted and life had flashes of peace, even if happiness remained unreachable.

He was grateful and hurried with eager purpose toward the bridge that spanned the small river.

Last night, he decided to find that merchant who had sought him out in the town square and apparently knew Lambard well. Thomas thought it interesting that the man had seemed uneasy, even slightly guilty, because Lambard was left alone with Thomas after too much drink. Did he know that Lambard was fond of men in his bed? Had he feared that the spice merchant would try to seduce a man vowed to God and felt he should have intervened? It was quite possible that he had either succumbed to temptation himself or knew others who did. Whatever reason, the man had been especially willing to help, and Thomas was grateful.

Of course, Thomas would ask him if Bardolph had a mistress and who she was, but he would also find a way to learn more about the spice merchant's reputation. He was determined to discover whether Lambard had any reason to kill Father Payn and Bardolph.

After a deep sleep, Thomas had risen this morning in a calmer mood and also resolved to be fair to Lambard. He would not be one of those men who pointed to the sins of others in order to hide their own faults, and he could not condemn a man for trying to tempt him, when he had been willing enough to sin. But he dared not ignore the possibility that the man had had a more sinister motive.

He breathed deeply until the air hurt his lungs. The pain made him feel oddly content, an inexplicable reaction. But he had no quarrel with any brief moment of calm.

It did not take long to find the helpful merchant.

When he saw Thomas approach, he smiled, albeit cautiously.

After the usual courtesies, the monk eased the conversation into what he needed to know. He began with the simple question about whether today had brought fresh rumors that the hanged man was still troubling the village.

"The death of Bardolph makes us all tremble, Brother, and men have concluded the phantom still roams. Yet no one yet claims to have seen him. Many pray he has satisfied his longing for revenge and returned to Hell—or at least chosen a far distant village to wander through. We would be glad if he did either."

Thomas joined him in that hope. "I was wondering why Lambard thought we might see this ghost so near the inn." He realized that was not a wisely phrased question so quickly clarified why he was interested. "Did the place have some significance for the brigand while he lived?"

The man shook his head. "He was not a man fond of much drink. When his wife was alive, he never went to the inn. She made their own ale."

"Might Lambard know any other reason why the spirit would so deeply hate Father Payn or Bardolph? Of course, one had denied the Welshman absolution and the other was his hangman, but most damned souls would not bother with such things, preferring to torment unfaithful wives or men who had deeply wronged them over many years. I ask the question so I can dismiss any other motives for this desire for vengeance against the two men."

The man thought for a moment. "I cannot say, Brother. You must ask Lambard. He had some private quarrel with Father Payn and might know if Hywel had a similar problem. I would not know if they ever spoke together about the priest."

"Were you at the hanging?"

"Aye. Although I usually don't go to executions, this one was different. I felt betrayed by Hywel. I was shocked by the verdict, for I never thought he would have killed Englishmen, especially in their sleep. His wife was a good woman of our village, and he had never expressed any anger against us." He gestured as if pushing those thoughts aside. "Now his brothers were different. If they'd been hanged, none of us would have been surprised. They have since vanished, and we all think they have fled to Wales."

"What do you remember of the execution?"

He shivered. "It was a strange hanging, as if either God or Satan was displeased by it. The gallows broke, you see, and some men believe that means God wants one or both condemned to be spared. Hywel, however, was already dead. Bardolph declared it."

"And his corpse was taken away for burial?"

"No, Brother. He was hanged again."

"A dead man? Yet the hangman surely saw no need?"

"Rainold ordered it. He said it was his brother's wish, lest there be any doubt the assassin of innocent men was dead."

"Did Sir William have any reason to doubt Bardolph's experience and judgment in such matters?"

"I have never heard of any problem with a condemned man being cut down, then scrabbling to his feet and praising God's mercy for saving his life. It happens elsewhere, thus I must accept Bardolph's skill." The merchant hesitated. "In the past, Brother, we did not have great cause to hang men from the village. Now, outlaws are everywhere, and treason against the king suggests we may have more executions in days to come."

"Then it seems strange, does it not, that Rainold insisted the corpse be hanged again for the reason he gave?"

The man nodded. "He had come on the sheriff's behalf to witness this execution and has done so before. When Sir William sends him, all know that Rainold speaks with his brother's voice. Perhaps the order was given to please the crowd, for the crime committed was a heinous one."

"Did you hear Father Payn refuse to give Hywel absolution?"

"I did not. I was standing too far back in the crowd, although I did hear the priest and the stonemason shouting. Then there was a roar of approval from those standing closest to the gallows. Later, I heard the tale."

Thomas was at a loss to come up with more questions. Stalling for time, he gazed around the square, then asked, "I do not see Lambard. Do you know where he is so I might ask further about any problems between Father Payn, or even Bardolph, and Hywel?"

"I have not seen him since the night we were all at the inn," the merchant replied with a slight flush rising on his cheeks. "I feared he had been taken ill, but his servant said he had been at the abbey church, praying for his sins. Apparently, he took a vow to spend a few days on his knees. You might seek him in front of the altar."

"If he has a tryst with God, I will not trouble him," Thomas said. Despite his duty to pursue answers to questions, he was relieved that he had an excuse not to speak with Lambard alone. He would still have to find a way to get those answers in the presence of another. It was quite possible that Lambard's time in the abbey church had far less to do with a penitential vow than why Eluned was also there. "But, if I may, I would ask one more question and then will take no more of your time."

With courtesy, the man assured the monk that he was happy to do anything to help rid the village of this plague of violence.

"Did Bardolph have any close friends or even a woman with whom he spent his time? I wish to seek information that only such people would know and might help my prioress chase away this vile imp."

"Although none of us hated Bardolph, we believed that he and Death stood too close together. We did not want to be any nearer mortality than a man must and thus avoided him." His smile twitched and faded. "As for a woman, there was one with whom he shared the bed." He pointed to a nearby house. "Mistress Maud lives there. We have no official whorehouse here, but she keeps a few girls in case they are needed by unmarried lads." He laughed. "A few of the women even leave when some of the virginal boys fall in love." He suddenly coughed. "Forgive me if I have offended by my sinful mirth…"

"You have not offended. This a small place, and I assume most of the women come from families all know. Might a few of those marriages even be blessed by both God and family?" Thomas hardly needed to ask. Just as the longtime bedfellow of the local village priest was often accepted as if she were his wife, the occasional local whore could be welcomed as a bride if the family ties were strong enough.

"Some," the man responded sheepishly.

Thomas briefly wondered if he had been one of those virginal lads, and then continued. "The founder of our Order, Robert of Arbrissel, often went to whorehouses to preach to the women there," he said. "I feel no fear or shame in following his example when there is a holy purpose at stake."

With that, he thanked the merchant, gave him a blessing, and went to the brothel. In truth, Mistress Maud's establishment offered him far less temptation than a walk down a dark passageway with a merchant who sold spices.

Chapter Twenty-Seven

It had been a long and sleepless night for others in the lodge. Eleanor and Sister Anne had taken turns sitting by the patient's side. Although the prioress trusted Sister Anne's judgment, she knew how perilous childbirth was for all women. Her own mother had died in bloody agony. If God wished a soul, He would take it.

As she bathed her sister-in-law's face and kept her shivering body well-wrapped that night, she prayed that this would not be the time for death. Her brother had found joy in his wife, and their babes were healthy. Eleanor prayed the children could grow up in the loving arms of the mother who bore them. Although her aunt, Sister Beatrice, had raised her with warmth and care, she mourned her mother's death even now and wished she had kept her just a little longer.

In the morning, however, the fever seemed to have broken. Elizabeth woke up, recognized those around her, and managed a smile.

Robert fell to his knees and wept with happiness.

Sister Anne was cautiously pleased and told her friend it was safe to leave Elizabeth's side. A servant could take her place. Eleanor finally agreed when her sister-in-law jested that her appetite had returned with such force that she might match her babe's eagerness for food.

Robert, however, decided that the local wet-nurse must be retained. If his wife's health required it, the woman would stay as long as the babe suckled. Sister Anne argued well that Elizabeth, who wanted to nurse, should not do so. Not only was there the danger of contagion but nursing might further weaken the mother.

Elizabeth, although her desire to nurse was stronger than her body, knew they were right and conceded.

Eleanor stepped outside and looked for the position of the sun amongst the drifting clouds. It was about the same time Eluned had gone to the abbey church each of the two days she had seen her. With luck, the woman would follow the same pattern today.

Since Brother Thomas was not here, presumably off to seek Bardolph's friends or a mistress, the prioress knew she could not stay idle. Weary as she was from the night of fear and vigilance, every part of her twitched. Sleep would be impossible.

Briefly returning to the solar, she told Sister Anne that she would be at the abbey church for a while and then return. It was understood that she must be summoned immediately if Elizabeth worsened.

Looking over her shoulder, she smiled pleasantly at the servant she had asked to accompany her. The woman's expression was humble and did not betray any reluctance to postpone her usual tasks in order to provide proper attendance to this baron's sister who had taken vows.

Eleanor hoped she was just as prudent. She did not want the servant to know how unhappy she was to have a stranger with her when she might be forced to conduct an unpleasant interrogation. But with neither her monk nor sub-infirmarian able to go with her, she had no choice.

The pair set off toward the village, the servant trailing a little behind. Across the bridge, Eleanor turned onto the path leading to the abbey church.

––––––––

Walking inside, the prioress saw that there was only one other person there, a young man whose dress suggested he was a merchant of some wealth. Was this Lambard? She had not met the man, but she decided it was noteworthy if his visit once again coincided with Eluned's.

She whispered to the servant that she must pray alone and suggested the woman remain outside to enjoy the warmer sun. Then Eleanor chose a spot sufficiently distant from the man for propriety's sake and in a shadowy area where she could watch the entry.

Eleanor knelt. First, she apologized to God for not giving Him her full attention. Since He found so many murders for her to solve, she felt some confidence that He understood why her prayers were not always as dutiful as those uttered by other women of her vocation. With due reverence, she then bowed her head and begged Him to forgive her myriad other faults and pleaded with Him to grant mercy to Elizabeth, her children, and her husband.

Eluned walked into the church.

Eleanor heard the footsteps, glanced to the side, and saw the maid framed by the doorway. Keeping her head down, she willed herself not to move. Fortunately, she had been inside long enough for her eyes to grow accustomed to the gloom. Lady Mary's maid would still be blinded by the outside sun and would be unable to see the prioress in the deep shadows.

Eluned walked slowly along the wall to the left of the altar, stopped, looked slowly around, and then vanished into the dark passage behind the sanctuary.

Rising, Eleanor cautiously followed, but, when she turned into the area, the maid was nowhere in sight.

Perplexed, the prioress turned back, yet knelt close to where Eluned had entered and waited for the woman to emerge. With the other penitent so close, she did not want to bring attention to herself or her purpose by searching the area.

Time crawled.

The penitent merchant remained on his knees.

Eleanor grew impatient. Unfortunately, her attending servant had clearly wandered an area very familiar to her as much as she could bear and was now waiting just outside the entrance to the church.

Finally, Eluned emerged.

Eleanor rose and walked toward her. "I see you have need to petition God as well as I," she whispered.

Putting a hand to her mouth, the maid bit back a cry.

With interest, the prioress noted that the maid held nothing in her hands. Then she realized she had not seen whether she did when she had first arrived.

"Please, my lady! Say nothing to my mistress or master about this!" Her voice, also lowered, shook.

Eleanor directed the woman deeper into the side passage for greater privacy, and then tilted her head as if confused by the plea. "Why should you fear disclosure? Surely you cannot have come here for any evil purpose."

"I pray daily for the souls of Hywel and his dead wife."

"That is no sin."

"It is if Sir William decided my orisons suggested I was disloyal to the king." She continued to whisper, but her speech had lost its tremor.

Unfortunately, the prioress thought, the woman has recovered herself. "Prayers for the Welshman's dead wife need no excuse.

Perhaps prayers for him need not either. He was hanged, but you knew him before his crime was committed. Thus you must have reason to offer his soul kindness after he was condemned for his vile treachery. If he is in Purgatory, he will be comforted. If he is in Hell, I fear the Devil will simply laugh at your compassion."

"He was known to be a virtuous man until then, my lady. Even if his soul is in Hell, I cannot imagine his spirit would beg leave of the Devil to come back and torment the village. He had no quarrels with anyone here, not even Bardolph or Father Payn. I know the one hanged him and the other refused to accept his plea for forgiveness, but..." She hesitated as if she could not find the words to explain further.

"Since you are also of Welsh ancestry, might you feel some obligation to another Welshman's soul? Is that what you fear most? That your loyalty will be doubted because you pray for a man condemned for killing Englishmen?"

Eluned nodded with marked trepidation.

"Yet all you need say, should you be asked by either lord or lady, is that you come to pray for your dead friend. You need not add that you do so as well for her husband."

Eleanor did not fully accept the reason given for the maid's fear of discovery. Eluned was clever enough to dissemble to her mistress over such a simple matter. As her deep fatigue seeped into her, Eleanor's patience with lies thinned, and she longed to resolve this matter swiftly. The sooner it was done, the sooner she could concentrate on the needs of her sister-in-law so they all might travel further from the dangers of war.

Forcing her irritation aside, she said, "I think there is another reason why you do not want them to know you are here."

Behind her, Eleanor heard a rustling and saw the penitent merchant rise. He gave the two women a long look and then left the church.

Eleanor wondered if he had meant to convey a message to the maid.

She looked back at Eluned and caught her newly determined expression.

"Do not hesitate to speak honestly, for I am weary of deceit." This time, Eleanor did not blunt her sharp tone.

Eluned took a deep breath. "Sir William and Lady Mary do not know that I had asked someone to allow the two brothers to use his property to prepare Hywel's body for burial. The night before the execution, I told the men to take his corpse there."

"Nor is that a crime, at least in God's eyes."

"The village would not agree, my lady, and so I kept silent. I did it for his dead wife, but few would understand. They would have preferred that his body be torn in pieces and fed to the wolves."

"That still does not explain why you come here daily." Eleanor dismissed the idea that the maid was leaving a bribe of money for whoever had let his land be used to cleanse a corpse. No maid had such wealth, and any stolen coin would be discovered by Lady Mary or Sir William.

Eluned bowed her head. "I visit his wife's grave. I vowed to do so because I know how her soul must grieve over her husband."

A blatant lie, the prioress thought and she retorted with rare mockery. "That is no sin, as you well know. Or did you find a way to bury him, unshriven though he was, with his wife in sanctified ground and now wish to do what you can to hide the evidence?"

The maid swiftly turned her head away. "I would not beg anyone to commit such a sin after Father Payn refused to accept Hywel's confession."

Spoken as if she hoped I would conclude she had done just that, Eleanor thought ruefully, nor would the brothers have needed begging to do it. Yet Eleanor had lost her advantage. She was flailing, and her suggestion about the grave was absurd.

"Please, my lady, let me return to my mistress before she decides I have been gone too long. If I bring attention to my absences, she will forbid me in the future to leave without knowing exactly what I am doing. I cannot betray my vow to my friend to pray for her…and Hywel."

"Go then," Eleanor said and watched the maid hurry away.

Her anger with herself for such incompetence was unquenchable. Yet she had no right to detain the maid and had no evidence of any crime, other than her certain suspicion that something indefinable was amiss.

———

After waiting until Eluned was well on her way to the sheriff's house, Eleanor went to the graveyard, grimly hoping her odd suggestion about a secret burial might hold merit after all, and sought any indication that a new grave had been dug—other than the expected one holding Bardolph. One other was clearly that of a child. Father Payn would have been buried in the abbey. Nowhere else could she see any signs of newly disturbed earth.

"A poor theory proven as foolish as it sounded," Eleanor muttered to herself as she hurried back into the church.

The confused servant bowed her head when the Prioress of Tyndal stormed past her.

This time Eleanor went into the area behind the sanctuary to seek answers. She found a side door made of wood that was rotting. It was locked, but the thing squealed like an outraged rat when she pushed on it. Even if the maid had had a key, she could not have gone through the door without Eleanor hearing the noise.

Close by was another, thick and sturdier wooden door, also locked. Eleanor suspected it led to a burial crypt but found no way the door could be opened without a key.

Annoyed and frustrated, the prioress marched out of the church and told the baffled but still respectful servant that they were returning to the lodge. As soon as possible, she would come back with Brother Thomas to examine this area more thoroughly.

Chapter Twenty-Eight

Maud the Bawd was as round as an apple and as pink as a gilly-flower, a woman more like a baker's wife than the mistress of a whorehouse. Her expression resembled a brokenhearted widow, not a businesswoman grieving the loss of a steady customer who always paid his bills.

"Bardolph was a sweet and loving man," she sniffed and raised a plump hand to pat the corner of her eyes. A waft of lavender filled the room. "I shall never find his like again."

As a man who understood how often common assumptions about people are in error, Thomas bowed his head in respect for the evident depth of her grief.

She looked away, squeezed her eyes shut, and clenched her fists. When she faced the monk again, it was with fury and determination. "I want justice," she hissed, but even in anger her dimples charmed.

"So does Prioress Eleanor," the monk murmured.

Mistress Maud gestured to a nearby chair. "Forgive my discourtesy, Brother. Please sit and let me pour you some wine. The air is cruel with damp, and your walk from the lodge must have chilled you."

Smiling acceptance, he sat, and Maud gracefully handed him

a cup of dark wine. When he tasted it, he was surprised at the quality. Instinctively, he pressed his hand against his heart as melancholy twisted a sharp dagger deep. Gritting his teeth, he drove the image of Durant, the wine merchant, back into the shadows.

"I know you came with questions," she said, "and I am sure someone in the village told you that Bardolph shared a bed with me for many years. Had he not been the hangman, and I a whore, we would have married." She smiled, her eyes looking into the distance as if seeing a happier day.

Thomas noted with surprise that she owned all her front teeth and they were as white as those of a far younger woman.

"He was concerned that I would suffer greater rejection than he in marriage. Men accept a bawd more than they do the town executioner. Despite all the promises our priests give us, Brother, death is rarely contemplated with joy. Sin often is, or at least until we know we must imminently face God. Otherwise, we would never delight so much in it. As for any mockery that I would daily put horns on his head, my beloved Bardolph knew I had been faithful to him since the day I owned my first house." She lowered her eyes, and then whispered, "As I shall remain until our souls are reunited in Heaven or Hell."

With gentle sincerity, the monk replied, "Then he was a man of rare understanding."

Her blue eyes sparkled. "And you are a rare monk to say so, Brother."

"We are all sinners, despite the likeness to God we may own," he said with a smile. "I fear men make too much of the resemblance and too little of our differences."

Her tears drying and a merry look teasing her lips, she refilled his cup. "What do you wish to know?"

He noticed that she did not drink herself. "Did Bardolph have enemies?"

"No more than any other mortal. Although he was not loved, neither was he hated."

"Then you have no suspicions about who might have done this deed."

She took a moment to reply, taking a deep breath and turning her face away to compose herself. "Definitely not some ghost. Hywel may have been hanged as a Welsh raider, but I knew him, not as a customer but as a stonemason who did repairs for me. He was one of the few who ever spoke to Bardolph when passing in the square. Welshman though Hywel was, he was kind and not the sort to return with the Devil's blessing to seek revenge. I would not say this to any of my neighbors, Brother, but I never believed Hywel was guilty of the crime for which he was executed. Neither, in truth, did Bardolph."

An interesting observation by a woman of good wits, Thomas thought. "This crime was not committed by any spirit," he said. "Of that, I feel certain."

She pressed a hand against her mouth, silencing any cry and banning further tears. "May this monster, who killed my Bardolph, be hanged himself with less kindness than my dear one granted those he was commanded to execute."

Thomas waited.

"You do not preach how we must forgive those who trespass against us?"

Although she gazed into his eyes with penetrating intensity, and he trembled at what she might see in his scorched soul, he felt only an intense longing in her look and no malice. He chose to reply with a simple shake of his head as one frail mortal to another.

Reaching out to briefly touch the sleeve of his robe, her reply was surprisingly tender. "Thank you for your kindness, Brother, and I beg your forgiveness. You came for information to lead you to the killer, and I have distracted you. Please continue. I shall respond as best I can."

Thomas sipped his wine first. "Bardolph told me that he had seen Hywel kneeling by the body of Father Payn. He had no doubt that it was he, yet he said he did not believe in phantoms."

"In truth, neither of us did. Although a few of the souls he had sent to Hell over the years were vicious in life, I occasionally worried about vengeance but he always calmed my fears," she replied. "As for seeing Hywel that night, Bardolph was perplexed by what he had witnessed when we later spoke of it. He had been on his way home from visiting me. We had had a merry evening, but he had not drunk much. He rarely did. The moon gave off good light." She shook her head. "There was no reason to imagine anything or fail to see the man's face clearly."

"I have heard rumors that many claim to have seen the spirit, yet only one besides Bardolph has confessed it to me, and no one can tell me the names of others. Now, it seems that the sightings may be the result of market day chatter amongst wives."

Maud raised an eyebrow. "One? I doubt anyone else has seen anything. Men hear others say that something has happened, or is true, and they fear mockery if they do not aver the same. As for wives, they are blamed for everything from impotence to a bad harvest." She flushed. "Forgive me, Brother, but my views are born out of the sins of men."

Thomas laughed, then grew serious with his next query. "Bardolph did not tell others of what he had seen?"

"He had no close friends, unless you count me, nor was he inclined to idle prattle. When Abbot Gerald asked him questions about the priest's death, he replied honestly. He told the sheriff the same tale. Those men had the right to know. Other than that, he did nothing else to spread the tale." She studied Thomas for a moment, and then added, "Nor did I." But she could not resist curiosity. "Who was the other one who claimed to have seen Hywel's spirit?"

"Rainold said he might have seen the ghost the night Bardolph died." Thomas watched her face for a reaction.

She chuckled. "Rainold was the witness? Sir William must have told him what Bardolph said. Perhaps the man did think he saw something. More likely, he imagined it. One of my girls can confirm that he likes a little fantasy to keep him happy."

Thomas raised a questioning eyebrow.

Maud sat back with a playful display of feigned shock. "Really, Brother? You want to know what swells his manhood?"

"I came late to this vocation and am not ignorant of the world," he replied with a grin, "but I know nothing of the sheriff's brother." He did not tell her why he was interested and most certainly nothing about the troubling conversation he had had with Rainold after examining Bardolph's corpse.

She wiggled her hands in amusement. "It is a common enough game. He likes to pretend he is a great lord and my girl his helpless servant. He never hurts her, or I would drive him out of my house." She sighed. "He is a foolish man, yet I sometimes pity him. It must be hard to be the younger brother of a man he neither loves nor respects."

Thomas took note but had another question for her. "Did Father Payn have any enemies in the village?"

She pondered a moment. "He was never very good at being a priest. Like some, who find themselves doing something for which they have no calling, he suffered resentment and sought others to punish for his pain. When his lack of vocation weighed especially heavily on him, he could be cruel." She raised a hand dismissively. "Oh, we all know sinners need rebuke and penance, but he took against some more than others. For instance, all knew he had bedded the same mistress for many years, but he rarely lashed out at Bardolph and me as if he felt an odd kinship with us." She shrugged. "With others, however, he gave little hope for God's mercy."

"Was the spice merchant one?"

She looked surprised. "Little escapes you, Brother. Yes, he was a man whose soul Father Payn claimed was irrevocably in the Devil's hands." She sighed. "Master Lambard is pleasant, honest in business, and charitable to the poor, but his particular sins are ones my girls cannot satisfy."

Waiting for her to continue, Thomas remained silent. He did not need to ask what those sins were.

"Perhaps the young man will find a more forgiving priest when Father Payn is replaced." It was clear she had nothing further to say on that subject.

"Might Lambard have killed the priest?"

"He is not a violent man! As we all do, he surely owns a blackened soul, but, in my opinion, there are others far more wicked than he. According to tales told, he spends more time in front of the church altar than many others in our village. For all the arguments those two men had, I cannot imagine the spice merchant killing the priest."

Thomas hoped his face had not flushed too much. "Who is more wicked than the spicer here?"

"How can I reply, Brother? Am I not the most stained of all? I could give you a list of men whom I do not like, men prone to striking my girls or cheating their own customers. That would not lead you to the man who killed my beloved. I know of no one who would kill two men with such heartlessness. Even our butcher has been heard to utter the occasional prayer before he slaughters for meat."

Although he wasn't quite sure where this might lead him, Thomas decided to ask the question. "Sir William and his wife. What do villagers think of them?"

"Ah! You ask for good gossip!" She clapped her hands with delight. "Lady Mary is a silly poppet and has failed to give her lord an heir, despite the many times she claims he honors her bed. Sir William is stern with those who break the law, but he is fair about proving any violation." She grew serious. "When Hywel came to him in defense of his brothers, and apparently confessed to the murder of the sleeping soldiers, the sheriff sought objective confirmation of the crime."

"Rainold?"

"As I heard, the younger brother witnessed the raid and, despite hesitation because of the respect Hywel owned amongst us, he finally came forth to give his testimony to his brother."

"One more question," Thomas said. "Do you know where Hywel is buried?"

"No," she replied. "Nor did Bardolph. His duty ended when he released the corpse."

With that Thomas graciously thanked her and rose to leave.

At the door, Maud told him that, if he thought she could help, she would answer any further questions. Then, with a swift look around, she bent forward and, in a low whisper, assured him that he could return any time he wished.

Thomas replied with a grin and a blessing.

Chapter Twenty-Nine

Eleanor was happy that her monk was back with her again. No matter how jealous she might be of the carnal sin he might have committed that drunken night at the inn, she felt certain it was one unlikely to be repeated. Over the years, he must have been tempted many times by women without breaking his vows. The circumstances that night, she repeated to herself with increasing determination, were unusual.

Looking at him now, he seemed more at ease after the visit to Bardolph's mistress, a woman who owned the village whorehouse. Oddly, this comforted her. If Brother Thomas had actually lain with a woman, and suffered as deeply as he did the next day, the last thing he would have been willing to do was go into a bawdy house.

Perhaps he never did lie with any woman, Eleanor thought, but was merely tempted after too much ale. If that was his only transgression, she could easily forgive him. Hadn't she been guilty of lust?

She audibly sighed with relief. After napping for a short time after her visit to the church, it seemed she had awakened not only refreshed but wiser.

Thomas looked at her in surprise.

"I grow weary of knowing so little, Brother. Forgive my impatience." Eleanor hoped the truth of this would keep her other thoughts about him hidden.

"We have gained some understanding of those involved, my lady, and, for all her sins, I found Mistress Maud's thoughts and observations helpful."

This was the man she had always known, endowed with compassion, unusual perceptions, and a logical mind.

"I agree from what you told me." She laughed. "Her description of the Lady Mary as a poppet was the perfect image for her. And, wicked though it may be, I found Rainold's fondness for playing the mighty lord while swyving his whore quite funny." She grew graver. "Yet Sir William is called fair, albeit neither much admired or loved. And despite his quirks, pomposity, and fondness for posing as a man still in his youth, he is not mocked? That is interesting."

Thomas was tempted to tell her what he had learned about Lambard and his quarrels with Father Payn, then decided against it. If he did, he would have to explain why he was looking into whether the merchant had any involvement in murder, and he was still unable to justify it without telling the truth.

During his first agony over his sin, he had almost told her anyway, but she had made it clear, as was her wont, that any confession must be given to a priest. Had he lain with a woman, would he have confessed that sin to her? As his prioress, she had the right to know.

"Let us go to the abbey church, Brother. I wish to show you something and require your opinion."

Still lost in his thoughts, Thomas simply nodded agreement.

No, he would not have told her, he decided. She firmly believed in the right of a priest to hear confession, render judgment, and order penance. It was her duty to assume this had been done and to direct the other aspects of priory life, unless the sin was so heinous she was obliged to know. Many monks and priests broke their chastity vows. Look at Father Payn, he thought. Lying once with a woman might be shameful, but it was not monstrous.

What he had done, however, might well be considered abominable. He had let a man touch him in ways the Church taught God especially abhorred. Unlike with Giles and Durant, he didn't even have the excuse of love. Thus his fall from God's embrace felt like Satan's spectacular descent from Heaven to Hell in a flaming arc like the morning star which had given the former angel the name Son of the Morning.

Thomas felt the tears well up once again. Was he truly one of the irrevocably damned?

For the moment, it didn't matter. He had sworn to do nothing until they had returned to Tyndal Priory. Until then, he owed his prioress all the help he could give her.

Rubbing his eyes dry, he realized that Prioress Eleanor had hurried ahead of him, and he quickly followed.

———

Today, no one was kneeling in the ebb and flow of shadow and light near the altar.

The pair went quickly to the ambulatory surrounding the apse, and Eleanor showed the monk the heavy door she had previously discovered.

"It may lead to a crypt," she said. "I think Abbot Gerald told me that the abbots were buried here." She put her hand against the rough panels. "It seems to be locked. I cannot imagine this is where Eluned vanished, yet I could find no other solution. That other door, which probably leads outside, makes too much noise when pushed. I heard no sound."

"Sister Anne found that outside entrance when we were here." He turned back to the other one his prioress had pointed out. "Most crypts in small churches have entries through a moveable stone in the floor," he said as he stared at the door. "Sister Anne did not mention two doors to the outside, and I see no light through the cracks in the paneling."

He knelt and examined the lock and round iron handle. Without much light, he used touch to do so. After a moment of wiggling the door, he rose and pulled it open. It moved quietly on its hinges. "The lock is faulty, my lady. I was able to loosen it without much effort by raising the door up slightly here and moving it a bit to one side at this point."

"A woman would be able to do this?"

"Easily enough if she knew how."

"We need light of some sort. I want to see what Eluned might be visiting behind this door."

————

It did not take Thomas long to retrieve a flickering cresset lamp near the altar.

With the monk leading the way, the pair slowly and carefully descended a few narrow stone steps to the brick-lined crypt below. The arched roof of the vault was so low that Thomas' head brushed the top.

The silence that greeted them was as solemn as Death itself. Despite the weak light, they were able to see a few stone coffins in an orderly row. Their simplicity gave credit to the vows these men had taken while on Earth. Unlike some abbots in more prominent abbeys, these men had apparently remained humble and knew their bodies would return to the earth from which God had made Adam. The only decoration chiseled into the lids was a simple cross.

Eleanor shivered. All mortals must face this truth, she thought. The body was nothing, the soul all. She bowed her head out of respect for the dead, to honor God, and to remember that the goal of one's short time on Earth was to be gentle, remain faithfully humble, and practice charity.

"No one is here," Thomas said in a hushed voice as if he, too, was subdued by the presence of those who had gone to face God's judgment and were now spending eternity under His verdict.

Eleanor suggested they walk around the crypt, seeking any evidence to answer why a lady's maid might visit here on a daily basis.

It did not take long.

"There!" The prioress indicated a spot on the ground between two coffins.

The monk hurried to where she pointed and knelt. "A mazer," he said, raising a small cup for her to see before replacing it and picking up another item, "and this box." He put it to his nose and sniffed. "Meat?"

She knelt as well and took the box. "Or a pottage of meat and pulses. I would also conclude that the smell suggests it was fresh." She ran a finger around the inside. "The meal was eaten not long ago. The wood is still damp."

"Then Eluned is bringing food to someone here?"

"So I believe." Eleanor looked around. "Yet no one is here."

Thomas jumped up and hurried from one coffin to another, trying to see if any of them remained unoccupied. Finally, he leaned against the last coffin and thudded his hand on the top. "None have been left open."

The pair quickly walked through the small crypt again, seeking any hidden door or loose bit in the stone floor or brick wall that might lead to a secret hiding place. Satisfied that no one was able to hide here, they retreated to the spot where they had found both mazer and box.

"It is a mortal who has been hiding here," Eleanor said. "Ghosts do not need food and drink." Her laugh at the attempted humor was brief.

"Hywel's two missing brothers?"

"We cannot discount that, although there is only one mazer and one box of food." Eleanor knelt again to look but found nothing more.

"Eluned comes at approximately the same time every day, presumably carrying food and a little drink. Why here, other than the ability of Eluned to come to a church without question? Do they share the meal? The men must vanish after, since no one is here now. If so, where do they go?"

"We do not know whether she comes a second time, although that might be difficult considering her responsibilities to her mistress," Eleanor replied. "If the brothers are hiding nearby, they may not come here together. Or one may have hidden himself elsewhere, and someone else feeds him."

"The question remains: where could they possibly hide?" The name of the spice merchant immediately came to mind as the possible second person to help the brothers.

"Or is it just one person?" She threw her hands up in frustration.

"The lamp is dying, my lady," Thomas said at last.

"Then we shall leave," Eleanor replied, "but we must find an answer to this enigma soon."

With that, the pair climbed the stairs, shut the door, returned the lamp to its niche, and walked back to the lodge.

When the door shut, and darkness fell once again on the dead, a loud sigh filled the crypt, a sound heard only by corpses.

Chapter Thirty

Sir William was angry, as only a man can who would rather be warm in bed with his wife than hurrying through a cold night.

"May Satan fry Wido's balls," he muttered. Why the innkeeper insisted on meeting him at the bridge instead of coming to the sheriff's house was a mystery. The relayed message gave no reason, only that it was urgent and dealt with the killing of Bardolph.

Stopping to catch his breath, Sir William put a hand to his chest and felt his heart pounding. His physician had recommended that he eat less and spend more time walking or riding. For an instant, he wondered if the man was right, then stubbornly concluded that he was a fool as all lanky, pale-fleshed physicians are.

A man needed his wine and meat to heat the blood. As for exercise, he had his wife to swyve. He grinned at the thought of her plump breasts and felt a pleasurable twinge in his manhood. It had failed him of late, but this troubling murderous spirit was surely the cause. The problem would be wearisome for a man of any age. He had no reason to think he was old enough to fear impotence.

Taking in a deep breath, he hurried on.

Since their marriage, he had made sure to satisfy the marriage debt as often as possible, although his many duties as sheriff sometimes took him away from her. Yet his wife had no cause to look elsewhere for satisfaction, and he truly had no reason to suspect she did. Now that Hywel was safely dead, Sir William was convinced that his concerns about the stonemason were unfounded.

When he caught her looking at the man and wetting her lips, he had grown hot with jealousy. She quickly explained that she had been engrossed in deciding what the cook should prepare for dinner to please her husband, that she was staring at nothing but her thoughts, and wasn't even aware that the stonemason was within view.

He tried hard to believe her. The noon meal, as she promised, had been especially good, and he never found reason to suspect her of adulterous thoughts again.

Yet he had remained angry with Hywel for causing him to doubt his wife at all, and, when the man came to protest the innocence of his brothers and suggested he had been the leader of those who killed the sleeping soldiers instead, he was overwhelmed with a strong desire for revenge.

Now he wondered if the man had actually confessed. In truth, he could no longer remember his exact words. Was it a confession or simply a badly worded plea to free the brothers? Had his rage against the stonemason and longing for retaliation blinded him?

Surely the hanging was warranted, whatever he personally felt. Hywel had not protested his arrest, and even if he had put him in prison out of personal hate, he was a fair man. He never let a man be condemned without verification of any confession. After confirmation of Hywel's guilt was discovered, he did feel joy but also refused to attend the execution lest God disapprove of his delight.

The sharp mist from the river bit his cheeks and numbed his fingers, and he grumbled, again cursing the innkeeper. When Rainold told him of the man's request, his brother was apologetic. But it wasn't his fault, as he quickly told him, for not asking more questions to discover why the location of the meeting was necessary. Rainold suspected Wido felt it safer for him not to be seen speaking to the sheriff in a location well-known by the villagers. The innkeeper had always been squeamish about seeming to be too friendly with the upholders of the law.

"The innkeeper always has been womanish," he muttered. "I believe the tales that all of Maud's girls together have failed to stiffen his manhood."

When he approached the bridge, he slowed, trying to stare more deeply into the darkness. With no moon, it was difficult to see anything.

"Lord Sheriff!"

Sir William was startled, spun around, and gripped his sword. "Here, my lord!"

The voice was not one he recognized, although it was hard to hear anything clearly with the roar of the dark river water surging under the bridge.

"Where are you?" he shouted back.

"Come down the embankment to the path, my lord. It is drier here under the bridge."

"I hope the Devil rips off his balls, if he even has them," Sir William grumbled and inched his way down the very steep embankment. Once he slipped and uttered another oath as his hands found a root strong enough to keep him from tumbling into the river. Finally, he reached the path and stared in vain into the night.

"You had better have important information, Wido, or you will rue the day you brought me here."

"I do," the voice said right behind him. "I think you might like to meet the one who murdered both priest and hangman."

Sir William spun around and reached for his sword. But when he saw who had spoken, he cried out in horror.

His last thought, before the blow struck him, was that this was such a cold and lonely spot to die.

Chapter Thirty-One

The Lady Mary wilted onto the bench, pressed her fingers against her eyes, and moaned.

Although the news of Sir William's grisly beheading with his own sword was appalling, Eleanor uncharacteristically struggled to feel sympathy for this woman. Despite presumed grief and shock over the brutal murder, the grieving widow still managed to pose herself in a manner most pleasing to the eye. Even her moan was vaguely melodic. Uncharitable though it was, the prioress could not dismiss her observation and wondered if the new widow felt much anguish at all.

As the lady lowered her hands, the prioress noticed no redness in her eyes, common when tears of profound misery are shed. In fact, the woman's cheeks appeared remarkably dry.

"Fear not, my lady," Rainold said, his words as smooth as one of Sister Anne's balms. "Now that I am heir to your husband's lands and title, I swear to honor you as his widow." He touched her shoulder briefly. "You may never have given my brother the son he longed for, but you were his beloved wife and shall want for nothing as long as you live under my roof."

The Lady Mary waved at her maid with an impatient gesture. Eluned inserted a bit of cloth into her mistress's hand.

Pressing this soft cloth over her entire face, the lady uttered what sounded like a convincing sob.

Surely I am being unfair, Eleanor thought with determined sympathy, yet her mind refused to acknowledge any cause for a kinder assessment. She glanced at Sister Anne beside her.

The sub-infirmarian's face was admirably unreadable, but the quick look she gave back in response flashed a hint that she shared her prioress' opinion.

"That was our deepest sorrow!" From behind the cloth, the widow wailed at a pitch that succeeded in not offending sensitive ears. "I longed to bear him a son. I failed, yet he never once threatened to set me aside for a fertile woman."

This time, when Sir Rainold touched Lady Mary's shoulder, he let his fingers linger an instant longer. "He was a good man. All knew he was stern in defense of the king's law, but he was ever fair and charitable." Sir Rainold's dazzling smile displayed every one of his white front teeth.

The widow lowered the cloth and looked up at him with an expression of deep humility that was perfectly constructed to show a barren wife's gratitude.

Eleanor was not impressed by the performance of either Sir William's widow or younger brother. Both are hiding something, she thought. Might this pair have a more intimate relationship than what was allowed by the bonds of their particular kinship?

As if sensing her thoughts, Sir Rainold gave the prioress a questioning look.

Eleanor did her best to eliminate any trace of her suspicions from her expression.

The new heir returned to murmuring supportive platitudes to the bereaved widow.

Compared to Sir William, who was aging into a corpulent fellow, Eleanor recognized that the brother-in-law had his charm.

He is much fitter than the dead sheriff, she thought, as well as several years younger. I may find nothing tempting about him, but he is well-favored enough to spark lust in other women. And both Lady Mary and Sir Rainold are much alike, she reminded herself, a similarity that might well have drawn them very close together.

"My lady?" Eluned spoke with hesitancy and a hint of fear.

"What is it?" The mistress turned and glared at her maid.

"The furred gloves, my lady. You wanted me to see the merchant about it again."

"I did?" The woman shook her head with a confused look.

"Yesterday."

"Then go!" Lady Mary snapped and waved the maid off. "Tell him that his delay is crueler now that I suffer deep mourning for my dead lord." She uttered a low moan, one clearly appropriate in pitch and dignity for a lady of her rank and sorrow.

"I will return with little delay," Eluned replied and fled the room.

The glover is not your destination, Eleanor thought, and knew she must follow.

As the two religious began to offer consolation, the prioress caught Sister Anne's eye and relayed a silent message.

The sub-infirmarian discreetly nodded.

After she had deemed enough time had passed for Eluned to get the food and drink she needed to take to the crypt, Eleanor offered her apologies for needing to return to the lodge.

Sister Anne assured the grieving widow and Sir Rainold that she would stay to pray with them for the soul of the murdered sheriff.

With grave mien and somber pace, Eleanor left the room.

As soon as she was outside, however, she saw Eluned in the distance. Lifting her robe so she wouldn't trip, the Prioress of Tyndal ran with the speed of a child at play to the abbey church.

Chapter Thirty-Two

The crypt door was ajar by a crack.

Eleanor hesitated long enough to press her ear to the opening and listen for voices.

In her rush to catch the maid and reveal the woman's secret purpose, the prioress realized she had not only abandoned convention but common sense. Sister Anne had been left behind, and her vocation always required a companion for the sake of propriety. In this situation, wisdom also demanded the company of another for protection in case the revelation of what Eluned was doing was a dangerous discovery.

Nonetheless, I am here and must act, she thought, and quickly uttered a silent apology to God. *With three deaths, two of which were unquestionably murders*, she explained to Him, *I could not wait for another opportunity to confront the maid. I beg Your mercy and protection!*

Hearing no sound from the crypt and taking a deep breath, Eleanor inched her way through the open door, and slipped down the stairs.

A feeble light wavered below, presumably from a cresset lamp, but silence continued to rule.

Just before the last step, Eleanor carefully looked around the corner of the wall.

The light was resting in a niche above the area where she and Brother Thomas had found the evidence of food and drink. Eluned had put the items she had now brought on top of one of the coffins and was bending to pick up what had been left.

How does she protect the food from rodents, the prioress wondered, and why had she left the box and mazer on the floor before?

Seeing no one else there, Eleanor took the final step into the crypt. "Are you feeding one murderer or two, Eluned?"

The maid spun around, screamed, and froze when she saw who had spoken.

Realizing that she stood between the woman and safety, Eleanor braced herself lest the woman attack. In order to escape, Eluned would have to strike or kill her.

For a tense moment, the two women stared at each other.

Eluned slowly knelt and raised her hands in a gesture that begged mercy. "Neither, my lady. I swear it." There was no defiance in her tone, but there was an odd sadness.

"Not Hywel's two missing brothers?" Eleanor decided to trust her impression that the maid offered no threat and stepped a bit closer so she might study the woman better in the poor light.

"If God granted them clemency, they reached Wales long ago. No one has seen them since they took Hywel's body from the hangman."

Skilled though Eluned might be in the cautious evasions that wise servants soon learned with their masters, the prioress had met others far more adept at polishing a lie into the semblance of truth. Years of unmasking the vilest of sinners made the task of deceiving Eleanor a difficult one. She smiled at the maid's weak feint and pushed her harder for facts. "Yet you sympathize with them or you would not have suggested that God had reason for leniency."

Eluned sat back on her heels and bowed her head. When she raised it, her eyes now held that missing hint of boldness. "They have been found guilty of no crime, my lady, either under English or Welsh law. They may have expressed a phrase or two of protest about the king's insistence on following English law in Wales, as if we were a lesser form of God's creatures than those who inhabit other nations. Would it be wrong to complain about the treatment of Welsh traders by English residents of castle towns who cheated them and mocked them as barbarians?"

"They were not arrested by Sir William for such opinions, Eluned, but rather for slaughtering defenseless Englishmen in their sleep."

"For convenience sake alone were they cast into prison. No one saw them commit this crime. They were deemed guilty by the local men for nothing more than their race and their sympathies for kin treated like animals."

"Imprisoned only for the sake of convenience?" Eleanor felt a flash of anger over the accusation of unfairness. "Were they not then released just as quickly by the king's sheriff?"

Eluned chose to say nothing.

"When the killer confessed, he was arrested instead."

"Hywel was just as innocent!"

Curiosity and surprise took over, and Eleanor felt her anger fade. The maid's words had been spoken with a passion far greater than might be expected in defense of the husband of a dead friend. Switching to a sympathetic tone, she urged the maid to explain.

"He never actually confessed, my lady." Her voice caught as if clothed in a sob. "It is true that he did not protest when he was imprisoned. All he wanted was for his brothers to be freed so they could escape into Wales. He believed them to be wrongly accused." She swallowed with a hiccup. "None of us thought he would be condemned. Sir William was not a brute. He insisted on collaboration of any guilt at the trial. Hywel knew there could be no witness to confirm that he was there that terrible night, let alone that he was the leader of the band. He had faith that the sheriff would be fair and release him."

"I understood that he did confess."

Eluned's face colored. "With respect, my lady, Sir William alone heard what he said, and he claimed Hywel specifically said those words." She shook her head as if recalling whom she served. "My master must have misunderstood exactly what Hywel said. I have heard it told that the stonemason merely suggested guilt but did not actually say he had killed anyone."

"And you heard this from whom?"

Eluned bowed her head. "The brothers spoke with him in prison. Perhaps others as well. It was a story told on market day and had the ring of truth."

Gossip on market days did not convince Eleanor. "Rainold came forth as a confirming witness to this confession," she said, her voice kept neutral.

Eluned slapped her hand on the floor. "Was he even there, my lady? Ask yourself that question. He never came forth when the two brothers lay in a cell, even to say aye or nay. Why do so only when Hywel was on trial?"

To herself, Eleanor agreed that she had made a valid argument with that observation. Yet how did the question of Rainold's motivation for not coming forth until Hywel was on trial have a bearing on the murders? Hywel was dead. No one had seen the brothers since the hanging. And who but they would care to seek revenge on those who had hanged the stonemason?

Still, Eleanor was troubled. The two should have fled immediately after release, yet they remained until after the hanging. If they knew he was innocent, would they not have escaped? Once his scheme to get them freed was revealed, they surely knew that they might well be arrested again.

She expressed her belief and waited to hear how Eluned would respond.

"Of course, they knew he was innocent, but they could not leave him without kin or friend under the circumstances. After Hywel was condemned, they were ordered to lead him to the

gallows with his rope in hand as a cruel example to others who
might be traitors to King Edward. They did so, not out of humiliation, but to comfort him. Escape was still possible while the
crowds were celebrating Hywel's death."

"You insist there was no witness to the attack," Eleanor said,
trying another approach. "How can you be so sure Rainold
was not telling the truth and might have been the witness he
claimed to be?" She hesitated. "Perhaps he was still healing from
his wounds when the brothers were put in a cell and could not
come forth until later."

Eluned seemed to ponder that for a long time, then looked
back at the prioress. "There was a story that he had slipped away
that night of the murders, abandoning his post and his fellow
soldiers to meet with a woman."

"Yet he was wounded."

"That same tale suggests he injured himself to support his lie."

Men had been known to cut themselves, even severely, to hide
their cowardice, Eleanor reminded herself. "Does anyone else
know more of this tryst?"

"This is about the sheriff's younger brother, my lady. If anyone
knows more, they are unlikely to confess it for fear of retaliation,
and I am unable to give you names of those who whispered the
story. It was another I overheard in the stalls on a market day."

More gossip, Eleanor thought, or was it? She could not discount that this maid had better sources than that. She was too
intelligent to be convinced solely on the word of some fish-
monger's wife. Perhaps it was more probable that Eluned was
unwilling to give names. "Then, if you can, tell me who the last
person was to see the two brothers."

"I do not know for certain, but it might have been Lambard,
the spice merchant. It was he to whom they took Hywel's body.
The merchant offered them the use of a hut behind his house to
cleanse the corpse for burial."

Eleanor unconsciously took a step back. This spice merchant

whom Brother Thomas met at the inn? Yet this man had not mentioned this detail of his assistance to the dead man's brothers to the monk. The prioress had no doubt Brother Thomas would have told her had the spicer said anything. She would ask, of course, but the omission was odd after the man had told her monk he wanted to help in finding the answer to the ghost. Perhaps the detail was meaningless, but that was not up to Lambard to decide.

"Very well, Eluned, I shall seek him out, but, as you well know, you have something to confess." She gestured around the crypt.

The maid's eyes darted left and right, then focused once again on the prioress standing in front of her.

Eleanor took a chance, knelt before Eluned who had remained on her knees, and grasped her hands. "Child, I wish you no ill. You claim you are not feeding a murderer. Then who are you bringing food from Sir William's table to sustain?"

Eluned began to weep. "Please, my lady, I do no real harm in this. First, let me ask if it is a crime to suggest that our king could have come to better terms with the Welsh princes. I speak only of one's hope to end this war with honor and nothing of treason. Our king has been a strong advocate for good laws and a consistent adherence to them. Could he not show the same wisdom with his subject lords?"

"One might debate that without offending God or even his anointed king." Eleanor thought this was an odd question in response to her query and had no idea what Eluned intended with such a reply.

"Then is it a crime to protect someone who has committed no worse transgression than to voice a belief that peace might be restored if the king proved again that he is the lover of justice and law that we all know he is?" The maid shook her head to indicate she was not yet done. "If this man were found before he escaped the village, he could well be imprisoned and even executed for no greater crime than his hope of peace."

"Has he sworn violence or taken up arms against the king?"

This time, Eleanor controlled her anger over any perceived insult to the king's justice. Sir William was dead, a man most agreed was fair. Who knew who would take over his position and how he would render justice? And, as Eleanor knew, justice was often hard to obtain when blind passions, common during war, ruled.

"Never, nor would he. He has been unwillingly stranded here. His only wish is to reunite with his kin in Wales. Once there, he will avoid the war as best he can, having no longing to fight. He only lacks the way and time to leave. He will remain hidden here only until the moment he can depart."

"Do you know this man well and do you swear to his loyalty to the king?" Eleanor knew how risky this approach was. Eluned had not so much lied to her as avoided answering questions fully. Yet her instinct told her that the maid was honorable. Even if she was in strong sympathy with the Welsh cause, and the prioress had no doubt she was, she did not seem likely to commit or advance treason.

Were Eleanor truthful with herself, she, too, had some quarrels with the king's decisions, although they remained unspoken. Yet she was not Welsh, and her eldest brother was both a liegeman of the king and his friend. It was highly unlikely her loyalty would ever be questioned.

"I know him well, my lady, and I can swear that he wishes King Edward no ill in body, life, or rule."

Not quite the same thing as being loyal, the prioress thought, but set that aside for the moment and asked her most important question.

"Is he the ghost that men speak of in the village?"

"He is, my lady."

"Yet Bardolph was convinced the man who knelt by Father Payn's corpse was the executed Hywel."

"He resembles him well enough in the shadows that linger even in the light of the fullest moon," Eluned replied, "but I give you my oath that he has slain no one. If I lie to you, may the Prince of Darkness take my soul and condemn it to the worst torture possible for eternity."

"If he is not the murderer, who is?"

"That I cannot answer," the maid replied. "If I could point my finger at the one, I would. The three dead men were flawed, but they were no more evil than most of us. I cannot say they offended anyone deeply enough to invoke the rage to kill."

The prioress realized that Eluned had reached the edge of her endurance. She was taking enormous chances in stealing food and keeping this man's secret. Although she might have several reasons for hiding him, Eleanor suspected that the strongest one was love.

Eluned now bent forward and covered her face. "My lady, is there any way you can help this innocent man escape to Wales? I beg your mercy. He is innocent of all wrong, and yet..."

"You love him."

"I confess it, and he loves me."

Although she feared she might regret this promise, Eleanor's own heart understood all too well what the young woman was suffering. What would she not do to save Brother Thomas' life? She fought to retain her masculine reason and banish her womanish heart. The battle between her two natures was short, but neither side was victorious. She was forced to a compromise.

"I can promise nothing, my child, and must require further proof that this man is free of any hint of treason. I must also insist that you help in all ways possible to find whoever has killed so viciously. If you can do all that, I will also do what I can to help this man leave the village safely. I cannot promise, nor can anyone during a time of war, that he will reach Wales and his family without harm."

Eluned swore to help.

As the cresset lamp now threatened to go out, the two women rose.

Eluned took the dying lamp, left the food where she had placed it, and the two women climbed the stairs.

As Eluned turned to close the vault door behind her, she whispered to Prioress Eleanor, "Go to Lambard. If you say to him 'Eluned says Hywel wishes it,' he will know I have given him permission to tell you all he knows or even suspects. I think he can prove the innocence of the man I am helping to hide. He may even show you paths to investigate in your quest for this terrible killer."

And yet, Eleanor thought, he did not do so for Brother Thomas. Why would he now become more agreeable? Because Eluned approved? She chose to ponder the problem later. For now, she simply nodded.

With that, the prioress let the maid hurry off to her mistress.

Although she had to meet Sister Anne at the sheriff's house, Eleanor needed time alone to consider what she had learned and try to make sense of the contradictions and new complexities.

She also prayed she had not been criminally foolish and erred tragically by what she had promised the maid.

Chapter Thirty-Three

Eluned looked neither left nor right as she ran into the house now owned by Sir Rainold.

Brother Thomas and Sister Anne watched her, and then went back to the subject of their conversation.

"What a monstrous way to kill a man," Sister Anne said. "And the murderer used Sir William's own sword to decapitate him?" She shuddered.

Nodding, Brother Thomas took a moment more to catch his breath after returning from the bridge. "From what I was able to see when I examined the body, I believe Sir William was struck down first, just as Bardolph was before he was hanged. The sheriff was probably unconscious when the assailant took the sword and cut off his head. The blow was not cleanly finished but was enough to kill him."

Thomas winced. The memory of Sir William, lying on the blood-soaked earth with his head dangling by a few shreds of flesh and bone, would remain with him longer than most violent deaths he had witnessed. "This was an especially cruel murder."

Hearing footsteps, the pair turned to see their prioress approaching.

"I heard part of what you said, Brother. The form of this death appears to be symbolic, as were the other two," Eleanor said.

"I am so glad you have returned," the sub-infirmarian said. "The Lady Mary has accepted as much comfort as she could tolerate, and Brother Thomas has just come from examining the sheriff's corpse."

Eleanor frowned for a moment. "Did Sir Rainold take you there and return? He was here with the widow when we arrived. I assumed he had already had the corpse moved to the abbey."

"He sent a servant to tell me of the death and relay the message that Rainold could not accompany me. His duty lay in consoling the Lady Mary and assuring her that she had no fears regarding her future now that he has inherited. He gave orders for the servant to take me to the murder site so that I might better examine this latest corpse. Only then would the body be sent to Abbot Gerald for care." Thomas described in detail to his prioress what he had seen and concluded.

"As it was with Bardolph, no satanic imp needs to render a man unconscious before cutting off his head," Anne said. "I agree with Brother Thomas that this crime was an earthly one."

Eleanor's smile was grim. "I have spoken with Eluned, and she admitted that the ghost we have been seeking is a creature still owning flesh and blood."

"Then you have found the killer!" Sister Anne's eyes sparkled with happiness.

"Yet you allowed her to freely return to this house?" Brother Thomas looked at his prioress. "I do not understand."

"I have not found the murderer, or at least I do not think I have," Eleanor replied and told the pair about her meeting with the maid.

Sister Anne threw her hands up in disgust. "It is unconscionable! Even if this Welshman is innocent of all wrongdoing, surely a way could have been found before now to get him away. How could this woman allow the village to remain fearful? Who is this man she is feeding? And how came she to hide him in the first place?"

"Do you even believe her claim that he is innocent, my lady?" Thomas made no attempt to hide his doubt.

"I remain certain that Eluned is still hiding parts of the truth, although she has wit enough to realize that I could report how she has been stealing food and harboring a man whose loyalties, in this time of war, are questionable. Barring unusual mercy from her mistress, her thefts are criminal even if the man she is protecting is innocent. For that reason alone, I think most of what she has told me is factual."

"Thus she kept silent only on what she believes you do not know and cannot find out." Sister Anne's voice betrayed a rare anger.

"Quite probably." Eleanor looked up at her monk. "There is one more detail. She gave me the name of one she claims can confirm her story and the innocence of her hidden man. You have already had contact with him, Brother. It is Lambard, the spice merchant."

Thomas failed to hide his shock and squeezed his eyes shut to recover himself. "Indeed, my lady?" was all he was able to say.

The prioress did not remark on his reaction and only asked, "What was your opinion of the man?"

"I cannot say," he replied and quickly tried to decide what he dared reveal. "As you concluded with Eluned, I wondered if he knew more about this matter than he ever divulged, yet I am unable to explain why I thought so."

"He did say he would try to help you resolve the sightings of the ghost."

Thomas slowly nodded as if still pondering.

"He mentioned nothing about his readiness to lend Hywel's brothers his hut to wash and prepare the body for burial? He may have been the last to have seen the two men."

"He said nothing about that. Perhaps he thought the cleansing of the body was irrelevant?" The monk frowned. "Yet it was an odd thing for him to have done. Hywel had been hanged for killing Englishmen. None of the other villagers, despite the opinion held of the stonemason before the trial, would have allowed the brothers a location to cleanse the body of such a criminal."

"Take your time, Brother," Eleanor said. "Think carefully about that night at the inn. Was there anything he said that seemed odd? Might he have tried to find a way to discover if he could trust you? Many would take his willingness to help the brothers as an offense to the king and the dead Englishmen. Although you say he seemed eager to help, I can understand why he might be cautious."

There was nothing Thomas wished to remember about that night. He swallowed hard and tried to do as his prioress wished. "After I had spoken to some of the merchants, he suggested the two of us leave the inn and led me to a narrow alley where he said we might see the phantom. We did not, and we soon parted company. He most certainly did not mention his offer of the hut or any conversation he might have had with the brothers after the execution. Perhaps he decided, for some reason, that he could not trust me enough."

"I understand that he might wonder because you came here in the company of the Wynethorpe family, yet he knew that before he offered to help. Can you think of anything else that might have caused him to hesitate?"

"I cannot. We had both drunk too much ale, my lady. A man's judgment is not logical under those circumstances." Thomas longed for this discussion to end.

"Despite the good reasons he would not want to speak of this detail to villagers, his past failure to do all he could to help us troubles me. How willing will he be to do so despite Eluned's encouragement? We are dealing with murder, not treason as far as I know. Yet I wonder. Eluned may be wrong about Hywel's innocence. Perhaps Lambard is more involved in the crime for which the stonemason was executed than is known."

Thomas kept his eyes lowered to hide his thoughts. If Lambard had used seduction to distract him from discovering the merchant's involvement in the murder of English soldiers, he also made it impossible for him to speak the truth lest the merchant reveal the sin committed. If Thomas stayed silent, he became an accomplice in the crime for which Hywel was hanged.

To prove his loyalty to King Edward, he would be forced to reveal his sodomy. At best, that might mean sentencing by the Church to a life in a solitary cell. At worst, it could mean a slow death at the stake if the support for such punishment had grown strong enough. Even if he was prepared for either punishment, how could he bring humiliation down on his prioress for harboring a sodomite?

"We must speak with Lambard privately and hear what he has to say when he learns that the maid has given permission. Since you have spoken with him before, Brother, I want you to accompany me. Your observations and questions will be crucial." She turned to the sub-infirmarian. "And your insights will be needed as well, if you can spare the time away from my sister-in-law."

"I feel greater confidence that I can," Anne replied. "She seems to be healing well. If there is an urgent need to find any of us, we can leave word with a servant at the lodge. Someone can run swiftly enough to the spicer's shop."

Thomas could find no way to refuse his prioress' request. As he nodded agreement, he implored God to give him strength to endure this meeting, find a way to spare his prioress, and gain the courage to face what could be a horrible future.

Eleanor finally smiled. "Having been foolish enough to chase after Eluned and follow her into a dark crypt alone, I am grateful that you both will be with me for this meeting. Having once failed to use the wits He gave me, I dare not call solely on His mercy a second time."

May He show me that mercy as well, Thomas thought, and

did not dare count the number of times he had beseeched such a kindness.

The trio walked on. It was not a long way between the dead sheriff's house and that of Lambard the spicer, but, for Thomas, it felt like the walk he might have to take between prison and the stake where he would be burned.

Chapter Thirty-Four

The journeyman who greeted the monastic trio in the shop below the living quarters seemed not at all surprised by their visit, yet was hesitant to disturb his master.

"He is spending the day in prayer and fasting. He gave orders that he should not be disturbed unless it was a matter of dire urgency. If you wish alms, I have the authority..."

Prioress Eleanor smiled with appreciative sympathy. "It is not alms we seek, but our cause is pressing. I respect Master Lambard's vow to dedicate this day to God and promise that we will neither interrupt his devotions nor tire him unduly." Her expression shifted into one that clearly conveyed her message that any refusal was unacceptable.

With resignation, the man bowed, said he would return shortly, and then vanished up the stairs.

Knowing that her portrayal of unarguable determination was usually successful, Eleanor tried not to smile. Although her approach carried the power of her position as Prioress of Tyndal, she wondered how often the man's wife had used the same look with equal success.

The journeyman soon came back and led the trio into a room above where Lambard stood, his expression carefully composed into one of warm welcome.

Thomas deliberately stood at the rear of the monastic party. He trembled with dread and fury in equal parts but was relieved when the spice merchant ignored him as he bowed to Prioress Eleanor and Sister Anne.

"I have called for refreshment," Lambard said cheerfully. "My man servant will be here shortly."

Both good spirits and smile are forced, Thomas noted, and wondered if his prioress and sub-infirmarian had concluded the same.

"I fear this matter requires privacy," Eleanor replied. "Although your servant may be trustworthy, it is imperative that we four speak alone."

For the first time, the merchant glanced over the prioress' head at Thomas. Alarm was unmistakably present in his eyes.

Briefly, Thomas felt his anger melt away, and he discreetly shook his head in response to the unspoken question. I may be a fool, he thought, but perhaps Lambard has as much reason as I to hide what we did in that alley.

"I shall tell him." Lambard excused himself and left the room. When he returned, his face was gray. Shutting the door quietly behind him, he invited his guests to sit.

Giving permission to the others to do so, Eleanor remained standing. "I bring a message, after which I have many questions. Or, if you prefer, you may tell the whole story without omissions or shadings to hide truth."

The merchant tensed, and then nodded.

"Eluned says Hywel wishes it."

To Thomas' ear, Lambard's sigh was one of relief rather than regret.

"I hope she explained that, in giving you that message for me, you have agreed to take no action against any of us in this matter." The merchant's tone was respectful.

"I told her only that I would agree as long as treason against the king is not involved and that the man in hiding is no murderer. I need proof of both, Master Spicer, not allegations."

"Some define treason more narrowly than others, my lady. Do you allow disagreement where there is no intent to commit any form of bodily harm or to overthrow a duly anointed king?"

"Eluned and I discussed that. In principle, I do. Yet I also know that men are known to twist meaning to suit their purpose and often try to make even murder sound like a loving act."

"I swear on any hope my soul may have of God's mercy that the only sin in what I am about to tell you is one man's wish to join his family in Wales and a belief in his right to think King Edward might have avoided this war if he had been more generous with the Welsh after that last one."

How often had she heard that, Eleanor wondered, and yet this was from the lips of an Englishman. "Tell your tale, and truthfully, but know that I shall make my own judgments."

Thomas noted the sweat on the merchant's forehead. Then he wiped it from his own. Lambard must have smelled Death's corpse breath as strongly as he.

Lambard cleared his throat. "If Eluned trusted you, then I must as well."

Eleanor now sat, folded her hands in her lap, and waited.

"Abbot Gerald is right in one part of this sad tale. The ghost, who haunts our village, is indeed Hywel."

Sister Anne gasped and then pressed a hand over her mouth.

"He is not a phantom, however. He is a living man."

Eleanor's face was a study in calm and patience.

"What happened the day of the hanging, my lady, might be counted a manifestation of God's mercy. Despite the roars of approval when Hywel was marched to the gallows, few of us, in our hearts, could believe that the man we had grown up with, a man whose wife helped other wives bear children, and one whose word could always be trusted, was guilty of leading a band of marauders to kill soldiers in their sleep. Yes, he was a Welshman, but King Edward has loyal Welshmen fighting in his army. Hywel could have left the village after his wife died to join Dafydd. He did not. That supports his loyalty to our king, or so I believed and still do." He looked around at the monastics. "In any case, what happened at the gallows was most certainly a miracle. There can be no other explanation."

"Hywel survived the hanging?" Sister Anne looked doubtful.

"Two hangings," Lambard replied. "Bardolph pulled him up first, and, while the stonemason was thrashing for breath, he hauled up the second condemned man, a common murderer. It took two men to do the latter for the man was grossly fat. After a short time, the beam broke under the weight. The two felons fell to the ground. Bardolph declared Hywel dead, announcing that his bowels had loosened and his bladder had voided. The other man was alive, screamed for a reprieve, and claimed the breaking of the beam meant God wished for clemency to be granted."

"Which Bardolph denied?" Eleanor tilted her head with a mildly curious look.

"He turned to the sheriff's brother and representative for a verdict. Rainold said that the hanging must be completed for the second felon and that Hywel's dead body must be hoisted up again as well. So, after the beam was finally replaced, the live felon was hanged again, and then Hywel's corpse briefly raised, until Bardolph declared the first man dead."

"Was his judgment on that accepted or distrusted?" The prioress looked at her sub-infirmarian, but Sister Anne seemed lost in thought.

"Rainold merely glanced at the fat man's corpse, nodded, and passed on to Hywel's. Bardolph pointed out additional proof of death on the stonemason's body: the protruding and blackened tongue as well as blood around the neck and in the mouth. Indicating satisfaction, the sheriff's brother let Hywel's brothers take the corpse away. Bardolph was offered the clothes, as is often a hangman's due. Perhaps he had lost all desire for them after hanging a dead man, but he refused. The second felon had no family here. I think some soldiers removed that body, and may

God have mercy on their souls for what they might have done with it. As I have heard the tale, the dead man had raped and killed the wife of one of the men."

Eleanor's gray eyes grew dark, but she said nothing.

"Were you a witness to the hanging?" Sister Anne asked.

"I have no love of public executions. My servant went and told me in detail what had happened."

The sub-infirmarian glanced at her prioress, then asked, "Could Bardolph have deliberately failed to hang Hywel long enough for him to strangle?"

"If he had done so, he would have been hanged on his own gallows, Sister. The law demands that to keep hangmen honest and immune to bribes. Hywel wasn't hanged long the second time, however."

"Why was Rainold not satisfied he was dead the first time?" Sister Anne still looked perplexed.

"I cannot explain why Rainold demanded that Hywel's dead body be hanged again. My servant said he did not indicate he questioned the verdict of death. But the crowd cheered the decision. Perhaps that was the sole cause. Rainold often chooses to do the popular thing when he acts on his brother's behalf."

Thomas raised an eyebrow as he wondered if the younger brother did so to cast the sheriff in a more favorable light or to do so for himself. As far as Thomas was concerned, the latter was the more likely conclusion.

"Your servant returned with an excellent memory of the execution," the prioress said.

Lambard paled, then nodded.

Remembering the cold demeanor of the servant when he first came to this house, Thomas briefly wondered if Lambard had once lusted after Hywel. Out of jealousy, had his servant gone, not only for the satisfaction of seeing the stonemason dead, but to convey all the grisly details of the death to the spice merchant?

"How came you to offer a place to wash the corpse?" Whatever her thoughts, Eleanor's tone was flat.

"When Hywel was condemned, Eluned came to me and asked if I might allow his brothers to use a hut I own behind my house to wash his body and prepare it for burial. For the kindness that Hywel had often shown me, I agreed. But it was after they brought his dead body there, the miracle occurred. Eluned ran to me, begging me to follow her to the hut. I found that the corpse was breathing freely. Hywel even moved a leg."

"How could he have survived?" Anne murmured as if to herself.

"God's mercy, Sister. That is the only explanation," Lambard replied. "Eluned told me she had been in the process of bending a penny over his corpse to invoke a saint's mercy when she heard him moan. In shock, she looked down and discovered his eyes were blinking at her." Still in awe, Lambard fell silent.

The prioress gestured for him to continue.

"We all agreed to say nothing to anyone else about this out of fear that the sheriff might conclude, as his brother had done, that Hywel must be hanged yet another time. In truth, I may be wicked beyond redemption and a vile sinner, but I am convinced God meant Hywel to live."

"Few mortals are beyond redemption," Eleanor said, "but your conclusion about God's mercy has merit."

"We did not dare call on a local healer, for we knew we must keep this miracle secret, but I have herbs and some knowledge of their use in cures. I tended him, as did Eluned when she could leave her mistress. It took many days for Hywel to recover enough to speak. On the fourth day, he was able to swallow a little meat, not just soup. As he gained strength, Eluned and I decided that we must hide him elsewhere until he could escape. My hut was not safe enough."

"His brothers?"

"Gone to Wales, I think. Eluned told them to flee when Hywel seemed to recover. I did hear her tell them, if Hywel lived, she would find some way to get him out of the village safely. I assume she and they agreed to a location where the three brothers could reunite. I swear I do not know where, nor did I ask."

"So you chose to hide him in the crypt where the abbots were buried?"

Lambard nodded.

Eleanor smiled. "A clever spot, I confess. Abbot Gerald seems in fine health, thus unlikely to need a tomb, and I assume the vault has few if any visitors."

"There is always an empty coffin for the next abbot, my lady. Hywel hid there until Eluned came with food. If he thought anyone else was coming to the crypt, he pulled the lid over him to make it look like the coffin was sealed. Since he was a stone-mason, he was strong enough to raise the lid from inside and kept it slightly ajar with a flat stone."

And thus he hid from us when we searched, Eleanor thought. In the dim light, the small space between lid and coffin would not have been noticed by Brother Thomas.

"She cared for all his needs, dangerous though that was."

"Because she loves him," Eleanor said.

Lambard hesitated, then nodded.

Love him she must, to hide all evidence of his presence at the possible cost of her own life. Should she be caught thieving as well as hiding a condemned man, she might well be hanged herself. "Yet she made one mistake," she added. "We found proof that someone was being fed in the crypt."

"She feared you suspected something when she noticed you had followed her. In order to make her excuse for being at the church more believable, she did not wait to take the containers away after Hywel ate. It was a mistake."

"Then Father Payn and Bardolph did see Hywel." This was the first time Thomas had spoken.

Lambard started at the sound of the monk's voice. "Another error, one that was mine. I thought it safe enough for Hywel to go to the abbey church that night, but I did not imagine that Father Payn would return from his mistress at the same time. Hywel told Eluned that the priest fell to the ground dead, presumably thinking that Hywel was a spirit returned from Hell to seek vengeance."

"And Bardolph saw Hywel kneeling by the body," Sister Anne added.

"Hywel had just confirmed the priest's death, then saw the hangman and fled when Bardolph turned away for just a moment."

"And the murders of the hangman and Sir William?" Eleanor carefully did not reveal her opinion on who had committed these.

"The lock to the vault is faulty, as you have discovered, but once the door is closed, no one can leave from inside the crypt. It can only be opened from without." He looked at the now silent monk. "You can easily test it."

"Eluned could have let him out," Eleanor said.

"These murders happened at night. As I explained, Hywel could not have left the crypt without help. Since the hanging, the Lady Mary has insisted that Eluned sleep in her chambers. When her husband comes to share his wife's bed, Eluned remains outside the door until he leaves." He cleared his throat. "After he is gone, the Lady Mary requires mulled wine and her maid to return to sleep at the foot of her bed for the remainder of the night."

The prioress pondered this, seemed to come to a conclusion, and said, "She also insisted you had proof that Hywel was innocent of the crime for which he was hanged."

Lambard smiled. "That is the easiest, my lady. As you noted, the pair are in love. Eluned and Hywel had taken advantage of a rare opportunity to lie together that night when the raid against the English soldiers occurred. It would have been impossible for him to leave her arms, lead a band of raiders, and then return to the village by morning when others saw him at his work."

"She might have lied to you," Eleanor countered.

"It is not just her tale I am telling, my lady. That night, I..." He hesitated, swallowed, and continued. "Unable to sleep that night,

I dressed and went out to walk. I saw them go into his house. The moon had just slipped toward morning. The raid, as the story was told at the trial, was already underway."

"You said that Hywel had been kind to you. Perhaps you owe him a boon in return." Eleanor's suggestion that he could be lying hung in the air.

Lambard did not indicate that he resented her suspicion. "Hywel may have shown gentleness to me," he said, "and thus I owed his corpse a place to be cleansed, but I have no reason to offer a false excuse for a man who commits such a crime against sleeping men. As God is my witness, I am a loyal subject of King Edward, and Hywel is innocent of the crime."

"Yet you did not testify on his behalf at the trial," Thomas said, "while Rainold came forth and confirmed that Hywel was the leader of the brigands. The sheriff's brother even expressed some regret that he must do so. Why did you not speak up as an honest man would?" His words were sharply spoken.

"He testified first. Eluned and I knew that we would not be believed. If men must decide whether a sheriff's brother tells the truth or a Welsh maid and a common merchant, whose testimony do you think they will choose?" Lambard looked at the monk with a sorrow that seemed much deeper than warranted.

Thomas glared in return. "The Lady Mary offered testimony that Hywel was innocent. Would that not allow you to speak?"

"And men smile when a highborn lady begs for mercy as she is wont to do. Lady Mary's testimony was a simple declaration of his character. Hywel had been a good Christian, an honest stonemason, and a faithful husband to his English wife. She said nothing more than all men in the village had once believed before Hywel was arrested. She did not claim he had not committed the crime for which he was accused."

Thomas felt the sweat coursing down his chest and back. Even if Lambard was innocent of any involvement in the murder of the soldiers, and what had happened that night at the inn would not be mentioned, the monk suspected that the merchant had still seduced him for some uncaring and calculated purpose. Had the reason been loneliness, Thomas could have forgiven him. Had it been lust, he could have as well. What he could not bear was someone making a mockery of his fragility and humiliating him.

"Why would Rainold lie?" Thomas knew there was more bitter anger in his question and only hoped Lambard did not detect the hurt behind it.

"You must ask him why he did, Brother. He may have cause, as men often do, when lying in bed with someone they should not."

Thomas fell back into silence, his face pale.

"And who might that be?" Eleanor smiled and seemed in no doubt about the answer.

"The Lady Mary," he whispered, "but I cannot offer proof. Since Eluned has shown I can trust you, I will say that it is she who says that may be the case. She has been unswervingly loyal to her mistress. The only reason she told me is that we have been friends since childhood, and I would never speak of it unless she approved. I think it best if you ask her for the details."

Eleanor nodded, rose, and thanked the merchant for his testimony.

He bowed his head, then begged a blessing from her but not from her monk.

Confused, she glanced at Thomas.

His eyes remained lowered.

She gave the requested gift.

Lambard accompanied them to the shop entrance. He stood in the open door for a long time, watching the trio walk away. Tears flowed, and he did nothing to stop them as he looked at the departing monk.

Thomas did not look back.

Chapter Thirty-Five

When the trio arrived back at the lodge, Brother Thomas and Sister Anne both saw that familiar look on their prioress' face and knew she needed time by herself. Each told her where they would be and then slipped away.

Eleanor turned her back on the lodge and walked toward the forest edge just below the hill crest.

Although chapel prayer was both her duty and comfort, there were times when she sought another place for contemplation, one devoid of all mortal men. At her priory, she often walked in the gardens, after the lay brothers and sisters had finished their work, or else the cloister garth. On occasion, she shut the door to her private chambers and sat with her cat in her lap, a creature to whom she talked and even imagined understood her words. Silence was not obligatory. Arthur, the cat, purred. Birds sang, and the wind rattled anything loose. What she did not want was the sound of other people.

In the beginning, when she first realized that God required a different kind of obedience from her than He did most religious, she discovered that need to escape the children of Adam and Eve. They distracted her from fresh thinking and kept her from giving form to her wordless thoughts. As the years passed, she became confident that God saw no sin in her chosen methods of reflection or He would have expressed displeasure early on.

She did not wander deep into the forest but soon chose a fallen tree trunk on which to sit. The bark was damp and rough, but she did not mind. Her back to the lodge, she took in a deep breath and shut her eyes.

Some might call birdsong raucous or even undisciplined. Others might complain that the touch of a soft breeze on the cheek was wickedly erotic. To the Prioress of Tyndal, none of that was true. These were small gifts of perfection that God gave the world, gifts offered for delight and utterly devoid of sin. Only in the children of Adam and Eve was there the possibility of evil.

And which of the flawed mortals in this village was the most likely to be Satan's minion?

First of all, she thought, we have the dead: Father Payn, Bardolph, and Sir William. All were assumed to be victims of an angry soul belonging to the condemned man, Hywel, released from Hell to wreak vengeance on those who wronged him.

Yet through some miracle, Hywel seemed to have survived, not just one hanging but two.

Although she had not seen the man, she was willing to assume he lived. She was even willing to accept, for the moment, that he was not the killer of the three men. If not, then someone else must want everyone to think he was.

Each of the dead men died in a way that was symbolic of a wrathful spirit's vengeance. Father Payn, a man who showed heart-lessness by denying a condemned man's final confession, died when his heart failed from the shock of seeing a ghost. Bardolph, his hangman, was found dangling from his own gallows. And Sir William, who had accepted the judgment of Hywel's guilt and condemned him, was found with his head chopped off. Since the head was the seat of both soul and reason, the murderer had rendered the sternest revenge on the sheriff.

It was a clever tale, meant to distract all from seeing the truth.

But with Hywel still alive, and Lambard's tale believed, then Father Payn died a natural death as Sister Anne was convinced he had. Perhaps it was the sight of a man he thought was dead that killed the priest. Sister Anne had told her that the heart often suggests its willingness to end its work before it actually does and will seek any reason to do so in its own time. Father Payn might have died from the exertion of running back to the abbey after visiting his mistress, even if he had not seen what he assumed was a ghost.

According to Brother Thomas, Bardolph was struck unconscious before he was hanged and Sir William was as well before he was decapitated. To her mind, and her fellow monastics, those were the acts of a mortal. Imps can hang or chop heads with the simple wave of a clawed hand.

Eleanor opened her eyes and stared at the sky through the treetops. The death of Father Payn was a fine inspiration for someone who had been hoping to find a way to achieve some purpose and now saw a way by blaming a ghost.

She laughed. "If so," she said to the murmuring of insect and avian life around her, "the death of Father Payn was an accident, and poor Bardolph was killed solely because his death would help further cast the real intent into shadow. The intended victim has been Sir William all along."

Although her heart now raced with excitement, she forced herself to consider alternative conclusions but found no other that fit what appeared to be the motive quite so well. The only doubt that remained was whether the sheriff's death was the end point or other murders might occur.

So who was the murderer?

Loving Hywel, Eluned might have reason to seek revenge for his condemnation, if not his death, but she could not have struck either Bardolph or her master hard enough to stun them. Nor was she likely to have the strength to hoist one man up on the gallows beam or strike another's head off. Then there was the detail of Lady Mary demanding her maid remain within call at night since the hanging. That might be an odd request, one to which Eleanor would give further thought, but neither did she have cause to cast it aside.

Had Hywel helped the maid? A man twice hanged, but who still lived, was unlikely to stay around for a possible third hanging if he had the chance to flee to Wales. From what she had learned of the man, he truly did not seem inclined to violence. It seemed more likely that he had chosen to accept his survival as a precious miracle and hide until he could safely escape.

Indeed, Eluned seemed a weak suspect.

She could not entirely dismiss Lambard, who had certainly contributed to this tangled story of alleged treason, God's mercy, secret lovers, and as yet incompletely answered motives for murder.

It did seem that the spice merchant was viewed with some unease. Bardolph's mistress praised him for his charity, and other villagers would likely do the same, and yet her comment that he did not take advantage of her whorehouse did not sound quite like the virtue it should. Although Eleanor had not heard how Mistress Maud had phrased it, she had seen Brother Thomas' look when he repeated the conversation. There was an inexplicable shadow that crossed his face. At the time, she had not questioned him further and now regretted her failure.

Yet she had no good reason to think the merchant was disloyal to the king, and Eleanor was inclined to believe the tale of Hywel's innocence. Lambard gained nothing from the death of Sir William. He seemed to have some quarrel with Father Payn, but Sister Anne believed that to be a natural death, a conclusion against which there was no rational argument.

The prioress shook her head. Lambard might have his secrets and his transgressions, but she did not think he was guilty of murder. She was inclined to set his name aside as she had Eluned.

That left the Lady Mary and the new heir, Sir Rainold.

There was reason enough to assume that the younger brother

had lusted after the title and lands. It was not an uncommon tale, and he would not be the first younger son to find a way to prematurely inherit when he might especially enjoy the wealth from land and rents in his comparative youth.

In addition, there was one more detail that pointed to Rainold as the killer. If revenge had ever been the motive, he should have died after Bardolph. He was the most instrumental person in guaranteeing Hywel's guilty verdict. All Sir William did was order the trial and confirm the result of the verdict. In short, the wrong man had been killed after the hangman.

But Eleanor was not sure Rainold was alone in this quest. She had suspected the brother-in-law and sister-in-law were lovers. They were much alike and too close in age. Yet she was not sure just how deeply the young widow had been involved in the plot.

At no point had Eleanor seen any cleverness in the woman. Maybe her only guilt lay in the still grievous sin of adultery. If she was as frivolous and self-absorbed as she seemed, the true planning had to have been done by her ambitious lover. The only one who should hang was Sir Rainold. Although an adulterous woman could be burned at the stake for her sin, the king usually left the punishment to the Church. Thus, penance would remain the duty of Lady Mary's priest.

The prioress stood, brushed off her habit, and looked back over her shoulder at the lodge. Birdsong ceased at her movement and even the breeze hesitated.

"Now that I must return to the world of mortals," she whispered into the sudden hush surrounding her, "I must find a way to get the man to confess since I have no good evidence and am unlikely to find any."

With determined stride, she walked back to the lodge. Since the sheriff was dead, and no one had yet been chosen to replace him, Robert must take on the authority of the local lord and provide the men she needed. As representative of Baron Hugh of Wynethorpe, her brother was also the best witness to what she hoped would be a confession by one who had not only given false witness at the trial that condemned an innocent stonemason, but was also a double murderer.

It remained Eleanor's responsibility to make sure there was at least one person, perhaps two, to arrest.

Chapter Thirty-Six

"Lies. All lies." Sir Rainold folded his arms and gazed at his accusers with mocking smugness.

The Lady Mary stood near the wall with her maid beside her and away from the assembled group. Although her head was bowed, and her expression unreadable, her stance suggested that she did not understand why she, a simple daughter of Eve, had been asked to join this gathering of men and the highborn Prioress of Tyndal.

"Who dares to tell such tales?" His tone was less a question than a taunt.

"I would not come here with my brother and his men if I did not have good reason," Eleanor said in a voice that would freeze the resolve of most mortals.

Rainold was not deterred. "Forgive me, my lady, for I honor your vocation, but your concept of reason is still that of a woman."

She smiled with the warmth of ice.

Robert, who had been watching her, winced.

"Proof!" Rainold snapped his fingers.

"Statements will be given at your trial," she replied, "but I shall begin with this: there is no ghost in this village. Father Payn died of a failing heart when he saw something that startled him, but the deaths of Bardolph and Sir William were caused by a hand made of flesh and blood."

The man pursed his lips with churlish disdain.

Ignoring his swaggering attempts to unsettle her, Eleanor chose to reply in the manner of a mother dealing with a truculent child. "For that conclusion, there is sufficient evidence. Lest there be any doubt about my ability to recognize this, Abbot Gerald will confirm that imps do not need to render their victims unconscious before killing them."

"You have revealed nothing that points to the hand being mine."

"You asked for a logical conclusion, Sir Rainold, and I am starting by giving you the facts on which it is based. Patience is a virtue that is often rewarding."

He nodded but looked heavenward, clearly suggesting he was showing virtue enough by enduring a woman's typically torturous route to any conclusion.

"The death of the priest, and Bardolph's testimony that the ghost of Hywel had been seen kneeling by the corpse, gave one man the idea for how he might disguise murder. Indeed, it was a clever stratagem to use the tale of a damned soul bent on vengeance."

Rainold blinked and briefly smiled.

Eleanor noted that and continued. "Bardolph and Sir William were first rendered unconscious, or even killed, and then their corpses were carefully posed. The hangman was hauled up on his own gallows, and the man who rendered judgment was decapitated. It appeared the stonemason's tortured spirit murdered each according to the act committed that had sent him to Hell."

Rainold sighed.

"I confess that I need your help with one matter, something only a man of your preeminence can do." Eleanor tilted her head and gave the man a look of almost blinding admiration. "While I have been in this village, I have heard many say that you are a popular man, known to be possessed of unusual cleverness." She hesitated, then smiled with evident appreciation. "It is never immodest to admit to a fact."

Rainold's eyes brightened and he puffed out his chest. "It is true that I am noted for my superior wits."

"How sad that you were not the older brother. To his credit, however, Sir William did seem to acknowledge that you were far more capable than he."

After a brief hesitation, Rainold nodded although he looked perplexed.

"He counted on you to manage the estates, and, I believe, often asked you to be his representative when he could not perform some duty as sheriff?"

"That is all true." Rainold frowned.

"You were at the hanging of Hywel and the other felon, were you not?"

Again, he nodded.

"And, when the beam broke, you ordered Bardolph to hang both men again, even though Hywel had been declared dead and his body was covered with urine and feces. Why hang him twice?"

"I committed no crime in that. The Welshman had been condemned for crimes against innocent Englishmen. The crowd loved my decision. They deserved to see him hanged again and mocked for the crimes he committed."

"Yet, in so doing, you put yourself in great danger. Should Hywel's soul return from Hell to seek vengeance, it was you who ordered his corpse be treated with such contempt. In fact, you were in greater danger of revenge than your brother. Sir William tried to obtain objective proof that the stonemason was guilty, even though the man seems to have confessed. Of all those involved in Hywel's hanging, Sir William was the least guilty because he tried to be fair."

Rainold looked horrified. "That means I would have been the next to be killed!"

"Why, then, was Sir William killed first?" She tilted her head and watched him. "And, in answering that, let us not forget that there is no ghost."

He paled. "I do not understand your point in this."

The Lady Mary had raised her head and was now watching this interchange with much interest and an odd smile.

Eleanor waited a moment longer before responding. "The answer is that the wrong man was killed after Bardolph. If revenge was the motive for the deaths, it should have been you for your testimony at the trial that condemned Hywel. But your brother's death had always been the objective. When Father Payn died, and Bardolph said he had seen a ghost kneeling by the priest's body, the killer realized how he could arrange a death he had long hoped for. There was no reason for Bardolph to die, other than to make your brother's death look to be part of a pattern." She glanced around and knew she had everyone's attention.

Rainold's forehead glistened with sweat.

"Thus no one would question it when you inherited everything as you had long thought was your due. Well done, Sir Rainold! No one else in this village could be so skillful in hiding murder."

"That is not true. I loved my brother."

The high-pitched, sharp laughter from Lady Mary caused the hair to rise on more than one neck.

Only the prioress did not look surprised, and she turned to the woman with an encouraging smile.

The widow pointed to her brother-in-law. "You lie. How often have you boasted to me that you were the best steward, that my husband was a ninny who could do nothing without you? You even told me what you would do if he should die without an heir, something you were sure he would never have because you claimed he was impotent."

"Be careful," Rainold growled. "You have sins enough to hide, and I know them all."

She stepped forward and slapped his face with impressive

force. "Where were you the night of my dear husband's murder? I sought you for advice on an urgent matter, but you were nowhere to be found. When Bardolph was killed, you claimed to have been visiting an old friend. Yet he told me, when I met him in the market square, that you had only stopped for a moment before explaining you had a task to perform for me. Another lie, for I had begged no such favor."

Rainold's face turned purple with rage.

Lady Mary ignored him and turned to Prioress Eleanor and Robert of Wynethorpe. "I will gladly provide witness to all this and give you the names of men who can confirm what I tell you. I was not the only one to whom he said he hoped my husband would die and he could inherit."

"Whore!" Rainold screamed and lunged for the widow.

One of the soldiers grabbed him. He and another man dragged Rainold back.

The Lady Mary looked around at the others in the room. "Did you hear what he called me, this man who murdered my beloved lord?"

"With cause!" Rainold shouted. "And I add to that an accusation that you are a witch!" He held out his one free hand to Robert and Eleanor with an imploring gesture. "She seduced me and begged me to free her from her husband's bondage. She put me under a spell and, while I lay in her bed, said I should kill her husband. If I must hang for committing such a crime while I was under a spell, then she must burn at the stake for adultery and witchcraft."

Eleanor shut her eyes with gratitude. The man had just confessed.

Despite the grim threat, the widow laughed again with honest merriment. "Burn? Adultery? My lord and I enjoyed a loving marriage. Only rarely did we not share a bed, and when he was absent, or I was suffering my courses, my devoted maid slept in my room to keep me company in my loneliness." She gazed with much fondness at Eluned.

"Indeed, that is true," Eluned replied. "Either Sir William or

I were in my lady's company each night. She could not have lain with any other man."

When Eleanor looked at her, the maid dropped her gaze. It was an appropriate gesture for a servant in such an assembled company of the highborn, but the prioress suspected there was another reason. For a moment, she wondered if she should pursue her suspicions, then chose to remain silent. It was wisest, she decided, to remain satisfied with the victory she had won.

The prioress turned to her brother and nodded.

Robert stepped forward and gestured to his men. "He has confessed to murder. Arrest him."

Rainold struggled and could not free himself. Finally, he turned to Prioress Eleanor, his eyes glittering. "Do not do this, my lady," he snarled. "You will regret your actions."

"That was a rash threat," she replied. "I serve the God whom you must soon face. It would be more prudent to spend your remaining hours begging forgiveness for your sins."

Undeterred, he grinned back at her.

Even though he was securely held, there was something in his expression that caused Eleanor a tremor of fear and made her step back.

"Oh, but I do have cause, my lady," he chortled. "How would the local bishop and your abbess in Anjou react if they learned that Brother Thomas was a sodomite?"

Robert stared in horror at his sister.

Eleanor could not respond. For that crucial moment, when she should have sharply retorted, the world seemed to tilt and she struggled to regain her balance. Fighting not to panic, she prayed silently for help.

Rainold knew he had struck a good blow, and he hurried to take advantage of it. "The night your monk was drinking with the merchants at the inn, he left alone with Lambard, a man who is suspected with good cause by many to be a sodomite. You need not take my word. Ask others in the village."

Eleanor felt as if she had turned to ice.

"I saw them walk into a dark passage, very close together. Since I feared your monk might not know of the man's wickedness, I was concerned and followed. The spot Lambard took him was well-known for evils committed and the presence of the Devil's minions. It was then I saw Brother Thomas, his robes raised to his waist, and Lambard on his knees giving your monk a form of unchaste pleasure most abhorred by God."

Eleanor began to feel the welcome heat of anger but hoped that her face remained expressionless.

"If you insist on my trial for murder, I shall announce to all what wickedness your monk has committed and you will lose a man whom, I believe, you cherish above all others." He snickered over his blatant hint that she was also unchaste.

Eleanor knew her face had turned red. Rainold may have thought he had humiliated her, but her reaction was based in rage.

How dare he presume that she could be bribed when God's justice was at stake? Whatever guilt she felt because of her love for Brother Thomas or even her shock at what Rainold was saying he had seen, she pushed all that aside and stepped forward with the expression of fury that would awe an archangel on the Judgment Day.

Not expecting this reaction, Rainold backed into the men who held him prisoner.

"Announce what you will to whomever you wish," the prioress said in a tone pitched so low it rumbled like thunder. "It was at my command that Brother Thomas met with the merchants that night. He warned me that he might have to drink more than he should. Knowing him well, I knew he would be as temperate as possible, confess any excess, and serve his proper penance."

Rainold continued to grin but his lips trembled.

"As for what happened in that dark alley, Brother Thomas told me the next morning that Lambard had led him to the passageway in hopes of seeing this alleged ghost. When they got there, the merchant, in his drunkenness, unexpectedly knelt before my monk, lifted his garments, and took hold of his genitals. Brother Thomas was frozen with disbelief but recovered and fled. He spent the night in anguished prayer. I have told him to confess and serve whatever hard penance he is given as soon as we return to our priory. Those are the circumstances you have tried to twist into a greater sin than occurred." She gazed at him with utter contempt. "Now it is you who must think carefully. Whom do you think my abbess and the local bishop will believe? A man who foully murdered his brother out of greed? Or a monk who has, over many years, honored his vows and proven his devotion to God's justice and service?"

In silence, Eleanor begged God to forgive her the lie she had just told and for the false certainty with which she claimed her monk's innocence.

Looking back on that morning after the events at the inn, she now understood why Brother Thomas might have been overwhelmed with guilt. Perhaps her lie just now would be proven true, and he had grieved over a sin unwillingly suffered. He may have fled after recovering from the shock of the merchant's touch. She simply did not know.

But this was not the time to dwell on discovering the truth of what occurred. God's justice took precedence. She turned to Robert. "Take this foul man away," she said.

Then Eleanor watched with grim satisfaction as the men led the shrieking Sir Rainold out of the house to which he had so briefly laid claim.

Chapter Thirty-Seven

Immediately after the killer had been taken to a dank cell, Lady Mary gave Robert of Wynethorpe the names of all who might confirm that her brother-in-law had shown resentment against Sir William, even expressing the hope the sheriff would soon die, and had not been where he claimed on the nights Bardolph and the sheriff had been killed.

One of those witnesses mentioned another, a man who told Robert that he had seen Rainold near Bardolph's hut the night of the murder. Yet another witness swore he had seen the younger brother walking toward the bridge the night of the sheriff's death.

When asked why neither had come forward before, each reminded Robert that everyone believed the ghost was the murderer. Damned souls were responsibility of the Church and men vowed to God, not worldly men of sinful nature. Once a creature of flesh and blood had been arrested, however, they had come forward immediately to honor their obligations as loyal subjects of King Edward.

Between arrest and execution, Rainold drifted into madness, screaming from his cell that a man should not hang unless a witch was burned. Feigned or not, he howled like a wolf, danced until his chains rattled, and did his best to portray a man under a spell.

In truth, it did not matter whether anyone believed he was mad or had been bewitched. He would hang, and he surely knew it.

When he was finally hauled up on the gallows beam by a hangman imported from another town, the villagers watched until his dance in the noose ended and then turned away with what some described as a collective sigh of relief. With evil men, all knew there would be an ending to their crimes, if nothing else in death, but the ire of condemned and vengeful spirits was eternal.

It was the day after the execution of Rainold that the Lady Mary sent a message to Prioress Eleanor, begging her to honor the widow with a visit before she permanently left the sad house she had shared with her dead husband. The new sheriff, once appointed, would take it over as one of his residences.

Eleanor was surprised, not at the woman's desire to leave but at her wish to speak further with a person so deeply connected with the tragic events. For anyone, not totally devoid of feelings, the time, albeit short, between the arrest of Rainold and his hanging must have been grueling for the widow.

Yet when Prioress Eleanor and Sister Anne entered the room, Lady Mary greeted them with unexpected grace, and then begged them to sit and enjoy refreshment.

Eluned, quiet and obedient as always, served a fine cider and retreated to the wall with eyes modestly lowered in a manner that was intended to make everyone forget she was present.

"I wished to thank you for all you have done, my lady. On the morrow, I leave this place forever, but I could not do so without expressing my gratitude and offering a gift to your priory." The widow bowed her head respectfully but not before flushing with an undefined emotion.

"Yet Sir William died," Eleanor replied. "I grieve that we were unable to discover the slayer until afterward." The widow's face had acquired a unique beauty, the prioress realized. She was also struck with another difference between this woman sitting before them and the woman she had first met. Lady Mary was no longer a simpering fool. She had acquired dignity.

"He has left me with a gift, however," the Lady Mary said softly. "I am with child."

Eleanor recovered herself before she betrayed her surprise and swiftly expressed delight with the news.

"Sadly, I was unable to tell my beloved husband that God had answered our many years of prayer, but I am sure his soul knows and rejoices. I most ardently pray that the news will ease his suffering in Purgatory."

Quickly agreeing, Eleanor's curiosity was too strong to ignore, although she had to be very careful with her questions. "I assume your brother-in-law did not know either," she said, "for I remember he said that you had not produced an heir."

"And, as I recall, I answered that we had not been so blessed." The widow fell silent as she looked at the prioress as if waiting for a response that failed to come. "I deliberately did not tell Rainold, my lady. As you noted, he was a clever man and easy with charm. In truth, I feared for my life with him and that of any child I might bear. To protect myself and babe, I pretended to be fooled by his attempts to win my esteem. As a consequence, he concluded I was witless, willing to do anything he wished, and foolish enough to think he meant it when he swore to do me great honor should my husband die and he became heir."

"Yet your pregnancy would soon become evident..."

"I had not yet decided how to escape to safety before my quickening was obvious." She glanced over at Eluned with affection. "My maid and I talked much of what plans we should make, but you brought matters to a close quickly and saved my life as well as that of my unborn child. God answered our prayers in you." She looked down and touched her belly with a loving gesture. "My son," she said softly, even her voice glowing with love. "And

I do believe that God has granted me a son, whom I shall name to honor my husband."

Eleanor tried to calculate when this pregnancy could have begun but decided she could not without asking. Nor was there any point in so doing. As she well knew, the widow's response would be wisely vague.

"Rainold was a truly wicked man," Lady Mary was saying. "He tried to seed distrust of me in my husband's heart by claiming I lusted after the stonemason." She shook her head. "I barely noticed the man, although I knew who he was. One day, my maid pointed him out to me as the one who had married her friend. That must have been when Rainold saw me viewing the man with a pleasant expression and concluded he could turn my innocent thoughts into something damaging."

"You were brave enough to speak up on Hywel's behalf at his trial."

Lady Mary glanced briefly at her maid. "If Eluned was convinced of his innocence, then I did all I was able as a favor to a very loyal servant. Testimony to the man's character was insufficient. Rainold's testimony was far stronger." Her interest in trials and murder slipped away as she again smiled down at her belly.

Eleanor bit her lip. The lady was far cleverer than she had realized and briefly felt aggrieved at how easily she had been fooled by the woman's tricks. She still suspected that the widow had lain with her brother-in-law at least once, whether or not she had done so to protect herself for a while longer, to gain a child, or out of simple lust.

Yet was this child fathered by Rainold or Sir William? Miracles occurred and children were begotten after many years of a barren marriage. The prioress doubted that was the case here. If Sir William had been unable to seed a child in his young wife's womb when he was younger and reliably virile, how probable was it that he succeeded after his manhood had likely weakened? Sister Anne once told her that a man's potency often declined as his belly swelled, and Sir William impressed her as a one who did love his meat and ale.

Yet the adultery was something Eleanor knew she was unlikely to prove. Rainold was dead, and there were no other witnesses to a night or more of passion. The widow had constructed a fine argument for her virtue, thanks to Eluned's cooperation, and the prioress was sure the maid's fidelity had been bought with a coin more precious than gold and too valuable to reject or ever cast aside.

Perhaps she did not care to prove it either. Rainold might well have killed Lady Mary once he discovered she was pregnant with the rightful heir to the estates. The Church would have prohibited him from marrying his sister-in-law without paying far more than any simple knight could manage. Thus he could not claim the child was his, not Sir William's. He had also killed two men to inherit and sent another to the gallows to protect himself from the accusation that he had left his post with the soon-to-be slaughtered soldiers to lie with his brother's wife. By mocking the alleged killer of English soldiers, he had gained popularity with the villagers who would then find no reason to question it when he found a clever way to kill his brother. Why would he let a widow and her presumed legitimate heir live?

Eleanor set her thoughts aside, and the trio of women exchanged polite remarks and meaningless observations for a short while longer.

Soon, the Lady Mary presented a paper granting Tyndal Priory some rents in perpetuity. The visit had ended.

Eleanor and Sister Anne rose.

The Lady Mary knelt and begged a blessing for herself, her dead husband, and their unborn son. It was a gift the Prioress of Tyndal was willing enough to grant, as was her promise that her nuns would add Sir William to their prayers so his suffering in Purgatory might be shorter.

But the day's surprises were not yet over. As the two religious approached the street door, Lady Mary turned to her maid and said, "I believe you have another visit you must make to that dreadful man who has yet to deliver that order for gloves. It must be cancelled. Perhaps you should leave to speak with him now and accompany our guests for part of their walk back to the lodge house." Her expression was a curious mix of sadness and amusement.

When the women left the house, Eluned turned to Prioress Eleanor and said, "Have I yet to satisfy you about Hywel's innocence?"

The prioress smiled. "I shall honor my promise to help in safely getting him on the way to Wales, my child. The trial delayed me. Although I am sure you understood, I grieve that it was necessary."

Eluned began to weep with joy.

"Dry your tears, child. I need you to use all your cleverness to help me."

As Sister Anne stepped back and remained alert to anyone approaching, Eleanor and the maid discussed what must happen and when.

Chapter Thirty-Eight

Abbot Gerald was confused.

"The exorcism must still be performed," Eleanor said. "The deaths of Bardolph and Sir William were done by human hand, but the death of Father Payn was not."

He turned grave as he pondered this. "You fear there is still a malign spirit at work?"

"A being that can now be put to righteous flight from the village. I suspect the failure to do so before was the distraction of evil done by a mortal. Brother Thomas is convinced the exorcism will now be successful."

The abbot actually bounced with joy. "An army of monks shall march against the creature! I will gather everyone in my abbey..."

"That will not be necessary," she replied with a solemn expression. "After much thought and prayer, I have been granted the needed guidance in this matter. Brother Thomas must wrestle this spirit alone in the night with the ferocity that Jacob showed in his struggle with God. Only I may accompany him. Since our Order believes that the duty of the abbess and each prioress is to represent the Virgin Mary on Earth, I must be there to offer her support so he may have the needed strength in the contest." She smiled. "Just as Jacob survived the match, Brother Thomas will be victorious but only if each of us does as is required." She paused to add emphasis. "Nothing more. Nothing less."

"Tell me what I must do," the abbot said. "I could wrestle with the cursed thing myself should your monk need respite."

"Your offer shows admirable faith, but I assure you that the Queen of Heaven will give Brother Thomas all the might he needs."

Despite his evident regret that he could not join in the battle, Abbot Gerald acquiesced. "What must be done?"

"As the light begins to fail this evening, you and your monks should accompany Brother Thomas and me to the abbey church. On the way, psalms shall be sung to alert the forces of evil that their presence here must end. Once we are inside, Brother Thomas will bolt the doors shut and examine the inside to make sure there is only one opening through which the spirit can enter and leave without coming too close to the altar. I will then call out to you from behind the door that we are ready."

"We shall maintain a vigil outside, kneel and raise our voices in ardent prayer."

She bowed her head with honest gratitude. "There is too much danger for that. Once I tell you that the exorcism is about to begin, you and all your monks must swiftly retreat to the abbey. No one is to stay behind or in any way linger on the way. If any man does, his very life and even soul are in danger. As we are all aware, cursed spirits, if thwarted, grow violent, and this one might choose to chase after a monk not surrounded by the holy walls of your abbey."

"All will be praying to God and would thus remain protected."

She hesitated. "The Prince of Darkness has agreed to abide by the results of this contest as long as we honor our word on how it will proceed. This news was part of the direction I was given."

"The Devil has a sense of honor? You truly think he will keep any oath?" Abbot Gerald frowned with evident doubt.

"Wicked and foul though he is," Eleanor said, "he has never

quite forgotten that he was once one of God's most beautiful and well-loved angels. Do we not call him Lucifer in memory of how he fell from Heaven with the brightness of the morning star? On occasion, it seems, he still longs for God to look on him again with favor and thus retains some flicker of honor."

Abbot Gerald blinked.

"When the contest is done, and the spirit returned to Satan's bosom, we shall emerge and send you word. Even then, you must remain in your abbey and offer hosannas in your chapel. Tomorrow, after morning prayers and the evening fast has been broken, I will send for you alone to come to the lodge. We have many matters to discuss."

"The villagers! Will they not be in danger as well if abroad?"

"Well noted, Abbot Gerald! My brother sent out his men to warn everyone that an exorcism will take place tonight and no one, including those who seek malefactors after sunset, should be on the streets until cock crow. Even Wido, the innkeeper, has agreed to shut his doors to trade." Albeit only after Robert promised him a bag of coin, Eleanor thought with displeasure.

Abbot Gerald clearly wanted to do more but knew he dared not insist if he wanted this imp gone. After all, he had begged Prioress Eleanor to help after he and his monks had failed. He owed her the courtesy of obedience.

With a nod and appreciative words, Abbot Gerald swore to obey her requests and left to prepare his monks for their duties.

Prioress Eleanor and Brother Thomas stood in the darkness of the abbey church and waited.

Although she had misled the abbot about what was about to occur, and grieved over the lies she could not carefully rephrase into truth, Eleanor had welcomed the prayers of the monks who accompanied the pair to the church.

Brother Thomas might not be preparing to wrestle with an accursed spirit, but they were both hoping to send a presumed innocent safely away from the village. In ways there was some truth in what was about to happen, even if it was she who had to wrestle with the resolution of this problem instead of her monk striving with a devilish imp.

She still had qualms. Was Hywel truly innocent or was she contributing to a treasonous act by letting a man who had killed defenseless Englishmen escape? Even if she was convinced of his blamelessness, was she wrong to allow him to go to Wales? Lambard, an Englishman, had sworn that Hywel had no wish to fight against King Edward and was a peaceful man who only wanted to return to his family. Was the merchant right?

Eleanor began to pace in thought. Her heart told her that there was much to support the conclusion that Hywel could not have been a murdering brigand. For years, he had lived in this village and gained not only the respect of his neighbors but the love of a woman all praised for her goodness. When the Welsh rose in arms against King Edward, he did not go to fight for the king, but neither did he join the army of Dafydd.

Yet the two who knew Hywel best, and swore he was no traitor, were a Welshwoman who loved him and a man Rainold had called a sodomite.

She winced. The sheriff's murderer had claimed her monk was as well. Looking at Brother Thomas in the shadows, she saw him as a menacing dark shape against a background of even deeper black. Then she shuddered, reminded herself that, to him, she might look just as ominous, and forcefully put all such distracting thoughts aside.

"I think it is time, Brother. The monks should be back in their abbey by now."

Brother Thomas walked quietly to the back of the church.

She heard him open the door to the crypt but heard no voices. When he returned, there were two shadows with him. The smaller one lifted a flickering cresset lamp up to her face. It was Eluned. Then the maid passed it to the taller shape next to her, and the light revealed the face of a man Eleanor had never met.

"I am Hywel ap Gruffydd, my lady." The man's speech was hoarse. He stepped closer and knelt, still holding the weak light high enough so she could more clearly see his face.

As he did, the prioress noticed the wide, dark mark around his massive neck where the noose had scarred his throat. And, too, the stonemason had impressive shoulders. Such a man would be hard to hang.

"Eluned has said that she told my tale to you. I would not blame you if you doubted both her word and mine. Yet I swear on the breath of the God we all worship and must face in judgment that I have never committed any act of treason against King Edward, nor will I ever do so."

"You think he was wrong to engage in this war against your kin." Eleanor knew her tone was brusque with suspicion.

"Have you never wished that war and bloodshed had never occurred? A man can wish that, yet know that blame is cast on one side as much as the other. I am a stonemason, my lady, a man unskilled with either sword or bow. I use a knife only to eat or, if need be, prepare a carcass for my meal."

She tried not to be influenced by the pleasing lilt of his accent or his eloquence. The latter was a quality her father had often noted in many of Hywel's countrymen, whatever their rank. "Your brothers? Are they equally innocent? If you return to Wales to be with them, might they not change your mind and persuade you to take up arms against the king?"

Eluned took in a gasping breath.

He reached out and touched the maid's arm. "An honest question that deserves a truthful answer, my lady. I cannot swear that they might not march with Dafydd or Llewellyn, for they believe the Welsh have been betrayed and cruelly treated. As for the murder of the sleeping men, they have given me their God-witnessed oaths that they were not there. Men must fight face to face, in their opinion. If they are forthright in their dangerous opinions about the justice of fighting for honorable treatment, and deny they murdered defenseless men, I think there is reason to conclude they tell the truth about both. My brothers and I share a horror over what happened that night to the soldiers."

"If not you or your brothers, who led the band?"

"I cannot say, my lady. Living here, we have heard rumors of many such raids by groups of men. The war may have ceased between princes, as Archbishop Pecham tries to bring peace, but the Welsh people remain angry here in the south."

Eleanor knew he was right. Had her brother not warned her and Robert to leave their manor because of this?

Yet the crime still angered her. Did the Welsh not tend to attack defenseless soldiers? Was there any difference between men killed by arrows shot from a heavy forest, as the Welsh often did, and sleeping men slaughtered with no chance to defend themselves?

However, her brother had told her that the English knew the Welsh fought from the cover of trees, and King Edward had taken precautions by cutting down the forests on both sides of the common paths in the north so arrows could do no damage to an army marching in the middle.

Somewhat reluctantly, she decided that there was a difference between a battle stratagem, against which an army might defend itself, and a wanton atrocity that men could not.

But she was not finished with her questions for the stone-mason. "Will you follow your brothers to war?"

Again, Hywel looked at Eluned. Even in the harsh shadows, his smile was soft with love. "Eluned and I have already told each other that we are wed in the eyes of God, and my wife believes she has already quickened with our first child." He looked back at the prioress. "As a Christian, I give you my word that I will not fight against King Edward and shall do my best to keep my brothers from doing so. I have given the same oath to Eluned."

He looked at Eleanor with such intensity she could almost feel it. "And if that is not sufficient, then I think you will agree that a man twice hanged, whom God must have saved for some purpose, or simply out of mercy, does not risk a third hanging if he is wise."

"I believe Hywel was saved by a saint, my lady," Eluned murmured. "As he was led to the gallows, I prayed for a merciful intervention."

The prioress nodded and decided, with some amusement, that the saint might well have been a Welsh one.

Men might not think her conclusion valid, Eleanor thought, but she was convinced the stonemason was honorable. Then she looked at Eluned. "When we spoke earlier, you said you would be here solely to assure Hywel of our good intentions, yet there is clearly more to your continued presence. You may be with child and have vowed marriage to a man going to Wales tonight. I think you plan to accompany him, do you not?"

The maid nodded.

"That was not part of our understanding."

"Forgive me, my lady. I am not abandoning the Lady Mary. As reward for my loyal service, she has released me to marry the father of my child." Eluned's voice betrayed her discomfort.

Eleanor caught the vague phrasing. "Does she know Hywel is alive?"

"Before you came to the house with your brother and his men to arrest Sir Rainold, she told me she had conceived and begged a favor that I was happy to grant. I told her that I, too, was with child and wished to leave her service to marry the father. She willingly agreed to grant me my freedom to do so and even gave me a fat purse of silver as a gift. I did not mention the name of the father, nor did she ask."

The boon asked was no mystery to Prioress Eleanor. Eluned was expected to confirm that there was no time when Rainold could have lain with the Lady Mary. In fact, as she now recalled, there was one night when Eluned had not been with her mistress but with Hywel.

"The night of the raid, where was Sir William?" Her question was gently asked.

Eluned paused, then said, "He heard rumors of a marauding band of Welshman on the border, my lady. He gathered his men and went to find them. Sadly, he found the dead Englishmen, but the raiders had fled."

If Sir William was absent that night, as the maid just confirmed, and Eluned and Hywel had been together as Lambard testified, then Rainold and his sister-in-law had had the opportunity to commit adultery.

With grudging admiration, Eleanor finally conceded that the Lady Mary had utterly fooled her into thinking she was a frivolous woman of little wit. Instead, she turned out to be immensely clever. And if Hywel could not have raided the English camp because he was with Eluned, then Rainold could not have witnessed the attack because he was with the Lady Mary.

As for adultery, she strongly suspected that Sir William, had he lived, would have accepted the miracle and rejoiced in his child. Rainold would not have dared to speak up for he was as dependent on his brother as the Lady Mary was on her husband. The sin of that one night, therefore, was up to the widow to repent and for God to forgive.

Eluned was still waiting for Eleanor to say something.

The prioress did not need to ask anything more. She had made her decision.

"Lambard has provided one horse and some provisions," she said to the pair. "They will have to serve you both, but you have time to travel safely and far enough before dawn. I cannot guarantee you will reach your family," she said to the stonemason, "but at least we have arranged a safe beginning."

The two wept and begged her blessing, a gift she swiftly granted. Then they swore they would pray for her for the rest of their days on Earth.

And I for you, the prioress thought, and urged them not to tarry longer.

Brother Thomas took the pair out a narrow back gate to the waiting horse.

Eleanor stayed where she was until she heard the sound of hoofbeats. Whatever misgivings she still felt, and loyal though she was to King Edward, her relief that the pair had escaped outweighed everything.

When Brother Thomas returned, he found her kneeling before the altar.

After a brief hesitation, he lowered himself to his knees and prayed beside her.

Chapter Thirty-Nine

When enough time had passed that Hywel and Eluned must have been well on their way, and dawn had begun its daily struggle to bring God's light back to the Earth, Prioress Eleanor and Brother Thomas returned along the path to the lodge. Only the joyful paeans of awakening birds broke the silence that surrounded them.

They often experienced a companionable and mutual quietness that was characteristic of the deep bond they had formed over their many years of working together. This time, however, Eleanor felt a tension between them that was as unsettling as it was unusual.

She knew the man walking beside her was fatigued, as was she, but his weariness seemed more acute, as if it had bored into his soul. Glancing at him with circumspection, she could actually feel the pain he was suffering, an agony so deep and vast she could see neither a beginning nor an end to it.

Although her heart longed to comfort him, there was nothing she could say. The right balm to heal his wounds and wisdom for him to follow were beyond any words known to her.

When her hunger to lie with him had burned like hellfire for years, she continued to have faith that God had all the answers but found He revealed them with excruciating slowness. Now she was again faced with decisions for which she possessed no competency and feared His solutions would come to her with even greater sluggishness.

She shut her eyes and briefly became lost in her own Gethsemane. She begged that this burden be taken from her, yet she knew it would not. Opening her eyes, Eleanor grew determined to face what she must with as much courage as she could.

Rainold might have been a murderer, a rank creature who remained unrepentant until the morning he was hanged, but she believed he had spoken the truth twice in his failed attempt to avoid justice. Even the Prince of Darkness was known to do so, albeit more rarely than hens were found to own teeth.

After much thought, Eleanor had no doubt about what had occurred the one night neither Eluned nor Sir William was in the house. Whether Rainold seduced her or she him, the Lady Mary had surely lain with her brother-in-law, hoping to beget the heir her husband could not give her. It probably happened only that one time. The act may not have given the lady more joy than lying with her husband, but it had filled her womb, whether with the son she longed for or even a living child was up to God. Eleanor could never prove the details, but she had finally concluded that none of it was her concern. God didn't need her help in the matter.

As for the tale of what had happened between Lambard and Brother Thomas in that narrow alley, Eleanor was equally convinced that Rainold had not lied about what he had seen. As she again fought back scalding, bitter tears, Prioress Eleanor knew that her monk had committed an act of sodomy.

When faced with the accusation, she had chosen to lie about what he had told her the morning after. At the time, she believed she had done so solely because she was outraged over Rainold's attempt to blackmail her. Once the moment of heated anger had passed, she had to confess to herself that she did it mostly out of the profound love she bore Brother Thomas.

It was clear to her now that he had been about to confess his sin when he was interrupted by the messenger. Had she encouraged him, he might still have spoken about it in private later, but she did not do so and said he must confess, not to her, but only to a priest.

Of course, she had been correct to say that, but just in part. A priest, not a woman, could hear confessions and order the proper penance. Yet Brother Thomas had the obligation to tell her, as his prioress, of any grave transgressions. She had denied him the chance, not just because of the problem with a ghost, but because she could not bear to hear that he had lain, as she then feared, with a woman.

Now, she wished she had not been so blinded by jealousy and then hidden the real reason for her willful ignorance by arguing that the dispatch of elusive phantoms took priority over his confession. Breaking his vow of chastity by lying with a woman required a hard penance. Doing so by committing sodomy with another man could mean far worse.

Sodomy of this nature was a sin the Church had always especially abhorred, but the majority of past Church leaders used to order only a lifetime of fasting as penance. In recent years, however, influential men had grown louder in their demands that sodomites be burned at the stake as a foretaste of Hell. Outside England, these executions were becoming more common.

Eleanor bit her lip and did not stop until she tasted blood. Perhaps her monk had engaged in this sin only because he had drunk too much and was not fully aware of what was happening until it was too late. The transgression might never be repeated. Perhaps Brother Thomas had fled before he and Lambard had consummated the act. If so, was it not a lesser offense, or was she merely blinding herself to the gravity of the act? These were arguments she had repeated to herself far too many times already and still failed to settle.

She truly thought that burning men at the stake for having sex with other men would become the new position of the Church. Yet she still believed in God's mercy. How could He want a man, who had done so much good in His name, tied to a stake, set on fire, and left to scream until his soul fell into Satan's arms? Had Brother Thomas no chance for penance, absolution, and the right to continue his good works, especially if his sin had only happened once?

"My lady?"

Eleanor had been so lost in thought that she did not realize they were back at the lodge. She blinked to chase away any disloyal tears, raised her head, and smiled at the monk she both loved and admired.

"I beg leave to finish my prayers alone in the chapel," he said, his voice rough with weariness.

She granted his wish and watched him walk away.

She ached to heal him of his pain. She might not have completely vanquished her desire to couple with him, nor chased away all jealousy, but her love over time had grown far more complex than lust. The thought that he might not always be by her side in all their endeavors to serve God was unbearable. She clenched her fists until her nails bit into the flesh. She could not, would not, let Brother Thomas die.

She looked back at the village, allowing herself a moment of angry resentment. Lambard may have been a loyal friend and a kind man in this matter of Hywel and Eluned, but Eleanor would never forgive him if he caused the downfall of the man she needed by her side so much.

Forcing these thoughts away, the Prioress of Tyndal spun around and marched into the lodge, called for a servant, and sent him off to summon Abbot Gerald.

The abbot would be relieved that his malign and destructive spirit, one that had so upset the village, had been sent back to Hell.

Hers had just arrived to take residence in her soul.

"Are you certain?" Abbot Gerald sounded very worried.

"I am," the prioress replied, and then noticed that he had something in his hand.

"We heard no sounds of the conflict."

"The battles between man and phantom may not reach distant mortal ears, but the noise is deafening to those involved. I can assure you that the roars of the damned soul, as it fought with Brother Thomas, were a taste of what we shall hear at the End of Days."

"And you, a woman…"

"In such hours, the Queen of Heaven drapes her mantle over those of us who must stand in her stead for justice on Earth, Abbot. Only afterward did I feel my mortal weakness." At least that was not a total lie. Were I forced to confront such a trial, she thought, the Mother of God would be my comfort and protection.

"We, and I especially, are much in your debt," he said. "You have done what none of us could."

"It is God we must always thank," she replied. "It is He who gives us the wisdom we need to find the answers to our just prayers."

He bowed his head in respectful agreement, then loudly cleared his throat.

"I see you have brought your treatise back, Abbot," Eleanor said, disguising her sigh of relief that the subject had changed from haunting to ambition. "I assume you have refined it and that this is a copy, not the original. I would not want to take your only one, lest some ill befall it."

His eyes widened, and then he grinned. "You will take this and make sure your brother hands it to the king?"

She gestured for calm. "Do not raise your hopes too high. I can promise little enough."

He nodded with grave solemnity, but the blaze of hope that caused his face to glow did not diminish.

"Take your time now, if you will, to give me a summary of your arguments. I shall read it myself, with the assistance of Brother Thomas, and I shall urge my brother to hand it to the king. What I cannot promise is that the king will accept it or even read it."

"But surely if I came to urge him..."

"He is in the midst of a war, Abbot. You have a far better chance of being heard if the manuscript appears without your special pleading."

Dejected, he leaned against the wall.

For a moment, Eleanor feared he was about to weep. "As you and I are aware, it is our duty to God to be far more effective at passionate prayer and service to Him than we ever could be at urging a plan of worldly concerns in the halls of kings."

Standing straighter, Abbot Gerald forced a resigned look. "You have promised me more than others have," he said. "Do not think I am ungrateful."

"Then please explain your proposals to me now. Of special interest to our king, I suspect, are your suggestions on governing the Welsh once they have been defeated."

As the abbot puffed his chest out with bright eagerness, Eleanor first called for wine to ease his throat as he argued for his positions and then settled on a nearby bench. *This will mean many hours to remain patient,* she thought, *but I am resolved to listen.*

After all the tragedies that had just occurred, and the sorrows she knew must yet be faced, Eleanor welcomed this comparatively brief time of peace and a chance to exercise kindness. When the will of princes and the greed of men turned the world around to violence, she knew such moments would be rare and ought to be cherished.

Author's Note

For those who fear I have really jumped the rails and wantonly exceeded all limits of acceptable fiction with the details of Hywel's double hanging and survival, I want to assure you that the story is based on a papal investigation that was quite detailed and well-documented.

In 1307, Pope Clement V ordered a canonization inquiry into the claim that Thomas de Cantilupe, a dead bishop of Hereford, might be a saint. The most dramatic proof offered by the bishop's supporters was that a notorious Welsh rebel, William Cragh, had been hanged twice on the same day, in approximately 1287, and came back from the dead after begging for the bishop's intercession.

William originally claimed to be innocent of the charges that he had murdered thirteen Englishmen during the rebellion of Rys ap Maredudd, but he was convicted nonetheless. As his relatives led him to the gallows, holding the rope that would hang him, Cragh said he prayed to the dead bishop for mercy.

Although I did change some of the details of the original story, I kept what I thought were the most intriguing and significant aspects. Like my Hywel, Cragh was hanged with another felon. The crossbar did break, possibly because the second man was very fat. When it did, both men were declared dead by the hangman who pointed out all the usually accepted signs of death.

By order of the sheriff, Sir William de Briouze, the second felon's body was released for burial, but the hangman was told to haul Cragh up once more on the repaired beam, in part because he was considered an especially vile rebel but also because the sheriff had an unexplained personal loathing for the man.

The chaplain, accompanying Cragh to the gallows, refused to hear his confession. This was not because the condemned denied guilt but because he could only speak Welsh, and the chaplain had no knowledge of that language. Apparently, the problem was solved by finding a Welsh-speaking priest, although this person was never identified. At the 1307 inquiry, the chaplain couldn't even remember who it was.

It is also true that the sheriff's wife, Lady Mary, unsuccessfully pleaded for the lives of both condemned men. She even asked to be given their bodies after the execution. She went so far as to insist her ladies in waiting pray with her to Thomas of Cantilupe for mercy and/or a miracle. Why she did this, despite her husband's ardent dislike and the verdict proclaiming both men guilty of homicide, is unknown. Even assuming she was simply fulfilling a noble lady's expected role of begging clemency, Lady Mary went further than was required or was even common. At the 1307 inquiry, she wasn't asked for a reason.

After the second hanging, Cragh's body was taken to the house of a local merchant so the corpse could be prepared for burial. While Lady Mary's lady in waiting was measuring the body for a candle to entrust Cragh's soul to Thomas de Cantilupe's care, the "corpse" began to move. One of the witnesses to this was the sheriff's son, who later testified at the 1307 inquiry. Another was the chaplain who confirmed the story and added some impressively gory details about the state of Cragh's body. (In my opinion, some of these details sound suspiciously enhanced to add greater justification for the bishop's sainthood.)

About ten days later, William Cragh regained his health, thanks in part to the nutritious meals prepared for him under the Lady Mary's direction. Because this was considered a miracle, Cragh was not hanged a third time. He publically gave thanks to Thomas de Cantilupe and was allowed to return to Wales where he remained a law-abiding man for years.

In 1307, William Cragh came back from Wales to give his extensive testimony at the papal inquiry, all of which was meticulously translated into English and recorded. The sheriff, who had condemned him and then demanded his body be hanged a second time, had died in 1291. The sheriff's son, who did not seem to share his father's personal animosity for the Welshman, appeared in his stead as a witness to the miracle.

It took until 1320, but Thomas de Cantilupe was canonized. By that time, William Cragh had really and finally died.

So could a man be hanged twice and survive? In the Middle Ages, people died of asphyxiation in hanging or compression of the carotid arteries, not a broken neck. However, people of the era would have had scant understanding of all the biological details. Instead, they relied on the presence of certain clearly observable signs to determine death. Today, we know it is possible to survive, depending on the position of the noose and the length of time actually dangling. We also know that some of those previously deemed accurate signs of death are not conclusive (voiding of urine and feces, for instance).

In Cragh's story, the details proving his death, reported in 1307, were all intended to establish the bishop's sainthood and never meant as a scientific investigation. The precise length of time for each hanging, how long the body lay on the ground between hangings, as well as the positions of the noose were not included in the testimony because they were irrelevant to the inquiry. Most medievals, as they did in 1307, would have concluded that his survival must have been a miracle. Whether due to a miracle or a combination of bad timing and a badly placed noose, the hanged man did return in 1307 to testify and was very much alive.

As backdrop to this story, I chose the part of the war between King Edward I and the Princes Llewellyn and Dafydd in which there was some lull and doubt about who was going to prevail or even the terms under which the war would end. That allows the reader to grasp the unease and fear which the characters living through such a time probably felt.

On March 21, 1282, Dafydd ap Gruffudd attacked Hawarden Castle, five miles from Chester. He not only ravaged the household, he burned the place and took the constable, Roger Clifford, hostage. In quick succession, Flint, Rhuddlan, and Aberystwyth were taken. Towns associated with the castles were looted, burned, and residents slaughtered. In the south, castles at Llandovery and Carreg Cennen were captured. Even the border town in England, Oswestry, was pillaged.

Edward I was caught completely by surprise and couldn't believe that the Welsh were doing this, convinced as he was that he had been admirably fair and even generous to them after the 1277 war.

The Welsh, both princes and the common folk, begged to differ. Dafydd and his brother, Llewellyn, had grown bitter over slights and outright insults. Dafydd resented Edward's failure to properly reward him for his loyalty in the earlier war. Llewellyn remained angry over what he believed Edward had stolen from him. English administrators mistreated the princes' huntsmen, messengers were arrested for no reason, woods belonging to Dafydd were chopped down, and Llewellyn had to sue for land he believed was rightfully his in an English court under English law. For the people themselves, they had to endure murders by Englishmen who were never brought to trial. They were obliged to trade only in towns run and populated by English but were forbidden to live there and often cheated. They, too, in their own land, had to obey English customs and laws.

The biggest complaint by everyone from top to bottom of the Welsh social scale was that Edward insisted that English law was superior to Welsh and must be followed. One of the rallying calls of Dafydd ap Gruffudd was to demand that Welsh law be honored as the laws in other nations were. In short, their customs and laws should be respected as valid. This rebellion was truly a national one, not just a squabble amongst princes.

Edward was apparently as oblivious to the high-handed tactics of his administrators as he was to the fact that evidence was planted in the coin clipping pogrom so innocent members of the Jewish community would be hanged. He was also not alone amongst the English for thinking the Welsh were backwards and barbaric. He saw nothing wrong in requiring a Welsh prince to plead for land in an English court stacked against him. When, after four years of getting the runaround, Llewellyn asked him to give him the land he believed was his right, Edward was peeved and retaliated by assigning a particularly offensive administrator in Chester who proceeded to constantly outrage Llewellyn's brother, Dafydd, whose own lands bordered on those of Chester.

Edward's reaction, to what he perceived as an egregious lack of loyalty and appreciation for his kind generosity, was swift. As is often true with swift and somewhat undigested orders, there were glitches that allowed the Welsh to continue their victories for a while longer. English nobles resented being ordered to provide troops outside the common practices of the feudal system. Supplies from military to food stuffs arrived sporadically.

Yet, by the early summer of 1282, Edward's armies were recapturing castles and it seemed the momentum was swinging to the English.

Then Llewellyn finally joined his brother, Dafydd.

His prior hesitation, despite having significant grievances, was that his wife, Eleanor, was pregnant. Llewellyn was also sixty years old. If the child was a boy, he saw merit in supporting Edward (or at least not fighting against him) for the sake of his son's future.

If the child was a girl, he might be better off with his traitorous brother, Dafydd, who had once even attempted to assassinate him.

On June 19, 1282, Llewellyn received a double blow. His wife died in childbirth, and the baby was a girl. He opted to fight with his brother. Llewellyn's choice to join the war against Edward gave the Welsh a fresh spurt of hope and somewhat dimmed English confidence.

By the autumn of 1282, however, Edward was still making some inroads. A boat bridge to Anglesey had been constructed and the south of Wales was secured, although small raids by the Welsh continued to be common and locally devastating.

But his success was muted by the Archbishop of Canterbury, Pecham, who insisted on conducting peace negotiations despite Edward's ardent disapproval. Although the Archbishop's motives were reasonable (he thought the Welsh princes might have justification for their grievances), he discovered by early November that both sides were adamantly opposed to compromise. He gave up on any hope of settlement.

This uncertain period, where the Welsh were still victorious in local skirmishes but Pecham had stalled the effectiveness of Edward's plans, is the period setting for this book. In hindsight, we know that, despite some devastating and humiliating losses by English troops in the early winter of 1282, Llewellyn was perhaps lured to his death and killed in November. Dafydd was captured in June 1283. Edward was triumphant. The Welsh hopes for any better treatment were dashed.

For those of you who are suspicious about my Abbot Gerald, you are partially right. I did base him on Gerald of Wales, a man who died almost sixty years before this book takes place.

I emphasize the word base. My abbot is not a total clone, and I did not give the real man several more decades of life because I thought it might be fun. My character is intended to represent the difficulties any person of mixed ancestry faced at a time when England and Wales were at war, as well as the uncomfortable choices of loyalty they had to make. There are major differences between him and the dead Gerald of Wales. For one thing, the real Gerald was known for his biting humor on matters ranging from clerical malfeasance to stories from the king's court. Sadly, my abbot lacks all mirth. Unlike the historical Gerald, my abbot runs a small and obscure abbey, and his life story is far from impressive.

Gerald of Wales, also called Giraldus Cambrensis (c.1146-c.1223), was a noted archdeacon and historian. He was the author of many works, but the two most readily available are Journey Through Wales and History and Topography of Ireland. There is some belief that Edward I may have read his book on the Welsh to better understand how to conquer and later rule them.

Born in Wales at Manorbier Castle, his father was of Norman descent and his grandmother was the daughter of the last king of South Wales. Gerald himself was firmly loyal to the English kings. He was educated in Paris, employed by the Archbishop of Canterbury to much praise, and, in 1174, was rewarded with the archdeaconry of Brecon. Two years later, however, politics reared an ugly head.

In 1176, Gerald's uncle, the Bishop of St. David's, died, and the nephew was nominated by the monastic Chapter to succeed him. Unfortunately, King Henry II was wary of him, especially after his own quarrels with Thomas Becket. He rejected the nomination, possibly because of Gerald's Welsh ancestry and family ties through his grandmother, but also because the king feared he would support St. David's desire to be free of Canterbury. St. David's, fearing the king's disfavor, caved in and ultimately approved the king's choice instead.

Gerald, terribly disappointed, spent the next several years in the study and teaching of canon law and theology before becoming a clerk and chaplain to the same King Henry II in 1184. Seems our Henry now thought our Gerald's Welsh connections might be useful in diplomatic efforts with Wales. For his efforts, Gerald was offered several bishoprics, all of which he turned down, either because he felt they weren't grand enough or he really only wanted the position at St. David's.

In 1198, he was again nominated by St. David's for the bishopric. This time it was the new Archbishop of Canterbury, Hubert Walter, who refused confirmation, even after King John said St. David's could elect whomever they wished. Gerald did take the position, but Walter refused to ever confirm the election choice. The battle was taken to Pope Innocent III, and Gerald, again for political reasons, lost the job.

Matters got almost fatally worse when Llywelyn the Great and Gruffydd ap Rhys II supported Gerald's right to the bishopric of St. David's while King John now took the part of the Archbishop of Canterbury. Gerald was actually put on trial for encouraging Welsh rebellion but was released and fled to Rome. He was later briefly imprisoned in France for passionately protesting the selection of another for the St. David's position.

During the rest of his life, Gerald believed his Welsh ancestry had been to blame for his failure to gain the position he most longed for and he even resigned as archdeacon of Brecon. It is believed he died in Hereford and may actually be buried in St. David's.

I hope he is. There would be some justice in that.

Finally, I couldn't resist including Son of the Morning, a name for Satan that I hadn't heard before. It is based on one of the many stories about his fall from grace that I found especially impressive.

In medieval times, the ruler of Hell was a figure that generated both fear and fascination, an interest that has continued to modern times. The fellow is very complex. His various names come from several traditions, each of which provides a different view of him as well as his connection to God. These often contradictory and even troubling aspects have generated passionate debates over centuries about how good and evil function as well their exact relationship.

No, I am not getting into all that. Quite apart from the need to keep Author Notes to a Note, I am not academically qualified to enter the debate. Nor will I get into the multifaceted origins of the terms Satan and Devil. I will keep to the story of Lucifer which generated the story of Son of the Morning.

The term Prince of Darkness needs no explanation, but to call Satan something that means light? Lucifer was the Latin name for the morning star, Venus, and originally had nothing to do with evil or devils. It only became linked through an apparent series of biblical passage confusions and maybe some mistranslations. Whatever the exact truth of that, the name allowed for the incredibly stunning imagery as the once formerly privileged angel is tossed out of Heaven in a flaming arc of light that matched the brightness of the morning star.

Being fond of vivid imagery as well as seeming contradictions, there was no way I was going to pass on including Son of the Morning in the books as one of Satan's names. It also fits the medieval love of the dramatic as illustrated by their artwork depicting souls being carted off to Hell.

Bibliography

The book on which I based my tale is a short one and well worth reading. The documentation in 1307 of both the events and the roles of the people involved in the 1287 incident is a fascinating snapshot of what was considered a fact (or not even considered at all), what was important in analysis, and what a logical conclusion would be at the time. That a man could survive two hangings, yet be declared dead by a presumably experienced hangman, is amazing but certainly not impossible. It also tempted me beyond all hope of deliverance to twist it into a mystery. If you read the Bartlett book, I think you will sympathize with my plight.

Included below are also books on Gerald of Wales, the Welsh war, and Marcher lands. May you enjoy as much as I have!

Gerald of Wales: A Voice of the Middle Ages, by Robert Bartlett;
    The History Press, 2006.

The Hanged Man: A Story of Miracle, Memory, and Colonialism in the Middle Ages, by Robert Bartlett;
    Princeton University Press, 2004.

Edward I and the Governance of England, 1272-1307,
by Caroline Burt; Cambridge University Press, 2013.

Eduard I's Conquest of Wales, by Sean Davies;
Pen and Sword Military, 2017.

*The Medieval March of Wales: The Creation and Perception
of a Frontier, 1066-1283,* by Max Lieberman;
Cambridge University Press, 2010.

Medieval Wales, by David Walker;
Cambridge University Press, 1990.

Acknowledgments

Patrick Hoi Yan Cheung, Christine and Peter Goodhugh, Maddee James, Henie Lentz, Paula Mildenhall, Sharon Kay Penman, Barbara Peters (Poisoned Pen Bookstore in Scottsdale, Arizona), Robert Rosenwald and all the staff of Poisoned Pen Press, Marianne and Sharon Silva, Lyn and Michael Speakman.

About the Author

Priscilla Royal, author of fifteen books in the medieval mystery series, grew up in British Columbia and earned a BA in world literature at San Francisco State University, where she discovered the beauty of medieval literature. She is a theater fan as well as a reader of history, mystery, and fiction of lesser violence. When not hiding in the thirteenth century, she lives in Northern California and is a member of California Writers Club, Mystery Writers of America, and Sisters in Crime. Visit her at www.priscillaroyal.com.